skeletal

/ˈskɛlɪt(ə)l,skəˈliːt(ə)l/

Katherine Hayton

Also by the Author

Found, Near Water
One Hundred Days of Noise

Contents

Watch this. Watch this now. Those men - the ones in the fluoro vests and the hard hats and the mud-caked boots. They've removed the bricks of the house, by hand. They've piled them up and put them aside in neat square packages wrapped in tarpaulin, ready to use again when the time comes. They're about to raise the house off its foundations.

It's amazing.

Before the earthquake, no one had ever really tried something like this before. It was a proposition of something that might work in a trade magazine that no one would ever have read. Except now it was read, and practiced, because there were so many opportunities to try out things people had never tried before.

Opportunity, and the potential to save money. A perfect combination for experiments. And this thing works.

Watch them. Right there. They're lifting the denuded house up off the foundations. It creaks and groans but it holds together. Amazing.

And look down in the foundations. Where they're cracked and broken and the floor on one side has dropped almost a foot in height because of the liquefaction souping up the earth. That bit, where it's broken so much the bare earth can be seen straight through the concreted silt. Even before anyone starts to try to crack it up. Broken along a prior instability.

That's where I am.

Watch them as they pull aside the hard clods, and now – that one – he's reaching forward, pulling one aside to expose a creamy

I

white bone. He's taking a step back now. He's calling over his shoulder to a colleague. His site manager is about to be wholly pissed off, and frustrated because he's not allowed to show it. Not in this situation.

But the whole site's going to be roped off and their work is going to be backed up and he's going to be on the phone for the rest of the day trying to shuffle everything around so he doesn't lose more than a day's wages for his crew.

It'll take a while before they know that it's me. There's going to be a stream of 'professionals' coming by. They'll carefully dig, and photograph, and exhume each bone. They'll lay it out on a board in a morgue, making sure that each and every little piece of me is tagged and laid out in place.

They'll drill into the bone, the femur, and try to get a read on the DNA left in the dried out marrow. They're going to find a match with a file on a missing person. And that missing person file is going to be me.

My mum's going to get a knock on the door that she's been waiting for, and dreading, for a decade. She's going to break down and cry with the easy tears of a drunk, even though her ten year chip takes pride of place in her jewellery box.

She'll cry, and won't hear half of what they say. But they'll be patient, and they'll go through everything with her again. And again.

I would cry too, if I still had something to cry with.

But for now that's all poised in the distance, a series of dominos not yet pushed into action. For now, there's just the hi-viz workers and the glimpse of something they know shouldn't be there. For now there's just my dead bones and the cold ground they've been stored in, hidden in, waiting for the puff of fresh air to caress their curves and lines. Waiting for the dirt to be brushed aside and their porous surface to inhale the warmth of the sun.

Waiting to be found.

III

part one - bully

chapter one

Coroner's Court 2014

By the time the coroner sits down, the court is close to half-full. A lot of people for an inquest, but there's a bit of public interest in this one, and a lot of witnesses.

The court isn't in a building purpose-built for the function. Instead, it's an old community hall taken over by the justice department for use as an ad-hoc venue now that the old District and High Court buildings are out of action due to earthquake damage.

Wood panelling reminds the participants that style belongs to the decade, and the seventies were a long time ago by anyone's count. Still, it matches with the pews that were hurriedly installed after February, and at least it's a room somewhere, which something can be done in safely. It doesn't take long in Christchurch before you're sick of your pathway being blocked by danger tape.

Hah! I've been looking around me for so long I've missed the start of the coroner's speech.

'I'll try to call you in a logical order, to fit in with the anticipated timeline, but I'm afraid this may mean I'll have to recall some of you at a later date.'

He's talking to the witnesses who've all gathered along the front benches. Funny to see how they group themselves together. There's no love lost between some of these folk. No love lost between me and them neither.

'Mrs Harrow if you need to vacate the room during testimony at any time please feel free to do so, you needn't seek permission. Has your representative shown you the facilities available?'

My mother nods her head. She looks so dignified in this setting. Nothing like the sloppy mess she was the last time I saw her in person. When I was a person, I mean. She would've had a hard time putting herself

1

together at that stage, but now her hair is arranged in a complicated knot at the nape of her neck, and it glows softly with care, conditioner and colour. Nothing like the last time.

'Okay. I want you to know that you can also ask questions through your rep at any time during the proceedings. Mr Anderson, you'll let Mrs Harrow know when you'll need to wait till the end, but otherwise?'

They nod to each other, old participants in this drama. Or similar dramas at any case. Mum looks content to know she's being taken care of. It's always nice to know that someone's looking out for your best interest. I presume.

'Okay, then we'll start the proceedings. This is to re-open the coroner's case file number 46782, the last verdict returned in this matter was manner of death undetermined. The transcript of that original hearing will be entered into evidence and will form the first part of this case.

'The first witness I'll call to the proceedings will be Ms Patricia Pearson.'

I settle back to watch the story unfold. It'll be nice to see everybody again.

***

Daina 2004

I don't know what it was about me that Ms Pearson the admissions secretary didn't like, but whatever it was she didn't like it a great deal.

The grimace of dissatisfaction her mouth screwed into when I appeared grew only deeper with distaste as I explained the reason for my appearance, late on a school morning, mid-way through term.

'My previous school confirmed they forwarded the records through,' I said and sat back in a hard wooden chair while she looked through the computer system for whatever the hell it was that she needed before I could be released into the horrors of the high school. This was the third high school I'd been enrolled at in a little under two years, and I believed I may have known just a tad more than she did about the process by now.

'We haven't received it through. We'll need your guardian to sign you in.'

'My mother isn't available today. I can hardly call her away from work just to sign me in, when it's all already been arranged. Isn't there another place you could look?' Experience mixed with desperation had given me some confidence.

'Stay there,' she barked and stalked out of the room on high-heeled shoes that would've labelled her a whore at my last school. Still, the woman could barely scrape five feet with them on. Who was I to judge?

'Knock, knock, Patricia.' A man stuck his golden-curled head around the corner, a smile on his face. 'Who are you, and what have you done with Patricia?'

'Sent her away,' I replied. 'She's hunting down a transcript from my last school.'

'What year are you?'

'Year ten.'

'Come with me, then. You'll be in my English class that is due to start in,' he made an elaborate show of looking at his watch, 'Ten minutes ago. Pat'll be ages if she's chasing down paperwork. It doesn't get on with her.'

When I remained seated, he smiled even broader. 'You won't get in trouble for actually attending a class, you know. On your feet.'

'Not until you tell me who *you* are.'

'I'm Bond,' he said, coming into the room with his hand extended. 'Jeremy Bond.'

He wasn't like any teacher I'd come across before. He looked tall, blond, and like trouble. But I followed behind him as he led me out of the main administration building and along to a wing that looked as though it had been added as an afterthought. Two prefab classrooms, standalone from the two buildings we'd passed to get here. And painted a brand new shade of neutral.

3

When he walked into the classroom, the whole room gave him their attention. A popular teacher, then.

'Class, this is our newest student,' he turned to me with raised eyebrows.

'Daina Harrow,' I mumbled, embarrassed as I felt everyone's eyes settle on me.

'Daina.' He rested his hand on my shoulder as he turned back to the room. 'Daina Harrow, just transferred in this morning so make her welcome. You may as well sit there at the front so that I can make sure you're okay.' He pointed and I slid into the seat. No relief from attention, as I could now feel everyone staring at my back instead.

'Right, where were we?'

'You were going to get a "sacred text" from the main office,' came a delighted yell from the back of the class.

'Oh, right. So I was.' He spread his empty hands wide. 'But I found a new student instead, and that's much better, isn't it? So where was I before *that*?'

There were half a dozen cries from around the classroom this time. All with completely different references.

'If I didn't know any better I'd think you were trying to trick me,' Mr Bond continued. 'So I'll just make it up myself.' He turned back to the board and wrote BLOOD in huge letters across it, then flourished it with a long line underneath. 'And whose blood would I be talking about?' he asked, turning back to the class.

'Lady Macbeth,' they chorused in unison.

'Well, not quite.'

'King Duncan,' came a lone female voice from the back of the class.

I wasn't the only one who turned to see a thin blond with a satisfied smirk on her face.

'Well done, Michelle. That's right. The blood was *on* Lady Macbeth's hands, but it was *from* King Duncan.'

He walked over to his desk, and looked puzzled at the lack of anything significant on its surface.

'It's in the office, sir,' came a helpful yell from the

back of the class.

Mr Bond's face cleared, and he nodded. 'Right, well I'll just be a minute then. I need to fetch something...'

He walked out of the room, and there was a patter of snorts and giggles from the back of the class. 'Bet you five bucks he forgets it again,' said the same voice that had reminded his teacher he still didn't have the book he'd gone to fetch.

I turned around to look at the back of the room again, and identified it as belonging to a short boy with a mess of long brown hair. He caught me looking and stuck out his tongue. I turned back to face the front of the class, my cheeks burning.

'Paul, you don't have five bucks,' drawled Michelle. 'And if you did you'd hardly pay up, welcher.'

'Well fuck you, Miss know-it-all.'

Half of the class broke into horrified laughter, while the remainder ignored the two of them and carried on with whatever activities they'd chosen to fill their downtime with. I could see more than a few smuggled cellphones half-hidden in palms. At least I presumed they were smuggled. Cellphones were certainly contraband at the other high schools I'd attended.

There was a few minutes of peace, and then I heard the distinct sound of fist hitting flesh, followed by a low groan.

'Fuck yourself, welcher,' I heard Michelle whisper just before Mr Bond re-entered the classroom with a coffee in his hand and nothing else.

'Now, where were we?'

***

Ms Pearson 2004

Patty left the office for a few minutes so the girl sat in there alone. She was a right piece of work. It wasn't hard to spot the troublemakers, not when you'd been at this job for as long as Patty had.

She walked down to the end of the corridor and let

herself into the staff room. It was gloriously empty, the whole coterie of teachers busy in their own classes. This was about the only time she used the room. Too much noise and too many people made her feel useless and alone. When she was actually alone, she felt neither.

There was a chair covered with battered leather that had her name on it. As Patty sank into it with a sigh of content she counted down the days until Friday and release into the weekend. Her garden needed some attention now that the days were longer and the sun was warmer. If she didn't pour herself into it now she wouldn't have the rewards of fresh vegetables and warm sun-kissed fruit in the height of summer.

Only one term left and then she could relax properly in the long stretch of summer holidays. During the term she felt constricted, but with a whole six weeks of freedom in front of her she could truly unwind. All the benefits of being a teacher and none of the marking or daily class planning. And her mother used to tease her for being stupid! Well, she was enjoying the last laugh.

Five minutes had gone by, but that was probably enough. For a girl sitting alone in a strange office in a strange school it would seem like longer. Patty stretched herself out to her full height – not that there was much of it – and got to her feet.

Already her toes were protesting, and they had a good few hours ahead. Patty walked briskly back down the corridor. Not a person in sight. She was stuck in a permanent tiptoe due to the heels, but she wasn't about to give in and turn into a flat-foot. Nature's oversight could be corrected, and god knows Patty was going to correct it.

She could see as she closed the distance to her office that it was now empty. Patty shrugged, and wondered how she could fill in her morning. There were still some payroll forms to be processed. Duty registers to be checked. If she didn't get that done by Wednesday then the substitute teachers wouldn't get their pay. So she would definitely do that for the ones she liked. The rest, and there were many, could play roulette with whatever else took her fancy.

The scent of cologne that assailed Patty as she walked into her office made her screw up her face with distaste. Mr Bond had been in here, then. Nausea brought a rush of saliva to her mouth.

There was a textbook filled with notes that he'd left in a corner of her office. He seemed to delight in dropping by whenever he felt like it, half the time when he should've been in class instead, making a nuisance of himself. A bully, that's all he was. A stupid great bully.

She hinted as such every chance she could with Mr Fitzsimmons, the school principle, but he either didn't get the hint, or didn't want to take action. Certainly his class response was positive, and the results from his level had improved under his tutelage.

Patty opened the cupboard behind her and pulled out the office shredder. She'd need to use a bit of force to tear through the spine of the book, her nails would be put in jeopardy, but it would be worth it.

Once she'd shredded the entire textbook she put the remains into the office wastepaper bin and put the machine back away. She'd had to use her own money to purchase the shredder – the school's budget didn't run to such frivolities – but it was worth every cent she'd spent on it.

Patty pulled the stack of time record sheets towards her and started to check them against the school register, a smile on her face. She could easily get everybody's cards through, she decided. No matter how much the subs had slighted her in the past. They'd all be paid on time.

No one could ever say that she wasn't diligent.

***

Daina 2004
Just before the end of class Ms Pearson knocked at the door and entered, not looking pleased. She beckoned

me out of the room with her forefinger, and a wit in back went 'Oooooh, new girl's in trouble,' in a sing-song voice as I obeyed the command.

'You shouldn't have left just like that,' she said sternly and handed me a clipboard. 'I've been looking all over for you.'

Mr Bond came out of the room behind me, and put a hand on my shoulder again. 'Sorry about that, Pat,' he said, as I tried to decipher what the form was all about. 'Thought she was better off learning something while you sorted out the paperwork.'

There was a sniff in response, and out of the corner of my eye I could see that most of Ms Pearson's face was fighting a sneer. God, she was awful.

'Sign there,' she said, pointing at the bottom of the form. 'We'd usually get your parent or guardian to sign, but we'll make do until your mother can come into the office.'

Fat chance that would happen. I fully expected we'd be on the move again several times before my mother would ever pull herself together enough to visit a school office.

'Is that legal, Patricia?' Mr Bond asked in a teasing tone.

There was a loud bell that made me jump, and he laughed. 'No need to be so tense,' he said as he gave my shoulder a squeeze and released it. 'It's only the end of period bell.'

I handed the clipboard back to Ms Pearson, and she handed me a handwritten timetable. 'Here you go. Your next class will be biology. Just follow this lot; you'll be with them for all standard classes, and you've been enrolled in graphic design and computer science for your two voluntary classes.'

At my raised eyebrows, she added, 'They're the only classes with room at the moment. You can try to select next year. If you're still here.'

She turned away, and gave Mr Bond a look I couldn't decipher. 'You left your textbook in my office. I put it in the staffroom for you.'

I tagged into the stragglers from class and followed them out of the prefab building and into one of the more solid-looking wing buildings.

'Hey Daina,' called a voice behind me, and I turned to see Michelle coming up behind me. I slowed my step so she could catch up.

'Looks like Mr Bond took a real shine to you,' she said, her smile revealing the whitest teeth I'd seen on a real person.

I shrugged, unsure of what response to give. I wasn't used to being approached. Teenagers tended to have formed into their social cliques well before I turned up, so I was used to being ignore or being stared at. Not being talked to.

'Hand on the shoulder and everything. He wouldn't go into bat with Patricia for just anyone, you know.'

I shrugged again, feeling less comfortable by the minute. It was almost a relief when I felt the sharp jab of her knuckles in my kidneys. It was a well-practiced shot, but I was well-practiced at receiving them.

Michelle leaned forward, so close I could feel her breath on my face. 'You'd do well to stay clear of him from now on, got it?'

I nodded. I got it.

Coroner's Court 2014
Jeremy Bond doesn't look like he used to.

The hipster appeal he exuded to his class ten years back has aged into seediness. His unkempt blond curls speak now of holding onto a look too far past its prime. Mutton dressed as lamb. They suit the shop window though.

His smile reveals teeth yellowed with nicotine, a habit that seemed daring and unusual at a different time, now just frowned upon by society everywhere.

His voice on the stand is hesitant. I remember his easy charm, the lilt of his voice matching perfectly to the teasing expressions that were his trademark, but now his voice tremors and he seems petulant when he would once have pouted.

Some things don't change though. Michelle is seated right in the front row, hanging off his every word. She married him, you know. After everything that happened, everything he did to her. Some dogs like being kicked.

She's sitting right next to my mother. As though she were family. As though she were someone who cared. The lying bitch. She's not there to make sure justice is done, or to find out what happened. No, she's seated right up the front there as a fanbase for Jeremy.

She's still thin and blond. She still looks like a cunt.

'Mr Bond, when was the last time that you saw Daina Harrow?'

Jeremy angles his seat towards the coroner. *He* seems like a nice man. Quiet voice, making sure that no one is feeling pressured. Aware that being in the front of the room could be hard for some people, and going out of his way instead to make it seem like a private chat.

10

'Oh, I think I probably saw her last about a month before her death.'

'Keep in mind that we haven't yet established a time or date of death, so you'll have to give us an approximate date, if you don't mind.'

'Well,' Jeremy screws up his face. Fine. So he knows it's a month before my death, but he doesn't know when? Could that possibly be because he's lying through his teeth?

'I'd guess around November or December 2004.' Jeremy notes the frown on the coroner's face, thinks back and hurries to amend, 'Around December. Definitely.'

'Okay. And how did she seem at the time?'

'Oh, much as usual. She was always quiet, introspective, you know. Maybe she was a bit pale.'

Listen to him. Just listen. A bit pale. I was down to 45kg and all he noticed was that I was a "bit pale". Sic him, Judge.

Except the coroner isn't a judge, and he isn't going on the attack. He just accepts this testimony the same way he accepts all the rest.

What I want is a trial. A good juicy trial. Have a prosecutor ready to jump to her feet and yell, objection! Not that they run a courtroom that way here. But still, would be nice.

'Well, thank you for your time Mr Bond. Unless there's anything further you'd like to add at this time you can step down. Keep in mind that I may call you back to give evidence at a later time if it becomes necessary.'

'Thank you.'

He stands and walks to the nearest bench to sit down. Not because that's the seat he's chosen as the most advantageous, but because that's the closest and he wants to get out of the limelight. Well, well, Jeremy. Events echo, don't they?

***

Daina 2004

'So what I want you to do is pull back the tables and chairs. We'll create a space in the centre. Shove all the tables over here, and line up the seats. Just like a theatre.'

Mr Bond directed the operation with a theatrical flourish, fitting in with the occasion he was trying to create.

'Right,' he said, clapping his hands together and rubbing them. 'Now all I need is a volunteer to play the Lady Macbeth. Don't all raise your hands at once.'

His irony was lost on the class, and they remained motionless. While helping to reposition every piece of furniture in the class I'd somehow managed to be in the front of the group. I tried to step back and behind the next person, but it was Jason who, completely in thrall to his fear of public speaking though there's little chance of him being chosen, gave me a shove that not only had me back in the front line, but falling forward a step.

'I'll do it, Jeremy,' Michelle said, stepping forward. He encouraged the use of his first name, but she made it sound like honey on her tongue. Beside her, Sharon stuck her finger in her mouth, completing the mime with a simulation of retching.

'We already have our volunteer,' Mr Bond said as he grabbed hold of my arm and raised it above my head. I tried to pull it back in horror, but it was too late then. I glared at Jason as I stepped in front of the class.

'Right, I'll take you outside for a five minute consult to offer you direction, and then you can come back through once I've talked these guys through the program.'

He pushed me gently between the shoulder blades out of the class, and I walked out. I even managed to resist the urge to just keep on walking.

'Right, so I just want you to mime the actions of Lady Macbeth,' Mr Bond said as he closed the door gently. 'I'll have the class read out the soliloquy on your behalf, so you just need to follow along with what they're saying. Okay?'

It wasn't okay. It was anything but okay, but I didn't have a way of telling him that.

Michelle had already been scrutinising everything I did. Being picked out for this role was probably as much to her horror as it was to mine. There was no way of retrieving the situation now, though. If I tried, it would only make things a hundred, a thousand, a million times worse.

And Mr Bond just headed back into the class as though he hadn't singled me out as a target. As though he hadn't just made my life hell.

I waited in the hallway until I receive the knock to come back through. I acted out the stupid charade of a stupid woman stupidly trying to take back something she never can. I acted it out, and tried not to catch Michelle's eye, even as I tried to keep track of where she was and what she was doing.

By the time I was allowed to sit back down, and it was someone else's turn to have a fool made of them, my head ached.

And that was the first class of the day.

***

At lunchtime, I walked down the footpath at the front of the school to go into the mall. There was a teacher standing on the path, and as soon as I saw her I got a bad feeling in my stomach, but I kept going.

'Do you have a note?'

'Pardon?' I stalled, trying to get by.

'You want to go through to the mall, so you have to have a note. If you don't, you can head back.'

'I didn't know. I'm new here.'

I tried my best to insert full little-girl-lost into it, but I think my expression may have tipped into full-bitch mode while my control wasn't looking. She glared at me as though I'd told her to go fuck herself.

'Well, you know now.'

She stepped to the side to stop another girl who was using my encounter as her own opportunity. I turned back to the school. It wasn't as though I could slip by her. The path was the same width as the footpath, and it led to the only gap for 100 metres in the chain-linked fence that bounded the school.

I still needed to get to the mall though. It was already ten minutes past twelve, and I was cutting it fine if I wanted to get to the bank before my mother woke up.

I slipped down the side of the school where the secondary bike sheds were. There was a six-foot wooden fence down this side. The joists were on the other side as well, so there weren't any footholds.

I trailed my hand along the rough wooden surface as I strode half the length of the school without finding a way to hoist myself up. There was a possibility that I could make it out through the back of the school, across the playing fields, but then I'd have to walk three blocks to get back to the mall entrance which was where the bank was located. If I tried that I'd be late to class, and that would draw even more unwanted attention to me. I was already the new girl: I already had a skank targeting me because of some bizarre crush. I really didn't need to be known for skipping class on top of that.

I looked back towards the front of the school. I couldn't see the path from here, but I had no real reason apart from absurd hope to believe that it was now vacated.

I looked at the bike sheds again. If I could get up on the roof, I could just jump down on the other side of the fence. They backed up almost to the fence line. But there was no handy way up onto the roof either.

I walked back anyway, an idea starting to gain traction in my brain.

It was within a metre of the fence. If I could manage to prop my back against it I could shimmy up the shed by my legs, then use pressure to move my back up again, and so on.

I didn't think about it for too long, otherwise I

wouldn't be able to try it. I pressed my hands and back against the fence, and placed my foot a metre up on the side of the bike shed. I closed my eyes and brought my other leg up as well. It felt like I was laughing in the face of gravity, but for the moment it worked. Now I just had to get up another couple of feet, and manage to wriggle over the top and I was home free.

'What the fuck are you doing?'

My eyes popped open, and I saw Michelle advancing upon me, with an entourage following close behind. Elvira, if my memory from home-room roll-call served me okay, and Alicia, also from Mr Bond's English class. In panic I pressed hard back against the fence and stepped up the wall to raise myself another foot.

'Oh, dear god,' Michelle snorted at my attempts. 'You know there's a road out front you can just walk down?'

I tried to hitch myself up again, but the constant pressure required was already making my arms shake, and my back twitch. I didn't get much further upwards, but at least I didn't fall.

'What are you going to do if I do this?' Michelle lunged for my feet, and I made another desperate move upwards, trying to get up and over before she could catch me.

I was still short of the top of the fence, but I avoided Michelle's outstretched hands.Her smile, and the tense line of her body let me know she was about to make another attack.

I pushed back hard against the fence, freed one of my legs, and as Michelle came at me again instead of placing it back on the shed wall I placed it firm in the middle of her chest and shoved myself back and up. Twisting I caught the top of the fence, pulled myself up to my middle, and swung my legs over. I held for a moment to try to ascertain I wasn't about to land in anything life-threatening. But my arms shook so much I couldn't hold for long and I dropped down, turning my ankle slightly on the soft bark, and scratching the side of my arm on some overgrown lavender, but otherwise safe.

'You fucking bitch!'

Michelle's head popped up over the side of the fence. For a moment I thought she would be on me in a second, and I stepped back. But then I heard the frantic scrabble of thick rubber soles failing to make purchase on the lichen-slippery wood, her elbow slipped from the top of the fence, and she disappeared with the thump of a hard landing.

I didn't need a repeat performance. I ran for the mall entrance.

***

I stopped outside the bank and waited until my breath had returned to normal before entering. There was a queue of people waiting for the tellers, but I stayed in the lobby and used one of the automatic teller machines.

I entered my mother's card and then typed in the pin. The hand around the keypad was a bit theatrical maybe, but there was someone in line behind me and I kept seeing news stories about people shoulder-surfing their way into your bank account.

There was a beep and the screen registered 'PIN incorrect – try again.'

I entered the number again. Fast fingers must have got it wrong.

The same message appeared, and I heard an impatient grunt from the line forming behind me. I should've stayed outside and used that machine instead. There was only the one user there.

My heart was thumping noticeably in my chest. I told myself that was simply due to my exertions, and entered the PIN for the third time.

And watched as my bank card was swallowed.

The man behind me in line laughed. I turned, cheeks burning, shoulder bumping him as I walked by. Arsehole.

'Steal it, did you?' he shot back at me as I reached the door.

I carried on without looking back.

My mother must have cancelled the card. So either I'd have to steal her replacement again, or just live in hope that she used the money for its intended purpose, unlike every other time her benefit was paid out.

Shit!

I couldn't believe I'd gone to all this trouble for something that was already a no go. My selfish mother. Okay, so it was her bank card, but now she'd just take the money out and waste it on her favourite hobby. I'd started to get used to having the money available to buy groceries so we could both eat, and pre-pay electricity so I didn't have to endure cold showers every morning.

When I was getting close to the fence I scanned the wood to see if there was a knothole anywhere. I could always go back through the normal pathway, but I couldn't imagine that I would be able to enact a re-entry with earning the third degree from Ms Simons in her sentry duty.

And, okay, my current situation didn't warrant a return visit, but that wasn't to say I wouldn't need it in future. I didn't want a teacher patrolling the pathway *and* the bike sheds the next time I needed to get across to the mall.

There was a gap in the fence further up from where I'd originally landed. I tiptoed through the bark and bush covered ground and put my eye up to it. I couldn't see shit. Or, should I amend that to, I could see shit. Whatever. There was no one standing directly in front of the knothole, of that much at least I could be certain. And it was further down from where I'd gone over so maybe I'd have a few seconds lead time even if Michelle and her friends were still hanging about.

I could hear the five minute bell go. Class was about to begin again anyway. No options left.

I grabbed hold of the vertical strut and put by foot on the horizontal and boosted myself up. I could clasp the top of the fence before I was even fully standing, and then I just had to jump up and swing my legs over.

It was as I passed the gravitational point of no return that I heard them running.

I tried to swing my legs back mid-turn but all I succeeded doing was hitching my skirt on the top of the fence leaving my backside and legs fully exposed.

There was a whoop of laughter as I struggled to free the fabric, and then I felt a hand grab at my underwear and yank it down.

The cool air against my buttocks. A flash of light. And then more laughter, running away this time.

I hung on one hand as I pulled my knickers back up. My skirt tore from the weight of me. It would be a hell of a repair job, but at least I was free now to drop to the ground.

There was no one in sight.

My skirt had torn in a vee shape down the side, but I adjusted my kilt pin to move the front further over, and that hid it well enough. The bell rang for class and I started to run towards the science wing. My mind worked through the series of events trying to make sense of them. A laugh, the pull on my pants, a flash.

They'd taken a photo.

The bitches had taken a fucking photo.

***

When I walked up the drive I could see that the curtains in the lounge were pulled shut. I tried to be quiet as I slipped my key into the lock, but every sound seemed to reverberate until it was all I could hear. With the door closed again behind me I could only make out the outlines of furniture in the gloom. There was a heavy fug of cigarette smoke, old fast food grease, and alcohol fumes that made me want to gag and cry at the same time.

If I had my way I'd stride through the house opening every curtain and window wide to let in the cleansing sunshine and clean, fresh air. I would vacuum up the ash and throw out the half-empty food containers, and pour every full and half-drained bottle down the sink. I'd throw my mother in the shower, and her clothes in the washer, and prepare something for the table that involved fruits and/or vegetables, and didn't rely on grease and salt for flavour.

If I tried that right then, I'd have a slap across the face before I was halfway round the room, and a punch in the stomach if I tried to go further. Not that my mum is violent by nature; she's not. But if she's in pain she lashes out, and nothing caused her pain during the day more than sunlight and noise. And me. Being present. Even quietly.

If I were a romantic I could try to pretend that she was a vampire. The sunlight would spell her death, so she drew the curtains as a barricade against mortality.

That would be the romantic version.

I tried not to make too much noise as I walked through the room and out the side. The stairs up to my room on the second floor creaked at my every step. I'd tried in the past to step at the edges, at an angle, at alternate sides, but there was no way around it unless I walked super, super slow. So I just got up them at top speed. The noise was pretty much the same, but at least it wasn't stretched out, and my nerves with it.

When I sat down on my bed I could hear the distant rustle of movement. I breathed slow and even through my mouth so I didn't make a sound, and listened as though it was a participatory sport.

The thump of my heartbeat, but little more. Five minutes, ten minutes. I stopped concentrating on how much noise my breathing made. I stretched out on the bed even though the slumped springs squealed with the change of pressure.

My stomach grumbled with hunger, but I was too tired to be worried about it now. I couldn't think what there'll be to eat anyway – I'd been counting on getting the money out of the bank to go grocery shopping.

Maybe some jam, with nothing to spread it on. Maybe some margarine. I was sure the eggs had run out. Too tired.

**

I came fully awake all at once. There was a deep thump of a bass beat issuing from downstairs. Oh great. Another one of mum's parties, and I was sure she'd remember that I need my beauty sleep on a school night.

I pulled off my uniform and had a look at the tear in my kilt. I'd need to fix it up before I wore it again the next day. It was already starting to spread further. If I didn't fix it straight away, it'd be unfit to wear by the next week, and there was no money to buy another one. I could only get this one by trading in another school's and pretending it had never been worn. Well, it had only been worn for six weeks, and that hardly counted.

The song shifted, and the volume increased. There were cries of admiration. A favourite, no doubt.

The neighbours'd be round soon to complain about the noise. If they did they'd probably be on the receiving end of a fight rather than gracious compliance.

I pulled on a sweatshirt and some sweatpants. If I was lucky, someone'd have brought some food along with them. Fish 'n' chips or Maccy Ds to soak up some of the alcohol. I trotted downstairs, taking no care about the level of sound. The bass beat had some audible notes now. And the cracked voices of people joining in without any true appreciate of tone, or rhythm, or melody, or the right words. It probably sounded great in their own heads. And they were unlikely to care about anyone else's.

Just as I was about to push the door open, there was a tinkle of breaking glass, and I paused, head to one side, trying to identify the sound.

A bottle. Definitely just a bottle.

Someone was out near the street deciding that what Christchurch needed now was broken glass strewn across the road for the morning traffic to appreciate.

I continued on through, and winced against the smoke in the room. From biology I'm aware that I should breathe through my nose when I'm confronted with pollution – the nose hairs help filter, or something – but stuff that for a joke. The smell'd make me retch.

'Love, you're home. You're home. Come and give your mother a hug. Mmmmmm.'

I was enfolded into the loose and fume-filled embrace of my mother.

'Caw, love – you're too young to have a grown girl, aren't you? Sisters, are you?'

My mother burst into appreciative laughter, and my insides groaned. She'd been turning on the flirt again then. I'd probably come across this one again tomorrow.

'Here, girl. Get yourself a drink then,' the man continued, shoving a half-empty bottle into my hand. Fill your own. Two litre. 'Cause that's appropriate, right?

'I'm good,' I say as I turn out of mum's gropey hands. 'Is there anything to eat?'

'Course there is love, course there is. I'll fetch you something. What d'you want? Chips?'

I nodded and followed Mum through to the lounge proper. There were about twenty people crowded into a space that usually felt confined when it was just the two of us. One of them was stubbing a cigarette out in a beer bottle cap, and then the carpet when it twisted to the side. Stubbing out our damage deposit.

The low table was covered by opened containers of Chinese food, the soy smell pungent even in the smoke-filled room. That, and the opened flowers of white paper with chips as their centre. Their floral scent grease.

I tore off an edge of paper, and scooped a couple of handfuls in, turning to take them back to my room. I was pulled into a rough embrace on the couch instead.

'Don't be leaving us, love. Sit here and talk for a while.'

Uncle Charles had to shout over the noise from the stereo and the impromptu backing singers, but that didn't seem to register as a reason his suggestion wouldn't work. I wriggled forward to the edge of the sofa, about to stand up, but he caught me roughly by the shoulder and pincered me back into place beside him.

'Whatchoo been up to then? Got a job yet?'

I resigned myself to staying seated beside him, and shook my head. I started to eat the chips. I could be here a while.

'Why not? Why aren't you helping your mother out?'

'I'm still at school.'

'So? You're fourteen now, aren't you? At your age I had a paper round and worked on the milk deliveries.'

'They don't have milkmen anymore,' I shouted back. 'And the only paper round is fully signed up.'

'Those are just excuses. You need to help out more. Your mother can barely get by as it is.'

I shrugged and continued eating, until the whole parcel hit me in the middle of the face.

I shrank back into the sofa, blinking, trying to grasp what had just happened. My uncle had hit the food straight into my face. My lips stung where the force of the blow had split it, the salt crept into the fissure and made my flesh scream.

''Bout time you learned some responsibility, girl,' Charles shouted at me.

I burst into tears and tried to leave the couch. It was late. I was tired. I was still hungry. I was sick of these awful people making their awful mess in my awful house. Why did my mother invite them? Why couldn't she drink alone like a halfway decent alcoholic would? Why was everyone out to get me?

A blow across the face shut me up. And then Uncle Charles' face softened. 'Oh, honey I'm sorry. You just get me riled when you don't pay attention. Here, let me get you some more food and you clean yourself up.'

He patted me on the knee, and headed off to the kitchen. I wiped my lip with the back of my hand – blood smeared across it in a wide crimson line. After a second it started to pull upon itself and form into droplets. Clotted.

I pulled the edge of my sweatshirt over my knuckles, and rubbed my eyes dry. A chip fell from my shoulder onto my lap. I swept my hand behind me and pushed another half-dozen onto the floor. They already smelt of cold grease. My stomach lurched once, twice, and I was running across the room out to the back bathroom. I retched over the toilet and some chips came back up. They hadn't even started to digest.

I tried to breathe through my mouth but the smell still overwhelmed me and I retched again. And again. I stopped when the effort grew too great for my stomach muscles to handle. I could still feel my throat trying to gag. Still had the sting of acid in my throat; my stomach. But I just couldn't anymore.

There was a pounding on the front door. The loud exchange of angry and indignant voices, and the volume being pumped up even higher on the stereo. I flushed the toilet and put my forehead against the seat while the cistern filled back up with a series of burps. There was an angry scream, and the soft sound of fist hitting flesh. Another neighbour learning the hard way.

He didn't have to worry. At this rate we'd be moving on soon enough.

I slowly walked back upstairs. My clock showed the time as being after two o'clock. There was noise, and I was agitated, but the tiredness gripped me even stronger, and I chased it down into sleep.

chapter three

Daina 2004

My lip was swollen, and a bruise shadowed my cheekbone. I tried to cover it with foundation, but the bottle was almost dry, and even adding in a few drops of water and shaking it didn't provide enough to offer any real cover.

So I walked into a door. Who was even going to ask?

There were three strangers asleep in the living room. I tiptoed past them, and then slammed the front door behind me as hard as I could, and ran down the driveway.

The tear in my skirt flapped gently against my knee as I walked down the cycleway at the back of the school. There must have been a rain shower overnight, and occasional drops from the tall oaks that lined the path dropped on my head.

I could probably "borrow" a stapler from first period social studies if I could get into the room early enough. Until I could find the time to locate a needle and thread, emergency repairs would have to do.

A fist in my back alerted me that Michelle or one of her cohorts was right behind me. I didn't bother to turn. If my mother ran through her current tenancy in as short order as she had her previous one, then I could at least get rid of one problem.

It would take another couple of months to run through a normal eviction proceeding, but last night sounded like it was close to drawing the attention of the cops and that would speed everything up.

'Hey bitch, looks like someone appreciates you as much as I do,' Michelle lilted as she walked past, 'Next time get them to do something about your nose, why don't you. Could use a lot of work.'

I slowed down so I wouldn't be right behind her, and walked over to sit on the wooden bench nearest to English. After form room I could get my skirt sorted, and then at lunch I might even be able to sneak into the home economics block to properly fix up my skirt. I snorted at myself. Dream big, sister. If I was truly lucky I could score some make-up from the year eleven personal presentation optional, and fix up my face.

'Hey, do you have a calculator handy?'

I turned to see a girl sitting next to me. She was part of a group of four, I knew the redhead was Susie Moore, but I hadn't learned the other's names yet. The one who'd spoken had the beautiful tan of Samoan skin, and dead straight black hair that looked natural. Unlike the friend to her left who looked like she'd gone full emo with black eyeliner, lipstick and nail polish to boot. The last girl had mousy-brown limp hair. Just like me.

I rooted around in my bag for my pencil case. It was stained from years of use, and the zipper got stuck halfway down where one of the teeth had melted in the sun, but at least it held everything I owned securely. I pulled it open and wriggled out a small plastic calculator that my mother had got free from the bank. The logo was still clearly emblazoned on the front, even though half the keys had worn away.'

'Cheers, big-ears. Mine ran out of juice.'

I smiled at her turn of phrase. Juice was a word that I'd only heard in mum's collection of seventies VHS tapes, not from an actual person.

'You're in Mr Nippon's maths class right?'

I nodded, yes.

'What did you get for number three? I can't work out quadratics to save myself.'

'Eight,' I answered from memory. I'd done the homework yesterday, during afternoon break. If I didn't do it then or at lunchtime, it wouldn't get done.

'You're kidding, really?'

I laughed at the plaintive tone in her voice, and so did the emo girl in a distinctly un-emo fashion. 'You're so bad at that I don't know how you manage to stay in school,' Emo Girl said. 'You'd be better off picking up an application for McDonalds.'

'Yeah thanks, Tracy,' she replied, giving her a push on the shoulder. 'I'll bring you into my next career counselling session so you can put paid to my parents' dreams for me once and for all.'

'Where're you from?' Susie asked, ignoring the two of them.

'I live just over on Sawyers Arms Road,' I replied, but at her screwed up face I laughed in realisation. 'From Timaru, originally. But we've moved all over in the past couple of years.'

'I've got a cousin, and an uncle, and an aunt who live in Timaru. Not together, but... They've split up. They still live round the corner from each other though.'

'Dude, *everybody* lives around the corner from each other in Timaru,' the mousy-haired girl joined in. She gave me a sly glance from under her lashes to see how I'd react, so I didn't.

'True,' I agreed. 'My name's Daina, by the way.'

'Shit, everybody knows who *you* are. You're the one Michelle's gunning for. Better you than me,' Susie stated with passion.

'I'm Vila,' said the girl still trying to figure out her maths homework. She'd already given up on my calculator and was writing numbers down by hand. She gave a pointed glance at Susie, who clicked.

'I'm Susie, that's Tracy, and that's Melanie.'

'Mel,' she immediately corrected.

I waved at them, and felt a smile start to form. It had been a long time since I'd spoken to anyone my own age for anything other than the shortest of commands, or politeness.

'Where the hell d'you get the split lip from?' Melanie said with interest. 'It looks like someone punched you in the face.' She glanced around then leaned in close to whisper, 'It wasn't Michelle, was it?'

I shook my head. 'I tripped going upstairs at home.

Caught the step with my lip.'

The look of admiration faded a bit, but then Melanie perked up again. 'I heard you booted Michelle in the chest yesterday, is that true?'

I was about to deny it when I reconsidered the attention I was now getting. I nodded instead. 'I used her as a springboard to get over the fence. I don't think she was very happy about it.'

There was a chorus of quiet giggles, and Susie looked around to make sure no one noticed our little group. *Our* little group. 'She'll be gunning for you even more now, then. I don't know how you managed to do that to her. I wouldn't have the balls.'

I shrugged. 'Well, my mum always said that if you get hit by a bully you hit back and they leave you alone.'

Vila shook her head. 'I tried that one with Michelle when we were back in year five. She beat the shit out of me.'

Tracy snorted at that one, and I turned to her in surprise, but Vila laughed and altered her statement. 'Well, she punched me much harder and made my nose bleed and me cry. That's practically the same thing when you're ten.'

Susie leaned in even closer and spoke even lower, 'I heard that she's been giving Mr Bond BJs after school. That's why she's so upset that he's taken a fancy to you.'

'Susie! That's not true,' Vila exclaimed.

Susie shrugged and leaned back against the brick wall. 'It's what I heard.'

Tracy just looked nonplussed so Susie helpfully mimed the action using her tongue and her hand, until Tracy looked appropriately disgusted.

'But he's a teacher. *And* he's good looking. Why would he ever let her touch him? It'd be like Brad Pitt marrying Roseanne.'

'She's thin and blonde. She's not charging for it. That's probably enough,' Susie said.

'Gross. If that's really true someone should report it,' Vila added.

27

'Are you going to?' Susie shot back. Vila shook her head. 'Well then, no one else is going to neither. Who needs that kind of trouble?'

The bell rang for home room, and we walked together through to our class.

'Here,' Vila said as we sat together in the middle row, offering me the calculator back.

'Are you finished? You can keep it if you like. Otherwise you'll get in trouble.'

Vila laughed, and waggled it for me to take. 'I'm already in trouble. I haven't understood anything in maths class since we stopped learning the times tables off by heart. I can't add up correctly even with this.'

I sat still for a minute, feeling a glow of friendship that I wasn't familiar with. It would be nice if I could keep hold of that for a while longer. 'I could help you if you like. My mum used to be a tutor for this sort of stuff, it's how I picked it up. I could take you through it.'

Vila smiled, and leaned her head forward. 'Really? You'd do that?'

'Sure,' I nodded. 'I'd be glad to.'

'I can't pay you, you know. My parents don't have that kind of money.'

'Neither do mine. I meant for free.'

Mr Dorman came into the room, and frowned at me as though I was the only one talking. Sometimes I wondered if I had a beaming light over my head, drawing everyone's attention to my massive flaws.

'I'll talk to you at lunch,' Vila promised as we settled down to wait for the long school-day to be over.

'Catch you then,' I replied. Smiling.

***

Vila plonked herself down next to me at the wooden bench by the tuck shop. 'What the hell are you doing?'

I was trying to manoeuvre the stapler into a position where it could easily pull together the two pieces of fabric on my skirt. 'I tore this yesterday. Didn't have time

28

to fix it last night, and I don't want it to get any bigger.'

'Come to mine after; my mum'll be able to fix that up for you. She doesn't work Wednesdays.'

'Except for sewing,' I joked back.

'Yeah, well looking after me isn't really a job, is it? It sure doesn't pay much.'

I clicked another staple into the line and then gave it up as a bad job as it jammed on the fabric, and nearly tore the rip bigger as I struggled to get it free.

'Leave it,' Vila ordered. 'She'll be happy to do it.'

I left it alone. It wasn't as though I was making any headway with it anyway.'Are you sure?'

'I wouldn't offer if I wasn't. Anyway, if you're going to be helping me, then I need to do something to help you back. It's not right otherwise.'

I shifted my weight. The wooden bench was too hard to be comfortable. Not to mention the peeling paint, and the high risk of splinters. We should get danger money for this type of stuff.

'Where's your lunch?' Susie asked as she plonked herself down hard beside Vila. 'Are you on a diet?'

'Yeah,' I replied. 'The diet of "I ran out of time to make anything this morning".'

'Really, do you want my sandwich? I'm getting a pie so it's just going in the bin otherwise.'

Susie handed it across the table to me without waiting for a response. It had meat, lettuce and cheese all layered between soft, white bread. I couldn't imagine why she would rather get a greasy pie with god-knows-what in the filling, rather than eat this, but I wasn't about to challenge her. 'That'd be great, thanks.'

She was already gone, queuing up in the tuck shop line.

Tracy sat down with a sigh and stretched out her legs. 'I'm so sick of school. I wish it were holidays right now. I could use the time to get a tan.'

'Sun'll kill you,' Vila said, an automatic response by the look.

'Something's got to. If it's not the sun it'll be the sex,

29

drugs and rock 'n' roll, bitches!' Susie said as she rejoined the table. She wavered her hand from side to side, the middle fingers tucked in, and her forefinger and pinkie making the horns.

I laughed until I was bent over in half gasping for breath. Melanie sat down next to me and gave me a pat on the back which started me off again. When I recovered and looked up there were four faces looking at me in astonishment. Then Vila started laughing, Tracy snorted and Melanie pulled a face. 'Youse don't get out much, then?' she queried. 'Or I missed something really good.'

I smiled and closed my eyes while I took a bite of Susie's sandwich. The sun warm on my face.

***

Coroner's Court 2014
I thought Vila would take the stand next, and reveal her secret thoughts of me. Instead the coroner calls a break. It's hard for me to fill in time while everyone else scatters to fulfil their base needs. I end up staring at the empty stand.

Boring.

There's something that happened next that no one bore witness to. It's hard to think of it, because the very nature of it was scattered and shattering. 'Cept it only lasted a few minutes, so what was the big hoo-hah, eh?

Rhetorical, that was.

I know what happened now. I know what caused it. At the time it was random, out of the blue, and frightening. And I thought my life had already descended to a point where little would frighten me. You'll see shortly that was a theory about to be tested, and was found wanting.

But this is getting us nowhere, is it?

So come closer now. While they're all out of the room stuffing their faces and voiding their bladders. Come closer, come closer and listen.

***

Daina 2004

There were five minutes from the first bell announcing that lunch was over, and the second bell announcing that you'd better be in class now.

I was busting, but I hadn't wanted to leave the table while I was having fun with people. Not just people, but people my own age. Having fun and talking to them like I was normal.

I slid into the third stall along. There was some paper clinging damply to the wall of the bowl. I looked away immediately. I didn't want to see any more. My bladder wasn't in the mood to fuss.

When I sat, the plastic seat mercifully cold against my rear, I saw a flash of colour out of the side of my vision.

I expected to turn and see graffiti on the wall. I expected it to be a crude drawing or a rude phrase in marker pen. Instead I saw a line of flame.

I jerked back against the cistern, but I was mid-stream and going nowhere. I held out a hand to the flame.

There was no heat. I could feel the wood of the wall through the flames. Could hear my fingertips scraping on the wood even over the crackle of the fire.

Finished, I pulled up my knickers and flushed. The line of flame continued to flicker its strange light. I inhaled through my nose, but there was only the usual strong smell of air freshener hiding the raw bodily odours beneath.

I shook my head, closed my eyes, and reached for the latch of the door.

I flicked it open and walked out, only looking back over my shoulder.

There was nothing there but the toilet stall. Exactly as it should be.

Girls were jostling each other for mirror room at the

sinks. Makeup was applied with the careful skill of girls new to the art, but with plenty of recent practice.

I waited on unsteady feet for the sinks to clear. I heard the second bell go, but while everyone else rushed out of the room I stayed. I moved to the mirror and looked at myself.

At first it was my normal reflection. I breathed out, only then noticing I'd been holding my breath.

And then the colours of my face started to run.

They spread out along the surface of the mirror as if they were formed of ink I'd just spilled water on.

My face was a metre wide, two metres. I tried to smile, but a yawning chasm opened up.

I took a step back and closed my eyes. I concentrated on my heartbeat. THUMP-thump-THUMP-thump.

And then I realised I could taste the sounds it was making. Orange and chocolate. My heartbeat, my pulse, it tasted like a giant Jaffa.

My eyes flew open again. The colours were everywhere. Dancing around my head. Spreading out across the floor.

The mirrors were a thousand beads of light reflecting across the walls, the floor, the ceiling. And I was part of it all. I could no longer tell where the floor stopped and I began.

And then I blinked and it was gone.

I looked at the mirror again, and saw only my reflection staring back at me.

I washed my hands and then quickly ran to my class. I was a few minutes late, but that was all.

The entire episode only took a couple of minutes from beginning to end.

***

I didn't say anything to anyone. I followed Vila to her house after school, not even bunking off. That experience was put right out of my mind.

Vila may have said that her parents didn't have the money to pay for a tutor, but after seeing her house it was harder to believe. It was huge. Not only huge but full-on opulent. When I walked between the Roman pillars (bloody pillars!) into the two storey entrance hall I felt like I was the downstairs part of 'Upstairs Downstairs' and I was out of bounds.

Even the street on the way into the house seemed magical and clean to me. There were concrete walls sweeping their way into the main street, *Northgardens* written a foot high on each side. The light fittings looked like gas lamps from the twenties. Wrought iron with tiny panes of glass.

'Showhome,' Vila whispered to me. 'Don't tell anyone, but my parents are renting and they got it cheap 'cause half the neighbourhood treks through each week. You should see the list of chores they have to do each day so it looks lived in, but not too lived in.'

I could handle chores.

The kitchen was all shining stainless steel and glassy marble. Beige carpets that no one would ever think about stubbing their cigarettes out on spread out across the floors, dotted with landing pads of varnished wood.

Not like my state house by any stretch of the imagination. I don't even know if they should have the same noun to describe them.

Vila put some plain biscuits on a tray, along with a couple of slices of some cake heavy with fruit, nuts and chocolate, and then pulled a bottle of coke out of the fridge.

She lifted her eyebrows at some glasses behind a display pane of leadlight glass, and I picked up two and followed her back through the entry area, and then upstairs to her bedroom.

It was also clean and big. Vila spread out a plastic rug on the floor and then put the food and drink down on it.

When I raised by eyebrows, she said, 'I can't run the

risk of spilling anything. Mum'd kill me. And we'd get kicked out.'

Okay, so maybe not so ideal.

I helped her with the maths questions from the day. We'd started to work through the beginnings of algebraic manipulation, made harder by Vila's inability to add, divide, subtract or multiply in her head. She whipped out the calculator so often that I started to get confused myself. But when I suggested doing it in her head she just looked at me with a startled expression as though I was talking another language.

'Vila? I've fixed up your kilt.'

We'd left my damaged skirt on the ironing board in the lounge.

There was a tread of feet on the stairs coming up, and I tensed, waiting for a glorious mother from a thousand sitcoms to come through the door and find her daughter's new friend lacking.

Instead, a mess of curly dark brown hair and thick obscuring eye glasses came through the door. An old cardy in a patchwork of colours that really shouldn't go together – David Bain anyone? – covered a T-shirt with the neck stretched out and black cords.

'Mum,' Vila said as she jumped up, 'Heard of knocking?'

'I called out. Who's this?'

She peered at me, took in my half-naked state and handed across my kilt. I stood up as well, took the skirt, and extended my other hand. Vila almost killed herself laughing and I nudged her in the ribs and pulled my hand back without shaking anything.

'I'm Daina. I'm in Vila's class at school.'

She nodded and smiled at me, while Vila apparently decided her privacy had been invaded and pushed her toward the door. 'We're doing homework Mum. You don't want to stop me getting a decent education, do you?'

'Vila! You know you're not allowed Coke in your room.' She twisted aside and picked up the bottle and the two glasses, mine empty, Vila's still half full. 'Imagine if you spilled it in here.' Her voice climbed a couple of notes and a couple of decibels. 'Imagine the stain. Water only, you know the rules.'

Vila coloured deep red and then suddenly shouted, 'Get out of my room. Get out! Who cares about your stupid rules?'

She started to push at her mother again, but with force and anger this time. Her mother, mindful of the dark-coloured liquid still in the glass moved back to avoid being jolted into staining something herself.

'Vila! That's no way to treat...'

The door slammed in her face and Vila screamed wordlessly with frustration.

I stood silent, not sure what I was meant to do. I was used to people behaving in strange and overly emotional ways, but they had the excuse of being drunk. Was this what teenagers were meant to be like? Is this why we got such a bad rap?

Vila sat back down and pushed aside the text book and exercise book. 'Sorry about *her*. She's a nightmare. I can't wait to get out of here and live somewhere on my own.'

I nodded in complete disagreement. If she hated her that much maybe I could suggest a swap. I stepped back into my skirt in case I needed to make an exit.

Vila swiped her hair back from her face, and took a couple of deep breaths. 'I don't want to do this anymore, it's too hard.' Her face brightened and she looked back up at me. 'Do you want to go to McDonalds? We could get fries.'

I shrugged my shoulders. 'I don't have any money so I can't buy anything.'

'I'll shout you,' Vila said as she stood up. Her voice was openly curious. 'How poor are you anyway? Don't you get any pocket money?'

I started to feel uncomfortable and pretended to pat down the front of my kilt while I hid my face.

'Never have done. If I want money I get told to get a

paper round, but there aren't any available.' I tried to be open and nonchalant, but at the last moment my composure jumped ship, and I sniped, 'Not everyone gets things handed to them on a plate.'

'Oh yeah. Call this prison a plate?' She headed to the door, then looked back with her fingers on the door handle. 'Well, come on then, I said I'll shout you.'

I wanted to say no. I wasn't hungry, I didn't need charity. I could just leave and go home.

I forced a smile onto my face and nodded. 'Thanks, but you don't need to. I'm full up so I'll just watch you eat.'

Vila shrugged and headed out the door while I hoped that my expression was set right, and my words had formed the right sentences.

Her mother was in the kitchen and came out as Vila opened the front door.

'Where d'you think you're going? It's almost tea-time.'

'I'm going *out*. With my *friend*.'

'No you're not.'

As Vila continued out the door her voice rose. 'No you're not! Come back here,' she started towards the door as Vila ignored her and continued on her way. I glanced a look of apology back over my shoulder as I closed it behind me.

'Is your mother like that?'

'No, she's not as nice as your mum.'

Vila laughed. 'My mum's a nagging bitch. I bet your mother doesn't get on your back the minute she gets home.'

I laughed and said, 'She has her moments.'

'Want to run away and join the circus?' Vila's genuine smile was back, her voice light.

'You betcha. I'd make a good lion tamer.'

She laughed and cracked an invisible whip.

***

Coroner's Court 2014

Miss Jenner walks over to the stand, and I would close my eyes and groan if I still had eyes. Or something to groan with.

I know what's coming next.

The room is half-full at the moment. People have wandered in and out all day. It surprised me. I thought that there'd be the few people directly connected with me, and that would be all. But there were people taking notes, people sketching details. Some had identity cards around their necks. I presumed they were press, but they could have been office workers taking a break from the monotony.

Public interest in little old me. Little old me. Little old me that no one gave a shit about at the time, but give me ten years lying in the cold ground and suddenly I'm a person of interest. Is it wrong to feel a thrill of pride at that? Hardly down to me now, was it. I shouldn't feel pride. I do.

But this isn't going to be pretty. It wasn't at the time, and unlike my frail corpse, this isn't a story that ten years is going to colour any way except embarrassing.

Miss Jenner shakes her head at something on the stand. Her head is a bounty of soft, brown curls that follow the movement with grace. She wasn't this pretty back then. Not when I knew her. In the intervening years she's really come into her own.

'Now, Miss Jenner. Could you tell us about an incident during your class, concerning Daina Harrow? I believe it was touched upon at the last hearing, but we didn't deem it relevant at the time.' The coroner smiles an apology. Terrible to drag her into the court twice. Terrible to make her give evidence this many years after the fact, with a memory that wouldn't grow any clearer with time.

Don't make her do it, then. You don't need to hear this. I could just let you know who was responsible, if you can't guess, and what picture it involved, as if you didn't know, and we could just move on from there.

Move on Mr Coroner Man, you don't need to bore all these nice people with this rubbish.

'I used to teach social studies at Northfield High School. During that time Daina Harrow was a student in my year ten class. She arrived mid-term in the third term in the year.'

She looks at the coroner for approval, and he nods for her to continue.

'Daina was a good student. Her school record was a mess, she'd moved twice before in that one year, but she had consistently good reports. And she had a great memory for facts and figures. We briefly looked at statistics, and I would've loved to spend more time with her on that. She had a real flare.'

Oh. Okay. This is nice then. I didn't know that she'd even noticed me, let alone remembered what my interests were. Maybe she was quiet but observing everything, same as me.

'In one class I took the pupils through a series of photographs of the area from settlement to modern day. I'd had to put them into the computer.' She turned to the coroner. 'They'd originally been on slides, but the bulb had broken in our last projector, and we couldn't get a replacement anymore. I still had the originals and a camera shop transferred them into a PowerPoint slideshow instead.'

Some dick in the back row, coughed into his hand. 'Bor-cough-ing.'

Miss Jenner colours, the blush running up from her cheeks to her temples. It makes her look so pretty. I bet she doesn't even know.

The coroner frowns at the back of the room, but Miss Jenner's already got the message loud and clear.

'Someone in the class had added a slide into the file. We're not allowed to password protect the computers in case we have to swap them out, so anyone could've done it if they had the opportunity.' She looked pointedly at Michelle who met her gaze full-on, eyebrows raised.

'The slide was of Daina Harrow. She was standing

next to a fence, her skirt was up around her head and her underpants were down. I didn't notice for a minute, I was reading the text for the photos from a sheet so it was only when the class started laughing that I realised something was wrong.

'When I looked up I was horrified. I turned it off immediately, and got the class under control. But that poor girl,' she swallowed hard: once, twice, staring fixedly at the floor, 'She was embarrassed in front of the whole class. It was an awful trick. Real bullying. I reported it to the headmaster straight after class, but he couldn't, or wouldn't, do anything about it without definitive proof of who was responsible.'

She trails off, and swallows hard again. I am quite touched. And quite relieved. It didn't sound nearly as bad as it had been to live through. In fact, it sounded like a small thing. A trivial thing.

'I left teaching at the end of that year. I was asked to reapply for my contract, but I couldn't face it. That poor girl.' Miss Jenner wipes her eyes with the back of her hand. Another trivial thing. Crying in a courtroom.

The coroner clears his throat. 'I realise this is an emotional event to recount, but would you be able to tell us what happened to Daina after that class?'

Miss Jenner looks up startled, and considers. 'She ran out,' she says after a while. 'I went after her once the class had settled, and found her in the cloakroom at the end of the hall. She looked really scared.'

'Scared?'

Miss Jenner nods. 'She looked scared. I tapped her on the shoulder and when she turned around her face was white and she was shaking. It was awful. I'd thought I'd be able to comfort her, or something like that. Tell her it wasn't as bad as it looked. But her expression...'

She looks back down at the floor again, as though the memory was hidden in the grooves and channels of the boards. As though if she looks hard enough she would see through the years to where it was all still happening.

'I couldn't think of what to say. All my words just dried up in my mouth. She looked... she looked *terrified*.' She turns to look at the coroner, shaking her head. 'I just told her it was okay if she left for the day. She didn't need to come back into class. I couldn't...'

Her throat works as she blinks hard, and then she coughs into her hand. 'She turned back up at the next class, and I just pretended that everything was normal. I didn't really know what to do. I'd hoped that the headmaster would come through and *do* something that would send a message, but he didn't.

'She attended my class each time until the end of term, and then I never saw her again.'

The coroner rubs a finger along the side of his nose, pushing his glasses up and down, up and down. The papers in front of him must be going in and out of focus, but he doesn't care or he wouldn't do it, would he?

'And how did she seem after that incident? In herself?'

In herself. How I loathe that phrase.

'I don't know, really,' she answers. 'After that day I tried not to look at her. I'd failed her, you see.'

She looks at Michelle again, seated in the room as though she belongs there. As though she'd earned her place.

Miss Jenner, my newfound protector, my secret admirer, the failed heroine of my sad story, stares at her and this time Michelle has to turn away.

***

Daina 2004
Michelle turned around and smirked at me for the third time this period. I mugged back at her, but I was starting to think that something was up, something more serious than her usual hatred.

Miss Jenner was droning on endlessly about the history of our fair lands, accompanied by some seriously dull portraits and still-lifes which managed to capture none of the supposed excitement of the time. Why did Victorian people always look as though the camera was about to kill them rather than just take their picture? Did that sometimes happen?

I sketched out a quick pencil scene of the amazing exploding camera causing mayhem in Victorian Canterbury. It wasn't enough to be in black and white. I pulled my battered pencil case towards me and hunted through for a red felt tip. Success! But it was dried to uselessness. I touched my tongue to the tip and managed to coax a little bit of colour into the scene.

Vila had just passed me a note under the table, when I heard the first muffled laugh. I looked towards Alicia who was already looking at me, and felt my mind shift into another gear. Her face ran wider, wider, until her mouth looked like a giant void and her eyes were stretched into deformity.

I closed my eyes, opened them, and saw with dismay that instead of correcting my vision it had made it worse. Colours bled into her face: neon pink and orange, Kelly Green and khaki. I turned back to my desk and saw it transform into a wide expanse of wood. A plank a metre by a metre. Then two metres by two metres.

I looked down at my hands holding the note. They looked gigantic. Like the Kenny Everett preacher who used to scare the shit out of me when I was a kid and snuck downstairs to watch the TV that my mother had passed out in front of, drunk. The nails grew and curled and reached up towards the ceiling.

There was the long echo of a laugh. I turned to my side and saw a Cheshire cat smile, snidely stretching. And then another. Another. And then they all closed in. Mouths gaping, teeth glinting, throats reverberating with laugh after laugh after laugh.

I looked towards the front of the class. Or where the front of the class had been. There was a tiny light shining. I squinted my eyes trying to make out the shadow outlines inside it. And then it blew up to the size

41

of a movie theatre. Gorgeous Technicolor. Deep and wide 3D. My bare ass the size of the whole world on the monitor.

My stupidly large hands covered my eyes, but I could still see the image. The laughter grew and grew and grew until I couldn't handle the noise of it without bursting. Without busting. I closed my eyes to gather my bearings and ran from the room.

It was only when I ran full-tilt into a wall that I stopped. My eyes still tightly closed, I put my hands out and felt the cool wood of a bench. When I moved my head to one side the cold hard metal of a coat hook scratched against my cheek. If I'd run into that a second ago it would've spiked me dead.

I opened my eyes a tiny bit. The world still swam with colour and I closed them again. I felt for the bench and sat down on it, the cool wood immediately wrapping itself around my legs and encircling my waist in a wooden hug. I brushed at my waist in a rising panic, but my hands met only the cloth of my uniform. The hug of the wood receded and my lungs opened up a little bit more.

It'll only last a few minutes I thought to myself in desperation. *Like last time, just a few minutes.*

I gripped the bench tight as though if I didn't I could go flying off. Perhaps I really could. I tried to open my eyes again, and saw the room morphing and changing. Colours running and pooling. I closed them again, but now I could see the random evil shapes on the backs of my eyelids. And after another minute it felt as though I had my eyes wide open despite also knowing they were closed and squeezed shut.

I heard the sound of running, thumping, heading straight towards me down the corridor and I turned and forced my eyes open to meet this new threat.

Miss Jenner's face twisted into the garbled beauty of a Picasso painting. Her mouth was moving, and a minute later words appeared in a steady flow in the air.

By the time I finished reading them she was gone.

There was a whisper and gargle from the corner of the room. I needed to get out before I saw what belonged to that far more than I needed the comfort of a steady seat.

I ran my hand along the wall and made my way out into the bright sunshine. Great cubes of yellow spun and danced around me, amid globs of bright, bright blue. I'm going insane, I thought, as I made it across to the science wing, to the safe guidance of a brick wall. My mind has broken and I've gone spinning off into madness.

I turned my face into the brick wall to give my eyes a rest. They felt too hot, too far out of their sockets. My forehead against the rough Summerhill stone felt too cold in comparison. My brain felt like it was leaking out from my ears. Maybe it was. Maybe that was why my world had turned into a Terry Gilliam horror.

In the end I had to leave, otherwise I would still be there when everyone left class, and I couldn't handle that. The world was an awesomely scary place all at once, but an empty one except for me. Other people? I didn't want to imagine what they would bring.

My feet walked home by rote. I could see, but what I saw made no sense and couldn't be relied on for any sort of navigation. There was another moment of panic when I tried to unlock the door and my key didn't seem to fit. Had I turned up at the wrong house? If I had, I would just have to collapse on a stranger's front door and weep until they carted me away. There was nothing left in me that could find my way home if I wasn't already there.

And then I pulled at the ranch-slider door and realised my key wouldn't turn because the door was already unlocked.

'Mum?' I called out as I closed it behind me. The living room pulsed and swayed, a bewildering hue of brown, ochre, green. 'Are you home?'

There was no answer, and when I made the endless trek into the lounge then the kitchen then the bathroom then her bedroom there was no one there.

She'd gone out leaving the front door unlocked. Open for anyone who wanted to pay a visit. That was a new one.

The taste of the purple colours in my room was soothing, like caramel, honey, and whipped cream. I lay on my bed and watched a slideshow of insanity on the ceiling. Watched the ceiling and walls watching me.

I needed to get to a doctor. I needed to find out what on earth was going on. I was so scared. I didn't know what to do until mum got home. I didn't have the money to go on my own, and I doubted that she would either. Even at the reduced rates that her community services card would command I doubted there was much money in the house at all now. And if there was it wouldn't be spent on me. Not when my mother already had a prescription lined up at the bottle shop.

The sound of waves crashing on a beach filtered through the walls. Calm, peaceful. Perhaps whatever episode I'd had was now fading enough that I could go back to being normal. I'd never be able to go to school again, obviously. But maybe a bit of my brain would be left intact and I could start again.

Maybe I could get a nice job at the supermarket. Stacking shelves, serving little old ladies who wanted to have a chat. Maybe I'd be good at it. Maybe I'd be so good at it I'd be able to get a raise. Move on altogether. Move not only out of this school, but out of this house, and maybe even out of this life.

Perhaps there was something out there waiting for me, and this was the sign from God that I needed to move on and reach up.

Or maybe my brain was sick, the random senses a final swan song, and in the morning I just wouldn't wake up.

That was the comfort that sent me to sleep.

***

I woke up to the front door being slid open. I listened for a few moments, and then when I heard footsteps followed by the thump of someone sitting down hard on the couch I let my breath out and sat up.

The world was a very different place than I'd left it. All of the objects were the same size as they appeared. All of the colour appeared to be stayfast. All of the things that were visible, were just visible. I couldn't hear, smell, or taste the pattern or colour of anything.

When I got to my feet my stomach growled a complaint. After having scoffed another of Susie's offcast sandwiches at lunch I hadn't given it a thing. Of course, I'd had other things on my mind - and my eyesight, and my body.

'Daina, you in?' came a call from downstairs.

I ran down the stairs with ease, liking the way they stayed exactly where they should be, and exactly the same size they should be, and didn't have teeth. 'I'm here. Is there anything for tea?'

'Nice to see you too, daughter,' she teased back at me. The fading twilight of the day caught her auburn curls, shooting them through with fire. A thousand times prettier than the sunset. 'There's some stuff on the table. I couldn't be bothered cooking.'

I laughed at that. My mum's idea of cooking at its best was heating something up in the oven. That was posh, after all. Not like sticking it in the microwave.

There was ham, tomatoes, lettuce, potato salad and crunchy fresh bread from the supermarket bakery. I cut an inch-wide slice and spread it thick with butter, and then draped an assortment of tomato and ham on top before biting in.

'Would you make me one too, dear?' she called out from the lounge, and I only took one more bite before obliging.

'Potato salad too please,' mum added as an afterthought. I spooned some onto a large plate and put the open sandwich down next to it. Then took it and the remnants of my own through to the lounge.

'Oh, thanks. I've been starving all day. There's some coke in the fridge as well if you want it.'

I did. I loved the sweet taste of cola, the slight kick

45

of the caffeine. But only when it was ice-cold and full of bubbles. The usual offerings around the house had lids left off and long hours to raise them to room temperature. It made it taste more like the cough mixture and general health tonic it had started out to be. Flat as a pancake, and too, too sweet.

I snuggled in next to mum, and after she finished with her salad she put her arm around me, drawing me in for a quick peck on the forehead. Her breath smelt of sweet sherry, and I relaxed even further. There wouldn't be any parties tonight, then. And sherry was a trouble-free drink for my mother. Not like when she was on the gin and I would be pulled into soggy embraces while she recounted every sad life story she could think of or make up. Or vodka, when she would sit still while she grew her fury, and then unleash it all at once on whatever or whomever happened to be available.

Sherry also meant that she must have run through her money even quicker than usual. There definitely wouldn't be money for a doctor then, but I couldn't really care less. I just wanted to have her sit next to me, and feed me, and look after me.

'How's your new school working out love?' she asked me later, while she stroked my fringe back off my face.

'It's fine.'

She waited for a while, and then prompted, 'It's fine, and...'

I laughed. 'And some of the teachers are really nice. There's a mad English teacher who made me play-act as Lady Macbeth the other day. And I met a really nice group of girls. I've been around to one of their houses to go over some maths homework.'

She turned her big blue eyes on me, her brows creasing together in a frown. 'Are you having trouble with maths?'

I shook my head. 'No, but she is. I thought if I helped her out with that, she might return the favour in some other classes. Since I missed the first half of term,

I'm not really sure where everyone's at.'

The slight jibe bounced right off her. 'That's a good idea. Make sure she doesn't take advantage though. If you're not getting anything in return, then you make sure you charge her for your time.'

'I will. But she's not like that.'

She nodded, and turned back to the book she was reading, still cradling me in under her arm. 'You'd be surprised what people are really like sometimes,' she said a good ten minutes later. As though the conversation had just kept on going inside her head.

***

When I arrived at school the following morning, I went straight to the counsellor's office and put my name down on her sign-on sheet. There was a school nurse that also made visits, but it wasn't her day and I didn't want to wait any longer or I might never get around to telling anybody what had happened. The details were already sketchy in my mind.

It was probably just something stupid. Probably had too little to eat, or got dehydrated, or became stressed out, and it triggered something weird that would never happen again.

Or it might be brain cancer.

It was the first appointment of her day, and she was due to arrive only ten minutes after my home room would start, so I just sat outside her office and waited.

'Have you got a pass?' Ms Pearson asked as she walked by me. She didn't even stop to check, just carried on through. Like an automaton hall monitor set to fast forward.

When the bell for home room rang out, the halls emptied and I waited alone. Thank goodness. I still couldn't work out how much of yesterday had been true or not, how much had been some weird brain fart, but given that Michelle or one of her skank-crew had taken a photo, it seemed reasonable to believe that part. Given that a teacher had chased me down a hallway to see if I was all right, rather than just reporting me to the headmaster, it seemed reasonable.

Mrs Aiello arrived on the dot of late.

She moved with the slow grace of a large elephant, and her motion wasn't where the similarity ended. Fabric strained in all directions as she sought to cover her forty-year-old flesh with her thirty-year-old clothes. One of the seams was starting to unravel, space showing between the interlocking threads. I wondered if she'd even noticed. I wondered if anyone had pointed it out to her. I wasn't about to, so I guessed the answer might well be no.

'Harrow? Is it Harrow?' she asked, squinting at the list on the door. Apart from an appointment in the late afternoon which I was fairly sure was a gag, there were no other voluntary signatures on the sheet.

'Daina Harrow, Ms Aiello. Daina.'

She smiled at me as she juggled her handbag, her satchel, what looked like a knitting bag - if there even was such a thing – but certainly a container that carried needles and wool - and her office keys, or what turned out to be her car keys.

'Let me get that for you,' I said, and jumped forward just as the whole caboodle started to make a break for the floor.

'Oh, thank you, thank you. I'm sure I've got my keys in here somewhere, I remember putting them in last night when I locked up,' she beamed a smile at me and then turned her attention back to her bag.

'Have you lost something Ms Aiello?' Ms Pearson said, standing in her own office doorway.

'No, no we're good,' she responded and turned back to the lock with a business-like posture.

As soon as Ms Pearson retreated back into her lair Ms Aiello picked up her bag with both hands, opened the lip as wide as it could go, and recommenced squinting. She tossed the whole conglomeration of items nestled inside as though she was tossing some hot onions in a frying pan.

I liked her. I needed to talk to someone and I liked her. Most of all, I needed to talk to someone I liked inside where there couldn't be the possibility of casual eavesdropping occurring.

I placed her belongings down carefully on the floor, and picked a long hair pin out of Ms Aiello's bun where it was trying, and failing, to hold the bounty of grey and brown hairs under any sort of control.

'What are you..?'

'I've got this. I want Ms Pearson to come back out like I want a roll in the hay with the headmaster,' I said, and she reddened and then giggled at the image.

I bent down to look through the lock. It was an old-fashioned turn-key style, like we were living in a Dickens novel rather than the modern day. It made it a matter of strength rather than dexterity though, and I only spent a minute poking around with the hairpin before I managed to trip the tumblers and carry them round.

'Oh dear, I can't thank you enough,' Ms Aiello said as she walked into the room. Leaving most of her possessions out on the floor where I'd placed them. 'I must remember your services the next time I misplace them. I don't suppose you can do that with a car, can you?'

I was about to ask her which model, and then thought better of it and shook my head. Some secrets it pays to keep close to your chest. I picked up the rest of her gear and brought it in with me, making sure the door was securely closed behind me.

'What can I help you with today, then? Are you settling into our little school okay?'

I nodded and swallowed hard. Now that it came time to speak I wasn't sure how to phrase it.

'Don't you worry, don't you worry. We've got time. You have a think about what you want to talk about, and I'll have a quick look through your file so that I don't mix your name up with the janitor.'

I bubbled up a laugh in surprise.

49

'Oh, it's been done. It's been done.' She squinted at me across the desk. 'I'd say not by me but who'd I be kidding, eh?'

She kept looking through my file, squeezed full of too many different papers, from too many different letterheads. I tried to think of a way to start that wouldn't make me sound as bad as I thought I was, but the words eluded me.

'It says here that you were a Cantamaths contestant for the last three years,' she said and looked up at me, 'A pity you arrived a few weeks too late for that one. We haven't submitted a team in donkey's years.'

'I was a contestant, but I never won.'

'It's a team thing though, isn't it? You couldn't win alone even if you were the best in the room.'

I snorted and nodded, 'Sure. It was all those other students holding me back.'

She looked at me for a minute longer, then smiled wide. 'Sometimes it's the things we don't like to say aloud that are the truest. You had something going for you, anyhow. Gosh, you move about a lot.'

'My mum doesn't like to stay in one place for too long.'

'So what is it?'

''Scuse me?'

'What's the reason? Let me guess, you're bright. I bet you're mum's got some smarts too. Drugs, or alcohol?'

I shifted on the seat. The wood seemed to have grown too hard and too hot.

'Don't worry. You don't have to say it if it makes you uncomfortable. Must be hard moving all the time.'

I just nodded. I didn't want to say anything now, just in case I started to talk and then couldn't stop.

'I heard there was some trouble yesterday.'

I relaxed and leant back. This was my entrance.

'Yes, I was in class...'

She cut me off, 'Yes, and someone had a nasty surprise for you, I see.'

50

'Well, that's not the only...'

'I know, I know. There's been a bit of talk around the staffroom. I keep my ears to the ground, you see.' She tapped the side of her nose. 'I can sniff out the truth in a single morning tea break. Secret power.'

'You're talking about me in the staffroom?'

'Well, not just you dear. Everybody. All the pupils. Have to make sure we're keeping an eye on you. And I know you've gotten yourself into some trouble.'

'I've?' What the hell had *I* done?

'Heard you gave Michelle a bit of a once-over. No,' she said putting her hand up in a stop signal. 'Don't tell me anything. It's safer that way. About time someone put that girl in her place.'

My face was heating up, and my heart was beating faster. I felt indignation, and not just for me. They sat around in the staff room making up gossip about us? Over their morning tea?

'I really haven't...'

'Yes. That's the spirit. You've done nothing wrong. Just make sure it all doesn't go too far and get too out of hand, okay. I know there's the old mantras about giving a bully a taste of their own medicine, but as I'm sure you found out yesterday that sort of thing can escalate out of all control. You don't want to keep this little spat going on too long, do you? I think you can probably be the better person, and put aside your differences.'

I stared at her for a long moment, my mouth dropped open. And then I snapped it shut, an audible clink coming from my two incisors where they came together.

No wonder her sign-up sheet was barren.

'I see you got into a spot of bother at your last school...'

'Yes, well I really should get to class.'

'Don't worry about that dear, I'll give you a pass that'll let you off the hook.'

'No, no, we're going to be doing some work I was looking forward to,' I said as I stood and slung my backpack over one shoulder. 'I've already missed out so much because I was late arriving.'

She was shaking her head no. 'I'm sure you'll be able to pick up anything. All your records indicate that you're very bright.'

For some reason this statement, that should've sounded like a compliment, started to feel like a threat.

'Not really, I have to study really hard. So I'd better...'

'Sit down, sit down. We haven't even started, and I've got most of the day free so you can talk as long as you like.'

I stopped arguing and just walked away. The temptation to jimmy the lock and keep her inside her room all day was strong, but I pretended I was the better man.

Outside I looked in at Ms Pearson's office. If she was my mother she'd make sure I saw a doctor. If for nothing else than it was the expected thing to do. But she wasn't going to help a pupil out with their stupid problems, and the person who should was barking.

Another brilliant idea gone down the gurgler.

It better not be brain cancer.

chapter four

Ms Aiello lumbers to the stand. The grace I remember is gone, lost to arthritis and varicose veins, but the wide smile is still in place. It looks incongruent in the setting.

'Now, I want you to tell us – in your own words – about a session you held with Daina Harrow.'

Ms Aiello nods. 'Actually we had several sessions. I think she came to rely on me.'

Ummmh. No we didn't. And, huh, no I didn't.

The coroner nods, and she nods back until she realises that he was trying to prompt her. She gives a trilling laugh, and places her arms on both rests to lever herself up to change position. She winces in pain. I could sympathise. It was hard when your body turned against you and started to inflict the pain that it was meant to protect you from.

'Well she signed up on my sheet. I'm usually quite busy, but I felt it was important to make the time to see her, being she was a new student and all. I set aside some time in the morning so that if we ran late it wouldn't interfere with the other students I'd booked in.'

I wondered if the lie ran off her tongue with such ease because she half-believed it herself. The genuine smile almost made the rubbish she was spouting believable to me.

'She'd been having some trouble with bullying. We took a hard line on that, and not just because of legislation. It's a no-win situation. Daina was a nice girl, but she'd rubbed some people up the wrong way, and then she'd escalated things by getting physical when she should've just backed away.'

53

Ms Aiello turns to the coroner and states, 'You should never get physical, no matter what the provocation. It can only make situations worse, but it's hard to get that across to a teenager when they're full of hormones. Daina was quite competitive as well, so it was expected that the entire episode would get out of hand if I didn't counsel her on how to handle it.'

She stops talking, and looks satisfied with herself instead. The coroner waits for her to resume, and when she doesn't he leans over to her, 'And what counsel did you offer her?'

'Oh, as I've already said. Don't let it get physical. Try to rise above, that sort of thing.'

'But it had already become physical, you said?'

Ms Aiello frowns and looks down at her hands. I can see a hairpin wandering free of her bun and wonder again how different a course my life would have taken except for that damn piece of bent metal.

***

Daina 2004

As though by agreement, nobody in my new little circle ever mentioned "the incident".

Perhaps it would've been easier to have it out in the open so that I could laugh about it, but at the time I was grateful for the opportunity to ignore it.

Other pupils didn't make life so easy. Not by confrontation – I think that would've offered me the chance to set things right – but by whispers behind hands. Whispers that stopped while I walked past, then resumed.

I got into the habit of having lunch with Vila, Tracy, Melanie, and Susie. We used the same bench and table each time; nothing like a teenager to stake out territory even in a public place, and I grew used to the company. On occasions when there wasn't any food in the house I grew used to the offers of sandwiches and the dreaded fruit that health-conscious mothers put in their daughter's backpacks, apparently unaware that unless I claimed it the apples, oranges and bananas they provided would go straight in the bins. Or, even worse, they'd sit at the bottom of the backpack for a couple of weeks and then go in the bins.

We started to sit near each other in class, in classes where the teachers didn't need to keep to a strict seating plan in order to remember each pupil's name anyway.

There was something for me to look forward to.

My mother continued to throw parties on the weeks she was paid out her benefit money, and continued to scrimp and save and go through the DTs on the week that she wasn't. I tried to lift her EFTPOS card again, but I couldn't find it anywhere. My mother may seem like an idiot when she was drinking, but all the booze hid a fierce intelligence that was more than equal to secreting a small plastic card away from her teenage daughter.

***

'Daddy. What are you doing home?' Vila bounded into her lounge and gave her father a big hug. Unilateral parental hatred, then.

Her father was a big man. Broad-shouldered. Well over six foot. He towered over me, and at five foot ten myself, that was becoming an increasingly rare occurrence for anyone, even a male.

He nodded at me, and I took another step forward into the room. 'I'm Daina.'

'She's the girl helping me with my maths,' Vila explained, still holding her Dad around the waist with one arm. 'Not that it's really helping.'

He gave her a kiss on the forehead, and pushed her back slightly so she let go. 'You don't have to be good at everything. As long as you're trying your best.'

'What are you doing home?' Vila repeated, this time a frown appearing and creasing her brow.

'I've got an all-nighter coming up,' he said. 'And I wanted to bring some stuff home, then go back into the office.'

He waved at his briefcase, which lay open on the side table. There was a flutter of pages as he leaned over and snapped the lid down shut.

'You're not leaving me alone with Mum for tea, are you?' Vila asked. The mock horror in her voice lifted it up into a higher octave.

He frowned at the television, ignoring Vila, and picked up a remote to pump up the sound.

'I don't want you fighting with your mother,' he said idly, his concentration diverted.

There was a picture on the TV of a crashed plane in snow. The 25th anniversary of Air New Zealand flight 901's infamous crash had spread the images across the airwaves so much it was as familiar as wallpaper.

Vila shifted her weight from foot to foot, then looked at the TV as well. There was an array of crash scenes, a Dash-8 on a foggy hilltop, with an Ansett NZ official tearfully breaking the news, then a Cessna 182 in a lake with a grey-suited man staring down the gathered journalists.

I felt a wave of sickness and turned away to steady myself against the sofa. Vila's Dad, his eyes still glued to the screen, stretched a hand behind him to feel the locks on his briefcase.

Broadcast over, he turned the TV off and kissed Vila on the forehead. 'I'll see you later tonight. No fighting, okay?' He picked up the briefcase and moved into the far corridor. 'Your mum works hard for this family.'

'He's got an office there,' Vila said to my querying look. 'Never stops working these days.' She stuck her lower lip out.

My calculator died halfway through the quadratic equations we were working on. There'd been a crack in the side of the tiny LCD screen for a while now, and after pressing in the latest numerals it went dark with a rainbow effect at the edge of the screen.

'Use mine,' Vila said and shoved it towards me. 'I still don't get how you just know what the answer should be.'

I took her through the method again, but my heart wasn't really in it. I'd already taken Vila through the steps a dozen times – she was well versed in the theory – but she couldn't make the leap to deduction. Part of it was her complete inability to divide or subtract in her head. Most of it was a general apathy towards the subject as soon as she realised the work it required.

There was the slam of a car boot from downstairs, and the rev of an engine. Vila leapt to her feet and went to the window. Her father's vehicle was reversing out of the driveway.

Even worse, her mother's car was turning in.

'Let's get out of here,' Vila said suddenly. She picked up the corners of the plastic picnic blanket we'd been working on, and lifted the whole thing onto her bed.

'I can't stand another moment of schoolwork. It's bad enough I have to do it all day. Let's go to the mall.'

'I don't have any money,' I reminded her, but she just shrugged her shoulders.

'I don't want to *buy* anything. I just want to get out of here.'

'But you haven't finished your homework,' I protested. 'You'll catch it tomorrow if we don't finish up.'

'That's tomorrow,' Vila said, and dragged me by the elbow to the stairs. 'Plenty of time to worry about it then.'

***

'Homework, ladies,' Mr Nippon said as he came to a halt beside my desk, almost clicking his heels together. Vila passed her exercise book across to him, and I offered up my sheets of refill.

He stared down at them fixedly for a good thirty seconds before speaking.

'Where's your exercise book, Miss?' He was good with names.

'I haven't got one yet. I only just started here.'

The loose pages continued to be glared at. 'You've been here for three weeks, young lady. That's more than enough time to equip yourself. I've given you the list.' He tapped his knuckles on the desk for emphasis. 'You make sure you get them or I won't accept any more work in from you. You need the right calculator for the end of year exams as well, or you won't be allowed in.'

I reddened as some of the kids at the front of the class turned to see what the problem was. I couldn't afford any of it, and there was no way that my mother was going to forgo a bottle of vodka to pay for a new calculator.

After school I went to the admin building.

'Excuse me, Ms Pearson?'

She smiled as she turned, and then frowned and sighed as she saw it was me. For some reason the purloining of me on the first day was considered my fault. I bet the golden-haired Mr Bond didn't get the long sigh.

'I was wondering if there was any assistance available to help with purchasing schoolbooks and equipment?'

'What do you mean, equipment?'

'Calculators, exercise books, that sort of thing.'

She stared at me for a long minute, and then snapped the book in her hand shut.

'There's nothing like that. Why?'

Because that wasn't immediately obvious to her.

'I don't think my mother can afford it.'

She continued to stare at me, a knowing look now working its way onto her face. 'According to your records your mother is on the DPB.'

I nodded. 'That's right. And things are tight right now. If I could just get some assistance, maybe even a loan?'

'We're already paying your mother to raise you. If you want school equipment then tell her not to spend the money on frivolous expenses.'

I bit back retorts, and wondered at what point in my

life I would be in an exchange with an adult where I wasn't judged and found wanting.

'She doesn't spend money on things she doesn't need to,' I answered. This was perfectly true, from an alcoholic's point of view. 'But we had a lot of expenses moving here, and this is just outside our budget at the moment.'

'You would've needed these things at your previous school.'

'We had to leave in a hurry. I don't think they were packed up, or we've lost them somewhere in the move.'

Ms Pearson sniffed, and walked behind her desk. She placed her hands on either side of the pristine desk pad that was centred on it, and leaned forward.

'Well, if your mother really does require some assistance perhaps we'd be able to help.'

I let out the breath I'd been holding, and relaxed. I nodded at her, 'Do I need to fill in some forms?'

Ms Pearson smiled. Wide. 'Oh no, you don't need to do anything.'

I started to feel as though I was on less sure ground. 'How do I apply for assistance then?'

'*You* don't, Daina Harrow. Your mother will need to apply for the funding. Once she comes into the office to complete the application we'll release the necessary equipment from the school stationery supplies.' She sniffed and shifted her weight back. Her hands folded neatly in front of her waist.

'While she's here she can complete the paperwork that she's failed to fill in for your attendance here. Get everything cleaned up and signed off.'

I swallowed hard and nodded. 'I'll let her know,' I said as I backed out of her office and turned away. One avenue I doubted my mother would be following up on anytime soon.

***

When I arrived home the front door was locked. I

went around the back of the house, and picked up the fake stone that held the spare.

Empty.

I went back around to the front, and put my ear to the door. I couldn't hear anyone moving around inside. Mum usually only locked it when she went out, and increasingly not even then. But the curtains were still drawn from last night so I couldn't be sure. Perhaps she was sleeping one off on the sofa.

I wriggled the door again to make sure it really was locked up, and not just caught. It refused to open. I stepped back and walked the perimeter to see if there was anything else open. The window to the bathroom was ajar, but when I tried to pull it open further I could see that the latch had been turned to the wrong side. It left enough of a gap to let some fresh air through, but there wasn't enough room for me to stick my fingers in and flick it open.

There was already a slight drizzle. If my luck held that would soon be a downpour. And we didn't have a veranda, or balcony. The art deco styling meant that there weren't even any eaves to shelter beneath.

The mist that formed on my clothing started to turn to droplets.

I tried to use the hairpin to open the lock, but I couldn't even get a feel for the tumblers, let along turn them. The rain was starting to come down more persistently now. Drops gathered in my wet fringe and then ran in tiny rivulets straight into my eyes. I wiped them clear with frustration.

I could throw a brick through the ranchslider. That would teach my mother to lock me out of the house. But then it would just mean cardboard over the glass, and an offer to every thief in the neighbourhood that it was open season at number fourteen.

I jiggled the front door again, pulling hard in anger, frustration and misery. It jolted and tipped on the long grooves of the fitting, and I could see that the lock mechanism was slightly ajar. I tried it again, sliding it

60

with force and exerting some downwards pressure to encourage it to slip more. I was rewarded with a wider gap.

Three more pulls and the tongue of the lock popped free.

I opened the door and looked around. No sign of mum so I pulled the curtains back to let in the grey sky shine in.

The spare key was on the lounge table, and I attached it to the clip on my backpack. Stupid idea to keep a spare where we could both access it. My stupid idea after a couple of incidents where my mother managed to lock herself out when she was the only one home. Not from this house. From another shabby state home. Well *she* could be the one who fended for herself from now on. You didn't need to teach me twice.

There was a sound from mum's bedroom that stopped me cold, and raised the hairs on the back of my neck. A howl, a moan, the unmistakeable sound of someone in pain.

I ran for her room and slammed against the door. It was locked as well. I pounded on it. Panic swarmed up my throat closing it shut. I had to exert my voicebox to get the sounds through. 'Mum! Mum, can you hear me? Are you okay?'

I pounded and tried to turn the handle but it bounced against the lock. My hand slid off, slick with the sudden sweat of fear. 'Mum! Can you hear me? Should I call an ambulance? I'm calling an ambulance.'

I ran back into the kitchen and reached for the phone when she came running up behind me. 'Get into you room right this instant, and close the damn door behind you!'

I stared at her. Relief lost to the ferocity of the anger I saw in her face.

'Get to your room. Now!' She slapped me across the face. The sting, the pain. And then she grabbed me by the shoulder and shook me. Pushed me towards the back corridor. Towards the stairs.

I looked over my shoulder at her in confusion as she headed back to her room. Then saw the man standing there with his hands on his hips. Naked. Erect.

I ran up to my room and slammed the door shut. As though that would erase the image from my mind.

***

'No, no, no,' Susie said as she grabbed the hairbrush from Melanie's hands. 'That's not the way. You have to backcomb it, otherwise it won't stay in place.'

Tracy sat and let them fight over administering her hairstyle. She didn't seem bothered either way. But then again she didn't seem bothered about much of anything.

Susie managed okay until it came to securing the twist in place. It held steady for about thirty seconds and then collapsed in slow motion. Now Tracy didn't have a hairstyle *and* had backcombed hair that stuck out like a white woman's afro.

'Guys, you can't leave her like that. She looks like a freak,' Vila said.

Tracy stuck her tongue out. 'Takes one to know one.'

'Here, let me try,' I said and grabbed the brush off Susie. When I was seven I'd dreamed of being a hairdresser and practised whenever mum was in the mood to let me.

I lightly brushed the outer layers, then twisted the rest into a knot, and secured it low on Tracy's head. It may not have been the complicated arrangement the other two had been aiming for, but at least she could go out in public.

'Now you look like a spinster,' Vila said with a laugh.

'What the hell's a spinster?' Tracy asked.

'An old woman who lives alone with a collection of cats,' I inserted. 'And no you don't. You just look a bit...'

'A bit...?' Melanie prompted, and Tracy raised her eyebrows.

'A bit like a middle-aged woman with only two cats.'

Tracy laughed again. Apparently unconcerned with how she looked. Something unique to her amongst female teenagers.

'Hey Daina,' Vila said and tapped my knee. 'We're up for maths next. Do you have your books sorted?'

I shook my head, and Susie looked over in confusion. 'What books? Did we need to bring something?'

Vila shook her head. 'Nah, she doesn't have any school stuff. Mr Nippon said he won't let her hand in any more homework until she gets the right equipment.'

Susie laughed. 'That sounds so rude: right equipment.'

She and Tracy mocked each other with pretend genitalia, and then Susie turned back to me. 'It's a pity it's not start of year. If you get a job as the stationery monitor you can nick loads of stuff and no one ever notices.'

'What do you mean?'

Susie shrugged. 'They have a stock of all the school equipment at the back of the music room. It's in the cupboard there, along with all the broken synthesizers and shit. They bring it out every January and have it all in one room so you can order everything you need from the school. They cream it in fees. The markup's nearly double what you can get it at The Warehouse.'

'Where everyone gets a bargain,' Melanie trilled in an odd moment of joy.

'Take this, anyhow,' Vila said, extending an exercise book. 'I can't help you with the calculator but seeing as how you're pretty much doing my homework you can at least share in my old offcasts.'

I took the book out of her hand. Vivid crossed through her name in pen. Half of the pages were missing.

'So generous,' scoffed Susie, leaning over to examine it in detail.

I felt a flash of anger, an emotion I didn't generally

allow myself. I was dressed in someone else's discarded blouse. St Vincent de Paul provided my backpack and my shoes. I had a rubber band tying my hair back. I couldn't afford a haircut, and I couldn't afford a frigging scrunchie because they only sold them in packs of twenty and I could at most afford one at a time. And now I was meant to be grateful because I had a discarded exercise book from someone who didn't even know how to add in their head. Grateful.

Vila nudged me in the ribs with her elbow. 'Sorry about the other day. I didn't mean to take it out on you.'

I nodded and looked at her. 'Your mother really didn't seem *that* bad.'

'Yeah, well. Sometimes what you see in a few minutes isn't what a person's really like.'

It could have been a barbed comment, but she softened it with another nudge in the ribs. And I got her point. My mother had once been the starlet of a dozen open days at primary school. She'd outshone every other mother there with her stunning hair and carefully applied makeup. She'd charmed and flattered every other parent in attendance until they hung on her every word.

And four hours later she'd be passed out cold while I'd be trying to work out how to feed myself. Hard to tell a lifetime of misery in a few short minutes. 'I'll trust you on that, then. Thanks for this.'

'Can't have you being kicked out of maths class,' Vila responded, standing as the bell went for class. 'I'm now fully reliant on you for any chance of passing.'

I laughed, but again I felt that firm flash of anger. I pushed it down and out and walked to class in step with Vila.

***

Once the coast was clear I slammed my locker door closed. One step towards the music class, and a man came in through the double doors. I turned back to my locker, trying not to look as though I was doing anything wrong.

An arm reached over my shoulder and I froze. I haven't even started to do something wrong, I wanted to protest. A helmet was lifted from the top of the lockers and the man walked back the way he'd come.

My heart was beating fast - thum, thum, thum – the sound prominent in my ears and the vibration visible in my chest. This was no good. I headed back to the exit from the prefab. This was stupid and pointless. I wasn't about to feel this bad just to get my hands on a calculator. I wasn't a thief.

My hand on the wired glass of the double doors I stopped. But what else was I going to do? If I couldn't turn in work during the year then my final results would be based solely on work already submitted. At different schools. With a total of eleven weeks missing already.

I had one chance to get away from this hellhole of an existence, and that was with a scholarship to university. That and a student loan, and I'd never have to live with my mother again. But they don't hand them out to dimwits. And they don't hand them out to students who stuff up entire years of schooling.

I could always beg and borrow to get the stupid plastic calculator. The one that had to have specific branding to be acceptable because otherwise the teacher might need to learn how to operate more than one. Or understand what it was they were passing on from the textbook. God forbid.

And if I succeeded at that, then I'd feel the same way I'd felt earlier today. Except double or triple and for a hell of a lot longer. If I wasn't allowed to just have something that was new and right, then I should take it. Better the guilty conscience than the burning anger. Eating away in me. I didn't want to die of cancer in my thirties because I spent my teen years seething with anger I wasn't allowed to express.

When I turned back around the corridor was still empty. I decided to take that as a sign and carry on carrying on.

There was a moment when I opened the music room when I thought that I'd walked in on a teacher. My mind spun through a half-dozen excuses, all of them lacking, and then realised that it was a music stand that someone had chucked a fabric cello case over.

There was a triphammer operating in my chest now. Knowing my luck with anything lately I'd pass out when I got my hand on the incriminating item, and then wake up in school prison.

But it was too late now. If I didn't get in and out soon the janitor would be heading around and locking it all up for the night. How the hell would I get out of that one, eh? I wouldn't.

I knelt down by the locked door, behind the piano, and quickly inserted the hairpin I'd been carrying since Ms Aiello's counselling session from hell.

The lock was almost identical. I wondered if the keys that staff held onto so dearly were actually just copies of each other, and could all be interchanged.

When I walked through the door I instantly saw the stack full of stationery. There was also a stack of sports clothing, branded with the school logo. I couldn't imagine having to pay for another uniform just so I could play a game. What a waste of money.

A pile of exercise books sat on top of a sealed cardboard box full of the same. I pushed and pulled a few boxes, and then found another cupboard with loose pens, staplers, rulers and – jackpot – scientific calculators. I pulled one out, and grabbed a slip of spare batteries to go with it, just in case.

It was when I turned to head back out that I heard a voice call out. I froze in place. I'd closed the door behind me but if anyone checked I'd be caught in the act. Ms Pearson would have a joyous celebration, but I'd be in the shit.

I scanned the tiny space. There was another door, which I presumed led to another classroom – the English room, if my spatial ability was up to par – but apart from that I was stuck.

I pushed a stack of boxes to my right, trying to make no noise at all and almost succeeding. It left a gap that I slid into and crouched down. I could just make out the door, and pulled my head back, tucking my legs and feet into the small space as best I could. I closed my eyes in case my not being able to see them stopped them being able to see me, and waited.

It was odd, but my heartbeat had slowed and quietened down. Maybe I'd gone so far into panic that it hadn't been able to keep up in the end, and was now just barely moving, like an overweight teen trying to make it through the last hundred metres of the 1k run.

There was no sound, followed by more no sound. I relaxed further back into my tiny trap, my spine becoming loose like jelly. Instead of the blackness behind my eyelids I could envisage my body as it changed into protozoa, into amoeba. Tiny and jelly. Jelly and tiny.

The door banged and my eyes flew open in surprise. Footsteps that sounded like thunderclaps. I pushed back against the wall as every part of body wanted to strain forward to peer around the corner and see. And be seen.

Shuffling. Closer, closer.

And then further away.

The door banged shut and I heard the lock turn. With the key inside it.

The relief of not being caught was short-lived. When I gathered the courage to walk to the door and peer into the keyhole I couldn't see light at the end of the tunnel. The key was still in there. How the hell was I meant to fidget it from the inside when it was blocked with the key? My limited lockpicking skills had only been born from necessity. They contained no finesse, no deep knowledge or dexterity.

If I'd felt sure that no one was on the other side I would have exploded, taken my frustrations out on the walls and the floor and the door. I would've pounded my fists raw and screamed my throat dry.

Instead I whimpered and began to cry.

The other door was the only possibility. I had no idea of whether the English room would be locked up: I didn't own a watch and my limited sense of time had been destroyed by anxiety.

I kneeled and pulled boxes away from the second door. With my eye to the lock I could make out daylight, but when I tried to work it the hairpin snapped from the effort.

I threw it on the floor with disgust and put my head in my hands.

When they found me tomorrow I would be in more trouble than I'd ever been in my life.

For so long I'd tried to hold everything together. Keep everything running as it had when I was smaller and my mother could still be depended upon to take care of things. But it had been crumbling, crumbling.

I didn't know what the hell I was doing anymore. I shouldn't have to. Now they'd find out that everything was a slapped together mashed-up lie, and my life would change.

It wouldn't be for the better.

My mother was no longer capable of looking after me. Hadn't been for a while. I'd now be in the type of trouble that would ensure I was taken away. Stored somewhere different. With the other broken kids.

And if I thought a spoiled teenage bully was a worry, it was nothing to what a truly fucked-up kid would be.

I was too high maintenance to live with CYF kids. Even at my low maintenance standards.

And then they'd try to place me in a home and I'd be left with some pervo who got his kicks off putting his hands down my pants - or her kicks. And then I'd be fucked. Literally.

I put the calculator into my backpack, and closed up the flap. There were some refills on the shelf in front of me, and some markers in the cupboard where I taken the calculator from. If I was in here for the long haul I may as well amuse myself. I could write a series of letters and put them in bottles. Leave the remnants of my current self and throw them out to the wind to let someone find in a day, a week, a month, a year. A lifetime.

I drew a picture of the home that formed my earliest childhood memory. The grass grew high around the steps leading to the front door, but at least the inside had been clean; spotless.

A bike that I'd been given to learn to ride on. Bright red paint that flaked off to reveal the hard crusting of orange rust. I'd fallen off a hundred times, brought home a hundred scraped knees, blood bright to match the paint. Bruises deep with crimson, purple, brown.

We'd moved so many times since then it was hard to keep track. The wooden house with the peeling white paint; the old red brick where I'd spent a day industriously poking out the crumbling grout until I was yelled at and dragged inside. They turned topsy-turvy in my head until they merged together into one old draggy house. Too old for decent folk. Too new to demolish. Just right.

And when I pulled the stapler off the shelf to seal my images and jottings away inside their own enveloped selves, a key dropped onto the floor. The key to the side door. The key to freedom.

Tears threatened again. This time in relief.

I packed up everything I could fit into my backpack, slung it over my shoulder, turned the key and walked into Mr Bond's English room. I'd been shut away for so long that shadows stretched across the floor. Soon the fireshow of sunset would begin.

The room was so dim that I almost missed seeing the figures standing on the other side of the glass panelled door. It was only movement that my eye caught. From the corner. My heart kicked into high gear again and I knelt behind the desk. This was all becoming too much. I just wanted to go home. Couldn't everyone just leave and let me go home?

I thought it would be the janitor, locking up for the

69

night. But then I caught the sound of a high voice, light and teasing, breathless. Michelle.

Mr Bond backed through the door, pulling her along with him. I crept further behind the desk, but they couldn't see me. They weren't looking.

He pushed her back against the door to close it shut again with them on the inside. He leaned into her and whispered something into her ear, wrapping a chunk of her hair around his hand and giving it a tug. She gave a long soft moan of pleasure.

There was no way this was right. When Susie had recounted her fantasy tales of what Michelle was up to with the English teacher, I thought they were just that. Spiteful gossip that no one should believe. But look at this. Look at this!

I peered around the side of the desk and did just that. For a moment I even wished I had a camera to record this moment for posterity. See how Michelle liked being the centrefold of the slideshow.

Mr Bond turned her now so his back was to the door; his hand still wrapped in her hair, using his other to pull apart her regulation white cotton blouse.

She laughed low in her chest, her throat open as she leaned her head back. Mr Bond laughed too, but even I caught the edge in it. There was something wrong here.

He gripped her hair tighter in his hand, curling it one turn closer in his fist. And then he slammed her back against the schooldesk nearest the door; bending her painfully back at the waist, pushing up her skirt.

Michelle gasped in pain as her pulled at her hair. Skirt up, panties down, he used it as a cruel throttle to flip her over on the desk so she was face down. He pushed her head down on the desk so she was pinned and then pulled down his fly, and pushed up against her.

There was a scream for help caught in my throat. Self-defence battled against self-respect, and by the time I knew which side should win it was over.

Mr Bond thrust inside her, looking down at his own erection as he forced himself into Michelle, still keeping her head flat against the desk, ignoring her small cries or perhaps motivated by them.

Once, twice. He pounded for a few more thrusts, and then groaned and leaned over her. He disentangled his hand from her hair. Pulled himself out of her and gave himself a quick wipe on her skirt.

'You're so good, baby,' he said as he pulled his fly back up and straightened his shirt, tucking in the side where it had pulled out. The only sign of disarray on him.

'Take a minute if you want. I can't have you walking out with me; we might be seen.'

He left the room while Michelle put herself back together again. I couldn't make myself known now. What would I say? Oh, I saw you and just thought I'd sit back and watch.

There were tears slipping down her face, but she wiped them clear and they stayed gone. Michelle pulled her pants back up, fixed her skirt, and started to button her blouse. Her fingers made hard work of the tiny pearl buttons, slipping again and again instead of finding the buttonhole.

But then it was done up. Michelle stood for a moment in place, staring at the schooldesk in front of her, then gave it a quick swipe with her sleeve. She turned and was gone.

I sat back against the desk, tucked out of sight for a few minutes more. And then I also left, taking care not to jostle my pack as I walked, then jogged, then ran. Trying to outrun what I'd just seen. Trying to outrun what I knew I would have to do now. Failing.

chapter five

Coroner's Court 2014

'I hadn't had much to do with Miss Harrow prior to that. I knew that Patty found her a nuisance, something to do with forms and signatures, but I considered that it was just an enrolment hitch. Not something I needed to keep an eye on.'

'So when did Miss Harrow first come to your attention?' the coroner inquires. He has straightened from the slouch he'd relaxed into as the day's proceedings trailed along. I'm sure Mr Fitzsimmons had that effect on a number of people during his lifetime. Military bearing with old-school propriety that resonated with men of a certain age.

'She asked for an appointment to see me. She didn't arrange it with Patty – sorry, I mean Ms Pearson – but had come straight through to me. Literally, I mean. She just barged right into my office one morning, as though I had an open door policy.'

He laughs to show how ridiculous the very notion is. I wonder how else he'd thought I'd get to see him. Wait for a year for his secretary to pass on a message?

'I told her to make an appointment. And when she just stood there I consulted my diary and made it for her. On the spot. As a favour, you understand?'

The coroner nods his head.

A favour. To me. As though an appointment with the School Principal was something that every teenage girl wanted, but few could aspire to. What a dick.

'So when she turned up I had no idea of what she wanted.'

Because you hadn't bothered to ask.

'And then she started spouting some...' He coughs into his hand and colours just a bit before he continues,

'...Sexual nonsense. About the English teacher, Mr Bond. I didn't believe her but,' he shrugs and holds his hands out, palms upward.

'Why?'

Mr Fitzsimmons turns in astonishment towards the coroner, who is looking at him intently. He may have straightened his pose, but he isn't bending to this man. Good for him.

'Well, because it was ridiculous, that's why.'

'What was the exact nature of the allegations?'

Mr Fitzsimmons shifts in his seat. He looks uncomfortable. He fingers the space between his tie and his collar, not pulling it out any – that would be gauche – but making sure that it exists. That he can draw air in without trouble, if he can catch his breath, that is.

'Well, I don't know that I can remember all the specifics...'

'You would have kept a record of this appointment though?' The coroner asks.

'No. There was no truth to any of it, of course we didn't keep a written record.'

The coroner leans back in his chair, and rubs the top of his nose with one hand, his eyes closed. 'A student made a formal appointment with you to discuss a sexual allegation against one of your teachers,' he sums up, and looks to Mr Fitzsimmons for confirmation.

'I wouldn't put it like that.'

'How *would* you put it?'

'Well, I wouldn't call it a formal appointment, for a start.'

'But you made the appointment yourself, with a pupil, because she wanted to speak to you urgently about a teacher and their inappropriate behaviour.'

'Well I didn't know that at the time I made the appointment, otherwise I...'

'Otherwise you would what?' The coroner seems to realise all at once that he is leaning forward in an aggressive stance, and pushes himself back in his chair. 'Sorry, I didn't mean to sound like I was attacking you.

Please explain what happened during the appointment, to the best of your recollection.'

Mr Fitzsimmons has lost his confidence. His voice sounds hesitant, questioning, as he continues with his story.

***

Daina 2004

I had my mouth open to blurt everything out when I realised for the first time that I didn't know what I should say. This was the only course of action that I'd been able to think of, outside of calling the cops and *that* was never going to happen. But I couldn't just let the whole thing go. If I waited I'd let my head rescript everything into a misunderstanding brought about by fear, brought about by indecision, brought about by my own aberrant behaviour.

I may have hated Michelle when she was treating me like shit, but even she didn't deserve what I'd witnessed. And there was no way that Mr Bond should have been allowed to get away with it. Not when there was a steady stream of adoring teenage girls flowing through his classroom. Not when there was every likelihood he'd done it before. And if the media hysteria about sexual abuse had taught me anything, it was that he'd do it again.

'I saw Mr Bond with a student,' I forced out. When I looked up at Mr Fitzsimmons I could see he had no idea where this was going. Damn. Why didn't we have a principal who'd been around the block a bit more? This guy wasn't even married. How on earth was I going to tell him without saying it all straight out? 'I saw Mr Bond having sex with a student in his classroom,' I stated.

Mr Fitzsimmons winced at the words, and his head was already shaking no before I had even finished my short sentence. 'I don't know what rumours you've been hearing, Miss... Miss.'

'Daina Harrow.'

'Miss Harrow. But there's no way that a teacher in this school had been having an inappropriate relationship with a pupil. You're mistaken.'

I stared at him in confusion. 'It's not a rumour. I saw Mr Bond having sex with a student. Last night. In the English room.' Mr Fitzsimmons continued to shake his head and I began to get angry. It made a welcome relief from feeling scared and awkward.

'It didn't look consensual,' I added. Then leaned forward to him to make sure he got the message. 'It looked like rape.'

The head shook no. A little waggle of denial. 'Miss Harrow. I'm not sure what is going on with you. Perhaps you've received a mark that you weren't happy with...'

'I'm not in here making an allegation of rape because I got marked down in a test,' I interrupted. 'I haven't *had* any tests in Mr Bond's classroom. He doesn't believe in them.'

That seemed to shock Mr Fitzsimmons more than any of my previous statements. 'Mr Bond is a fine teacher. We were lucky to have him sign up with our school. He has an excellent record and he's producing excellent results so far.'

I waited for some acknowledgement of my complaint, but the man just looked back at me as though he'd answered my question. 'This isn't about his teaching abilities,' I said, emphasis on each word. Just like you explain things to a retard. Which perhaps he was.

'Well, I don't know what this is about Miss Harrow, but you seem to have your wires crossed somewhere. You can't just walk in here and start making trouble just because you feel like it.'

'I don't feel like making trouble Mr Fitzsimmons. I came here because I'm scared and worried about a girl in my class who was raped last night by one of the teachers at *your school*. I thought you'd want to know about it before I called the police.'

He shot out of his chair and leaned over the desk at me. 'There's no need to threaten me with the police, Miss

75

Harrow. They won't appreciate you wasting their time any more than I do.'

All the frustrations of being a person without power in the world settled into me with a heavy weight. All the things I couldn't do. All the things I couldn't make people believe. 'You're the girl who left her class without permission last week,' he accused me.

'Yes.'

'And now you're in here making accusations about a teacher with no foundation and no evidence.'

As though there were any relation between the two events apart from me. I wished that I'd been able to go home and tell my mother what had happened and let her take care of it like any other teenager would be. Instead, I had to sit impotent in this stupid office with this stupid man and listen to his stupid mouth form stupid words that made stupid connections that meant nothing.

'There is evidence,' I stated back. 'There's a raped girl somewhere in this school, and I'm an eyewitness.'

Mr Fitzsimmons mouth pursed in as though he were sucking on a sour lolly. 'I meant evidence aside from your testimony. I think it's probably best that you go back to class. Is that what this is about?' he asked leaning forward.

'What?'

'Is this just a chance to get out of class? You've missed a lot of schoolwork already according to your transcripts. I think you'd better knuckle down and study hard if you want to make something of yourself.'

He sat back in his chair and looked out of the window, his back straight as a rod. 'I remember when I was about your age. I also wanted to lag about and wag school. There were children of my age who did exactly that. But I overcame those temptations. I studied hard and worked hard and now look at me! What do you want Miss Harrow? To be a layabout, and a beneficiary,' I could swear he was about to add *like your mother* but he settled for, 'Or be a contributing member of society?'

I swallowed and there seemed to be more bile than

spit in my throat. 'I understand that you've accomplished a lot, Mr Fitzsimmons,' I said, and tried to inject some respect and appreciation into my voice. It was so far from how I felt that I don't think I succeeded too well. 'It doesn't change the fact that there was a serious incident committed by one of your teachers yesterday, and as you're my guardian ad locum, not to mention Michelle's, I think you owe it to both of us to investigate.'

He picked up a pen that sat in front of him on his desk pad. It looked like an old-fashioned fountain pen, the sort that you had to pour ink into to refill, rather than just snapping in a cartridge. Given his other mannerisms, there was a good chance that it was. He focused on the side of it with intense scrutiny, and it wasn't until he laid it back down on the desk and it rolled to its side that I realised he'd been reading the inscription on the side.

'Very well,' he said, as he got to his feet and marched to his door. He pulled it open with so much force that I could feel the drift of air that rushed to fill the gap pull past my face. 'Ms Pearson,' he said. He wasn't shouting but there was something in his voice, the stern tone or the emphasis maybe, that carried the sound so well he may as well have been.

My second favourite person in the school appeared in the doorway. She saw me sitting there and had to fight with her facial muscles to keep the scowl away. I didn't bother. I was a teenager after all. I was meant to wear my displeasure with the world on my face.

'Yes, Mr Fitzsimmons?'

'Would you call Michelle...' He turned back to me. 'I'm sorry, what was the girl's surname?'

'Carrasco,' I replied and then frowned as I tried to think where I had heard that. 'I think,' I added to help.

He sighed, though not at the same volume as his previous command and turned back to Ms Pearson. 'Would you call Michelle Carrasco, if that is her name, to the office, please.'

Ms Pearson stared at me. Or glared at me more

accurately. I could've been in class right now. Working out some problems and getting a smile from the teacher when my answer was right. Getting a note from Vila with some sarcastic comment on it and struggling to hide my snigger. I could've wagged school altogether and wandered the streets trying hard to become the person that everyone expected me to be.

Instead I was sitting here trying to help someone who probably didn't want my help and fighting with someone who couldn't care less what happened in his school under his nose, as long as it didn't cost him any trouble.

'Do you really think it's appropriate to break into her class?' Ms Pearson asked.

I almost laughed when he responded, 'Of course I think it's appropriate, otherwise I wouldn't have asked. Do it now, please.'

He closed the door in her face, the rudeness of the gesture undoing the pleasantry he'd ended on.

'Thank you.'

'We'll see whether there's anything to thank me for, Miss Harrow. Don't think that if you've been telling lies as I suspect, that this will end well for you. You've already gone through one school this year, do you really want to jeopardise another?'

'I'd rather that than let this go without saying anything.' It was the truth if nothing else. Otherwise I wouldn't be here.

We faced each other down across the desk, waiting for Michelle to turn up and confirm someone's point of view.

When Ms Pearson knocked on the door and then entered I could see she was still smarting from Mr Fitzsimmons' behaviour. Her lips were pursed as she said, 'Michelle is here to see you.'

He nodded and said, 'Show her in,' as though Michelle wasn't already standing right there. In the doorway.

She scowled at me, but there was a small frown line

creasing her forehead. I wondered what she thought I was doing here. If she thought that I was trying to get my own back for her bullying. Whether I was making a complaint about her that she so richly deserved.

'Please take a seat Miss Carrasco.'

Michelle sat on the edge of the seat and stared straight ahead, not making eye-contact with him, but not looking away either.

'Miss Harrow has made some allegations against you,' he continued once Michelle had taken her seat. 'She alleges that there has been some sexual misconduct on your part.'

'No I did not!' I interrupted. I could feel the skin on my face heating up, the indignation made it harder to speak, and also made me want to cry. Was this whole thing hopeless?

I turned to look at Michelle, but she was glaring at me and so I turned back to Mr Fitzsimmons who was doing the same.

'I reported that I saw Mr Bond and you in the English room last night,' I said, my voice quiet. I looked down at the floor as the hopelessness of the situation swallowed me whole and drained my determination. 'I told Mr Fitzsimmons that it looked like you were being raped.'

There was silence for a long time. Mr Fitzsimmons cleared his throat, but then didn't follow up. My words echoed in my ears. A buzz started as the silence grew longer. Like the sound in your eardrums when loud music stops playing. I listened to the buzz and closed my eyes against the rest of it.

When I opened them again I saw that Mr Fitzsimmons was staring at the deskpad in front of him. I turned to Michelle and was astonished to see that she was crying. It was silent. The tears ran down her cheeks in a steady stream but she didn't make a noise. Until she sniffed. Long. Loud. She swiped the back of her hand across her face, gathering the tears up with her fingers and flicking the moisture off.

'That's a vicious lie. I've never had sex with anyone.'

'It wasn't an accusation Michelle,' I said as I turned fully towards her. 'I just didn't want to think that he would get away with it.'

'Get away with what?' she said and turned to face me. Equal. She was furious, and I felt my blood fizzle in fear.

'I...' but I couldn't follow it up.

'There's nothing to get away with, Mr Fitzsimmons,' Michelle said, turning her attention back to the principal. 'There has never been *anything* of a sexual nature between me and Mr Bond. He's a teacher for Christ's sake,' she said, and turned back to me. 'He must be three times my age and there's no way I would be stupid enough to meet up with an old man after school in an empty classroom. I don't know *why* Daina is making this stuff up about me,' she paused then, and rubbed her top lip with her forefinger.

She met Mr Fitzsimmons gaze again. 'Actually I do know why. I had a run-in with Daina a few weeks ago. I suppose this is her way of getting back at me. But this isn't true.'

She looked back at me, her eyes narrowed. 'I'm sorry that I teased you Daina. But this is no way to get back at me. Mr Bond is a teacher; he could get in a lot of trouble over your made-up stories. I think you should apologise.'

Mr Fitzsimmons leant forward on his desk, his hands crossed; fingers intertwined. The relief was written large upon his face.

'I think that's a good idea, actually. I didn't think it was true, but I have a duty to check Miss Carrasco, you understand. I'm sorry if I've embarrassed you or upset you in any way.'

Michelle nodded. A smile graciously accepting the apology.

'I saw you, Michelle. I saw him. It's not going to go away just because you wish it hadn't happened. What if you're pregnant?'

80

The smile dropped. Mr Fitzsimmons cleared his throat as if to speak again, but Michelle turned on me before he could open his mouth.

'There wasn't anything to see. It's all made up in your dirty little mind.' She looked at the principal again. 'I would never engage in anything like that Mr Fitzsimmons. I'm a virgin, you can test that, can't you? I've never, hmmm, *made love* with anyone and certainly not a teacher. I never would. I'm only fourteen years old, for goodness sake.'

I tried to protest again, but Mr Fitzsimmons leapt to his feet and waited while Michelle stood, then took her elbow to escort her out of the office, apologising all the way.

I sat frozen. The blood that had filled my face red pulsed in time with my heartbeat. My very fast heartbeat. I could see white lines in the same beat across my vision. A headache pulsed in my temples. I felt like a giant hand was squeezing my head in time. Thump, pump, bump. I felt sick.

'I think it's best that we contact your parents Miss Harrow. They'll need to know about this. We'll need them to come in and talk about appropriate disciplinary action.'

I gripped the arms of the chair tight; tighter. 'There's only my mother. She'll be at work right now.'

'We'll call her on all numbers we have available until we reach her. I don't think it's appropriate you go into class at the moment. It won't be fair to Miss Carrasco if you turn up in her class before we know how we're going to discipline you. There's a seat in the corridor where you can wait.'

'I really don't think you'll be able to get hold of my mother until...'

'That's not your concern at the moment, Miss Harrow. Please go outside and wait and let us worry about contacting your mother.'

He opened the door to shuffle me out, and crossed the corridor to Pearson's office with purposeful strides.

She would love this.

***

Ms Pearson 2004

Patty watched Daina sitting alone, waiting. She'd tried all of the numbers on file for her mother: there was one. Even repeated attempts. Patty was nothing if not thorough. But there was no answer. She didn't expect one. Fitz may sit in his office with his mind in the past and his head in the clouds, but anyone with a stick of sense could see that this girl was basically rudderless. Her mother was a wash-out. Patty would guess drink, but nowadays it could just as easily be P. Or H. That may be a stretch in the rest of New Zealand, but Christchurch and Greymouth retained their die-hard fans.

Patty had had a taste of it herself once. After her father died, her mother had started a new career drinking. Or new to Patty. Turned out it it was an interrupted career of her mother's. Interrupted by her marriage. Interrupted by Patty.

Her mother had spelt it out for her after the will was read and locked in. Patty had given her a lift home. She'd tried to be polite and not wince at her mother's breath, and had succeeded a bit. Waiting for a red light at the corner of Bealey and Papanui her mother had started an unexpected conversation by saying, 'I never wanted kids.'

Patty had just stared at the lights. She was a careful driver, but the announcement also hadn't been unexpected. Children grow up knowing these things.

'Your father wanted you. He talked me into it.'

The light had changed and Patty had turned into Papanui Road. It was a straight run through from there. The main road meant that the traffic flowed in stops and starts, but nothing to require much attention.

'So since he's dead now, I think that this should be the end of it.'

Patty had frowned. What had she missed? 'The end

of what?'

'Of us. Of me being your mother. I think we should just end it here.'

She'd turned to look at her mother. Her frown had deepened. 'End what here?'

Her mother had sighed deeply. An exhalation fraught with gin and coffee and mouldering foodstuffs. 'I won't contact you. You don't contact me.'

Patty was a good girl. She'd been raised to obey her elders. She'd been raised to obey her betters. She had dropped her mother off at the retirement village. She'd driven herself home. She'd cried that night. She sometimes still cried. There was no clear reason why.

Daina shifted her weight, and Patty wondered how long she would cry herself to sleep if her mother cut her off. The amount of running about and covering she must already have done for her.

Fitz stuck his head around the side of the door. 'Any luck yet? I don't want her sitting there all day.'

And yet that's what you told her to do, she didn't say. 'I haven't been able to reach her mother yet. I'll keep trying. What is it in relation to? Is it the bullying?' She may have been pushing her luck, but if you don't try you can't succeed.

'Some nonsense about Mr Bond. I don't know. Ridiculous. Make sure you contact her by the time I get back.'

Fitz went down to the staffroom to take his lunch. He thought it kept him in touch with the teachers, so they knew he was on their side. Instead it just made it easier to roster outside duties.

Patty walked outside, and motioned Daina over. 'I haven't been able to get hold of your mother yet. Do you want to come in the office for a minute?'

The set look on her face let Patty know that this request was far from welcome, but she followed anyway.

'Mr Fitzsimmons was just telling me that you were making a report about Mr Bond, is that right?'

Daina just stared back at her. Silent.

'Has he touched you inappropriately?'

A small crease flashed across Daina's brow, and then was gone.

Patty sighed, and smoothed her hair back. Everything was still in place. Just as it should be. It would never do to let her personal standards drop. Appearances were everything in her job. If she didn't look efficient, then pretty soon they'd bring in some smart software and she wouldn't be needed for anything at all. 'If Mr Bond has been inappropriate with you in any way, then I think you should tell me right now. If I call your mother and let Mr Fitzsimmons decide on a discipline then this is the last time that anyone will take a complaint from you seriously.'

Daina continued to stare at her. The deep study made Patty feel uncomfortable, but she met Daina's gaze. Inscrutable. That had been the one-word description on her standard four-report card. Inscrutable at ten years old. Let her look.

'It wasn't me. It was with Michelle, and she won't back up the complaint.'

'How do you know he did something wrong?'

'I saw him.'

Patty raised her eyebrows. And stared. Two could play the silent game.

'I saw him rape her.'

'But she says he didn't?'

Daina nodded.

And this was how cycles continued. The complainant wasn't believed, the molester was vindicated, the sexual assaults continued. A circle of pain and humiliation. But there wasn't any way to get off the merry-go-round once it started. No one could force Michelle to complain if she didn't want to.

'Your mother isn't answering the phone.'

Daina nodded.

'I have a number for your father on file.'

Daina looked startled, and Patty felt a grim satisfaction that she'd managed to get one over on her at last. 'Can I call him, or should I keep trying your mother?'

Daina shook her head from side to side. The slow movement was graceful. The girl had poise.

'Your mother's not going to come, and Mr Fitzsimmons isn't going to let you sit out there all day.'

Daina nodded. And then shrugged. 'Try him then. Even if you get an answer there he's not going to come.'

'You can go back out to the hall and wait.'

Daina left the office and sat down in the hallway again. She looked straight ahead, her hands folded softly in her lap.

Two weeks after Mr Bond had started at the school he'd backed Patty up against the file cabinets in the back room. He'd taken her nipple between his fingers and pinched, hard, scrutinising her face the whole time for a reaction.

It was hard to stop the cycle from happening if people wouldn't lay a complaint. But that wasn't Patty's problem. Right now she just had to contact a parent. She picked the phone up again and dialled.

***

Mr Harrow 2004

Graham slammed his arm out to stop his son flying forward as he also slammed on the brakes. It thumped heavily on the sides of the car seat and he shouted, 'Shit!' while he tried to manoeuvre the car to a stop.

Billy burst into tears, and Graham swore again. Under his breath this time. He didn't need a lecture from Emily when Billy started running around the home shouting 'Shit, shit, shit!' He was already getting cold stares because of a mishap with the grocery run. It was guaranteed to drop a few degrees if she found out he'd had to go to Daina's school to sort her out. Icicles would form if he had to bring Daina home with him.

Hard to sleep with an icicle, though god knows he'd still try at this point.

'Daddy, Daddy, Daddy,' Judy shouted from the backseat.

'What hon?'

'Daddy, Daddy, Daddy.'

Graham turned around to see that Judy had gotten free of her seat, and her belts, and was now trying to throw her leg over his seat back. 'No honey. Get back down. Sit down for Daddy.'

'Daddy! Daddy!' she responded, and tumbled forward, her leg caught on the elastic of the seat cover, her face striking the gear stick.

There was a moment where she went silent. She blinked. Once, twice. A line of red shone across her forehead where she'd hit. She blinked again. Then her face screwed up and tears sheeted down her cheeks.

'Daddy!' she wailed. 'Daddy!'

His arm was throbbing where he'd struck Billy's seat. He tried to encircle her small rigid frame with it, but she was at too awkward an angle for him to manage.

'Shit!' Billy shouted, and then burst into companionable tears. 'Shit!'

'Daddy! Daddy!'

Graham pulled the car to the side of the road, and looked with longing at the dead neon sign of the bar opposite.

He got out of the door, and closed it, the ten-second walk to Billy's side the only quiet of the day so far.

***

Ms Pearson 2004

Patty watched them arrive with interest. There was a small girl with an egg on her forehead pulling him forward. He was holding a boy on his hip. A boy who probably should've been on his own two feet, but had decided instead to let his father do the walking.

'Mr Harrow,' she called out when he looked lost.

He turned and followed her into her office. He didn't appear to notice his daughter sitting outside.

'Would you like to take a seat, sir? I'll just check and see if Mr Fitzsimmons is able to see you now.'

He slumped in his seat, catching the boy's leg between his hip and the chair. There was a wail, but only a half-hearted effort that soon cut off.

Patty knocked on Fitz's office door. There was a pause for a good thirty seconds, and then he said, 'Come in.'

'Daina's father's here for you. Should I show him in?'

Fitz nodded and stood. 'Please do.'

Patty went back to her office, and snatched the files the girl was tasting back off her. Mr Harrow's eyes were closed. His boy tugged on his tie, but he made no effort to stop him.

'Mr Harrow, it's just through here.'

He got to his feet and pulled the boy high on his hip again. Patty wondered for a second if she should offer to watch his kids while he was in the Principal's office, and then saw the girl reaching for her stapler with glee, and decided not.

He walked straight past Daina again with no acknowledgement. Patty studied her expression, but it was fixed. Still. Her relaxed gaze on the wall opposite her.

Patty nodded in appreciation. The girl had a good front.

***

Coroner's Court 2014

'Mr Harrow, I realise this must be a traumatic time for you.' My mother gave an audible snort from the front row, but the coroner gave her no acknowledgement. 'If you need to take a few minutes during your testimony just let me know, and I'll halt proceedings.'

My father nods. I could fully understand Mum's snort. He looks excited to be there, in a subdued way, but that is about it. I wonder if he'd be able to pick me out of a line-up at this stage.

'You looked after your daughter for a day shortly before she disappeared,' the coroner states. No one contradicts him.

Looked after – that's a good one.

'Could you tell us about that now?'

My father looks about the room instead. Trying to embed it in his memory, maybe. He crosses his legs, then thinks better of it and uncrosses them again. Then splays them. I wish I could still groan.

'Yes, I got a call from the school. It was unexpected. Daina and I hadn't had a lot of contact over the years, so I was surprised that they would still have me down as a guardian, but they weren't able to get hold of Rachael, so they came through to me.'

To give him credit he didn't seem to be rebuking mum for her failure. But given his lack of interest it was also entirely possible he didn't realise there was anything to rebuke.

'I was a full-time house husband at the time. I'd lost my job in telecommunications,' – a call centre – 'so my wife was out working full-time and I was staying at home and looking after my children.'

'From your second marriage?'

'Oh, Rachael and I were never married. It was never that sort of relationship. No, I've only been married once. And still am.

'So I was in charge of William – he's our youngest – and Judy – she's three years older. And they were pretty full-on I can tell you. William was still having trouble sleeping through, so I was up and down all night. And then I get this call out of the blue saying my *other* daughter's in trouble and needs help. I felt a bit like the gates of Hell had opened.'

He laughs. No one joins him. He doesn't notice.

Good on you, Dad.

'When I went to the school I couldn't work out what had happened. That guy there,' He nods towards Mr Fitzsimmons – I'm sure he was delighted to be referred to as "that guy" – 'He pulled me into his office and told me some long story about how he wound up as Principal of the school. Honestly, it took about an hour before anyone told me why I'd been dragged down there to begin with.'

'And what was the reason?'

'Oh, he,' my Dad nods his head towards Fitzsimmons again, 'said that Daina had been making some allegations against some girl or something. She was involved in some bullying as well, which I was surprised at, because Daina was always such a sweet wee thing. End shot was it was serious enough that they were suspending her from school for three days. He,' the nod again, 'also said if it happened again they'd exclude her.' He laughs all of a sudden, the noise unexpected. 'Told me I needed to sort out some counselling for her. As if I could just magic up some arrangement out of the blue. I looked at that for Billy a few years ago, and unless you're prepared to wait for six months then they expect you to pay for it. Like I could've afforded that!'

The coroner waits for a half-minute, but it appears Dad has just stopped his testimony. 'Would you be able to explain what happened then?'

Yeah, Dad. Concentrate.

'Oh, well, I was expected to take her home with me. Like looking after two kids under five wasn't enough to be dealing with. My wife would've gone mental. Not that I was leaving her out on the street or anything. She was quite happy that I just take her home – she said she had a key – and so I drove her round to Rachael's new place and left her there.'

'Did you talk to Rachael about what the school had said?'

'Well no. Not at the time. I had Billy and Judy with me, so I couldn't just wait around until Rachael got home. Daina said she'd inform her about everything, and I trusted she would. She's a good girl. And it was hardly like she was going to lie to her – a bit difficult to hide the fact that you're home from school for three days, isn't it?'

89

Not really.

'But you phoned her later to check?'

Dad shifts his weight, and shakes his head. 'It didn't occur to me at the time, and later I just thought it would all have been sorted anyway.'

Yeah, right. Later, like just now.

'And did the school contact you again?'

'What? No. No, that would always usually be handled by Rachael. I guess this was a once off and they went back to checking with her again.'

I thought how he looked that afternoon when he dropped me off and went back to his car. He'd come with me to the door, Billy hanging off one side, Judy clinging onto his hand on the other. There had been an expression of shock when I'd tried the door and it was locked. Relief when I'd produced a key and said Mum must be out.

He'd headed back to his car, shoulders higher now the burden of me was lifted. His duty was discharged. He didn't have to take me home, or have awkward conversations.

When he'd belted Billy into his car seat he'd ruffled his hair and kissed him on the cheek. More affection in a two-second period than I'd had in my life from him. And then he'd backed down the drive, attention on the road, attention on his other children, attention on the journey home.

I remembered waving to the car as it turned into the road. Dad hadn't even turned to look. Gone from his thoughts already.

***

There was a hefty knock on the door soon after four o'clock. I stiffened at the noise, then relaxed as I realised mum still wasn't home. I was expecting to see a salesperson, or a Mormon couple at the door. Even the dread thought of a debt collector flitted through my mind.

Vila was standing there instead. 'Heard you got booted out,' she said as she pushed her way inside. Susie stood behind her and waited until I nodded before coming in.

'It's only for a few days. They haven't excluded me or anything.'

'Why are you suspended anyway? We saw Michelle get called to the office, then she was back, and it wasn't till Susie had a word with Ms Pearson that we realised you were behind it.'

I turned to the kitchen, 'Do you want a drink of something?'

'No, I want to know what happened.'

'I'll have a glass of lemonade if you have it,' Susie said and came up behind me. 'Why d'you have all the curtains pulled?'

'You can open them if you like. Mum usually wakes up late so she doesn't want to see the sun much.'

'She work nights?'

Vila snorted. 'She's on the DPB. She doesn't work at all.'

'She's a nightowl,' I said with a bristle of annoyance. 'Always has been.'

There was some lemonade in the fridge, a mixer left behind. A supermarket brand. I poured out a glass and watched a few bubbles form with grim determination on the side of the glass.

'Here you go,' I handed it over. 'Vila?'

'I'm good thanks.'

She'd opened up all of the curtains, revealing the stained remnants of a dozen parties. There were cigarettes still ground into the carpet where an ashtray had overturned and people had kept on traipsing through, oblivious.

Vila wrinkled up her nose, but continued back through to the lounge and opened it up to let the sun reveal the extent of the damage in there as well. She brushed crumbs of god-knows-what from the couch and sat down with prissy precision.

Katherine Hayton

'So what happened? You know I'm not going until you tell me.'

Yeah, I had figured that. Oh well, safety in lying wasn't there. 'I told Mr Fitzsimmons about what you'd told me. About Michelle and Mr Bond.'

Susie spluttered and a mouthful of lemonade sprayed out of her nose. 'I told you that in confidence!'

'Don't worry, I didn't say that I'd heard it from anyone. I just said I'd seen it.'

'And what then?'

'Well, it doesn't look like Mr Bond came into any kind of trouble, does it?'

Susie frowned and put her glass down. 'Did they prove you hadn't seen something?'

'They asked Michelle to the office and she denied it.'

Susie still looked unhappy. 'I thought they'd have to do more than that. I mean, she's underage and stuff isn't she? Don't they have to report anything like that to the police just to be sure?'

That had been what I'd been expecting to happen. It was good to know that someone else was on my wavelength. Bad that it was nobody of any influence.

'Well, you just know how to make friends all over the place, don't you?' Vila said and stood back up. Susie looked surprised for a moment, but after a long look from Vila she got to her feet as well.

'We've got to be going, homework you know. I'll catch up with you when you're back in school.'

I nodded and showed them to the door.

Susie grabbed my upper arm and squeezed. 'You going to be okay?'

I nodded and tried to smile. It was the closest anyone had got to caring about me in a while, and I felt stupid tears trying to make an appearance. Self pity, mum'd call it.

Vila was almost to the footpath when she turned again. 'Oh, I forgot,' she yelled back to me. 'We're gonna have a small party in the park tomorrow. After school. Want to come?'

Friday. In the park. I tried to think if I had any other plans. 'Sounds good.'

'We'll pick you up around five. See you then.'

'See you.'

***

Coroner's Court 2014

Susie doesn't look as good as she should on the stand.

For some reason, maybe a lifetime of teasing, she's dyed her beautiful red hair mid-brown. It may stop the references to Gingas, but it does little for her appearance.

Her diminished height is emphasised with the weight she's gained. It's not much more than a stone over what she weighed in high school, but given her body's limited capacity to spread it out she looks like she's wearing a truck tyre's inner tube for a waistband.

She's still sweet though. She still looks concerned that she's doing everything right.

Her life really deserved to work out better than it has. A supermarket career doesn't have much room for elevated growth, but she's always been too kind to hand in her resignation and leave them in the lurch.

She reached the exalted heights of duty manager at eighteen, and there she's stayed. She should've gone to university; she was certainly bright enough, but I guess no one ever bothered to tell her that.

I certainly hadn't.

'You were involved in the incident in the park on the...' the coroner consults his notes before continuing, 'On Friday 14th November, is that right?'

Susie nods, and then leans forward to the microphone. 'Yes, that's right.' She looks like she's expecting to be arrested at any moment if she gets something wrong.

'Can you tell us what happened that night?'

Susie fidgets on the stand. She looks down into her lap where her hands are clenched together tight.

'We'd been invited to a party in the park. Just a get together, you know.'

The coroner nods in encouragement.

'When you're fourteen it's hard to go anywhere and do anything. They start charging you as an adult everywhere, but you don't get any of the other privileges. So we used to hang out in public spaces, restaurants.'

Susie had moved so far back in her chair that her voice stops being amplified at all. She leans forward again so her voice is caught by the sensors.

'Unless someone's parents were happy for a troupe of teenagers to invade their home we couldn't have a party. You don't get left alone at that age the same way the older kids do.'

The coroner nods again, a little more impatient this time.

'Anyway. Daina had been suspended from school for a few days. She'd missed out on the invite so we went around to her house to tell her.' Susie pauses and then adds another layer of truth. 'And to find out why she'd been suspended. No one told us anything at school.

'I thought it would be a nice night out.' She giggles at a memory. 'I wore some ridiculously high heels. I could barely walk in them. We met up at Vila's house beforehand to eat something before we went off to the park.'

Susie stops talking for a moment. She leans her head further forward, her hair covers her eyes like a curtain between her and the full benches she's facing.

'I thought it was going to be a nice night out. I didn't realise that Michelle had something planned.'

***

Daina 2004

Given a full day to contemplate what to wear I managed to work myself into a tizzy. My clothing options were limited, but as most of them were separates, I could combine and recombine them into an ever-growing number of inappropriate outfits.

My hair was midway between short and long, so that apart from a bejewelled hairclip there was little I could do. Unless I contemplated colour – and I didn't.

But what did you wear to the park? Was it a party? Was it a gathering? Would they be dressed up or dressed down.

Mum came home halfway during deliberations. 'School's over is it, love?'

'Teachers only day.'

She nodded and sloped off to her bedroom. At the door she turned back to me, 'I might have company tonight. Don't get in the way, right?'

'I'm going out.'

'Good. Make sure you remember your key. I'm not getting up in the middle of the night.'

'I will.'

'Wear your silk shirt. It'll look nice with that skirt.'

'I don't have a silk shirt.'

She disappeared into her bedroom then came back out holding a blouse in one hand and the portable iron in the other. 'You'll need to be careful with this, low setting. It's on the side.'

'Thanks.'

'Got a boy in mind?'

'Mum!'

She laughed and poked at my waist. 'Well, why else are you going out? Unless,' she paused and cupped her chin in one hand. 'You know if you're a lesbian it's okay to tell me, right? It won't make any difference to me. I love you unconditionally.'

'Nobody in that way. And I'm not.'

'Keep it in mind. Sometimes it takes a while to tell. And a bit of experience to know.'

She wandered away.

I ironed the blouse on the top of the table with a few teatowels under it for padding. It had never been mine. Mum must have been confused. The fabric had a sheen to it that caught the light and then threw it merrily

95

around the room; diffracted. When I put it on top of my old black jeans, with tears that had been placed at the knee and then genuinely worn through, it lifted them into elegance. It made accidental rips look like designer construction.

Even second-hand, or third-hand, it was nicer than anything else I owned. I went back upstairs and pulled a black cotton skirt with a crochet panel out of the wardrobe. It would be better still. Someone might even mistake me for a girl. Picking out an outfit ahead of time, *I* might even mistake myself for a girl.

'You look nice. You should dress up more often,' mum said as I walked into the kitchen later.

I rubbed the front of my right foot against the back of my left ankle. Mum gave me a short one-armed hug and then sat down at the table. A glass and a bottle were in front of her. Both half-full. Or half-empty.

'Where're you going?'

'Just to the park. Some sort of picnic, I think.'

'You be careful. Some weird people hang out in parks.'

I laughed. Some weird people hang out in our living room. 'I'll be careful.'

'Who're you going with?'

'Vila and Susie.'

She shook her head. 'I don't know any of your friends any more,' she said. 'You're growing up and away.' Her voice cracked on the last word, but she swallowed and smiled at me. 'I thought you'd stay little forever.'

I kissed the top of her head. 'No you didn't. You're one smart cookie.'

She laughed and squeezed my hand. 'Sure.'

There was a flurry of knocks on the door, and I pulled away and went over to open it.

'Be careful,' mum called out again, and I turned in surprise. I was going to the park. Not to a war zone.

I nodded and opened the door. Vila pulled me through and looked me up and down with a critical eye.

'You look nice. I've never seen you out of uniform.'

'You haven't really seen me out of school.'

Susie had on a pair of ridiculous shoes. High-heeled wedge patent leather sneakers. In white. She saw me looking and shrugged. 'I thought, what the hell. When else am I ever gonna wear them?'

'You're insane,' Vila said, laughing. 'We're going to the park, after. The park.'

'What do you mean after? I thought we were going there now.'

'Hell no. Girl's gotta eat first.'

I had a flash of worry. I didn't have any money to go somewhere to eat.

'Mum's put together a little assortment. She made me promise we'd eat at home first. She thinks we're going to the park to get blind drunk and she wants me to have a lining in my stomach first.'

'She thinks you're going to get drunk and she's still letting you go?' Susie asked, incredulous. 'My mum would lock me in my room if she thought that's what was going to happen. What about you, Daina?'

'I think she's only worried there are going to be boys there and I'll end up pregnant. Compared to that she'd probably welcome me drinking.'

'Carry on the family tradition.'

I laughed, but I had to bite back a retort. *I* didn't make fun of my mother, and I was the one who had to live with her and her bullshit. Damn if someone else should be able to make fun of her.

Susie gave her a slap in reprimand as well. Vila was acting more and more snotty with me, and it made me uneasy. If she didn't want me to hang around, then she didn't have to ask me. It wasn't fair to invite me places and then treat me like shit.

Half a street further and Susie started to hop on one foot then the other as she took her shoes off. 'They felt a lot more comfortable in the store.'

'You mean, when you were sitting down?' I asked. I grabbed her arm to steady her as she seemed about to topple.

'Something like that. Lucky I wore thick socks. Why do you live so far away Vila?'

'I don't live so far away. You and Daina live so far away. If you lived closer to me then we would be at my house by now.'

'Oh yeah. You make it sound so reasonable,' Susie retorted. 'But since Daina and I live close together I think you're in the wrong.'

'Are Tracy and Melanie coming?' I asked.

'They'll probably be sitting at my house making small talk with my mother the speed of you two. Race you.'

She shot off ahead. I looked at Susie's feet and then caught her eye. She shook her head and I nodded. We continued on at our leisurely pace.

'Vila's hyped up about something,' she said after a minute. 'She's been acting weird the last couple of weeks. Most of the time she's fine and then she'll go into full bitch mode.'

'I'd noticed.'

'I think there's something going on with her Dad, but she won't talk about it.'

'How'd you mean?'

'Something at his work. I think she's worried they may have to move. Like really move. To another city, maybe even country.'

'What does her dad do?'

'He's some sort of research doctor, or something. I don't really know. He depends on funding though, and if he can't get that here then he'll have to move on.'

'Shit. I've been moved around enough, but I've never had to go overseas or anything. Just stayed in Christchurch. That's hard enough.'

Susie nodded. 'I haven't even done that much. I'm still living in the house I was born in.'

'Home birth?'

She pushed me away, laughing. 'Shit, you know what I mean.'

'Imagine if she moves to a country where they don't speak English.'

Susie shuddered with theatrical exaggeration. 'She has a hard enough time understanding what goes on when everyone talks English. Can you imagine her trying to keep up in class if they were speaking another language?'

'Or she'd end up in one of those schools with all the army brats where they're from all over and the only thing in common is their language.'

She nodded, and then fell silent.

'Thanks for telling me though,' I said after another half block. 'I'd been thinking it was something to do with me.'

'Self-obsessed teenager,' Susie said rolling her eyes. I gave her another push, and then screamed as someone jumped out at us.

Vila shrieked with laughter and then grabbed us both around the necks. 'You two are so slow. I thought a bit of adrenalin would help matters.'

'Christ's sake Vila, we're almost there. Calm down will you. Nothing's gonna happen if we're a few minutes late to your damn *house*.'

'I wish I had a car.'

'You can't drive, can you?' I said. 'What good would a car do you?'

'If I couldn't use it to get places quicker, I could use it to knock down slowcoaches.'

She ran down the rest of the road to her house, and then leaned against the front door pillar looking pointedly at her watch. 'I told my mother we'd be here at five o'clock,' she yelled back to us. 'You know how I don't like to disappoint my mother.'

Susie burst into laughter at the lie, and then sat down on the footpath to put her shoes back on.

'Eww,' Vila called in horror. 'People walk on that Susie. It's bad enough you're a Ginga, don't be disgusting with it.'

Susie shot her the finger, and then stood with her

ridiculous shoes once again lifting her a good three inches off the ground.

'Let's go in and make your mother happy, then.'

***

'No more,' I said as Vila tried to give me another sausage roll. 'I couldn't fit another thing in.'

'No. You're far too skinny, you lucky bitch.'

'I don't know if it's my genes, or just that there's never any food in the cupboard,' I said. Since Susie had revealed what was going on in Vila's life I figured I may as well make it easy for her to make fun of me. I had nothing else to give her.

'You're about six feet tall, Daina. I don't think it's 'cause you've got nothing to eat.'

'Is that why you're wearing those shoes, Susie?' Tracy said as she looked at them, her face lit up with admiration, 'Trying to keep up.'

'I'm only five ten. There's not that much difference.'

'That depends on which end of that difference you're on.'

'Right, well if we're all finished then we should be going,' Vila announced. She'd been hovering by the doorway fetching and carrying, an odd choice for her. Now she tapped her toe to an unheard beat. A rapid beat.

'Ohhhh,' Susie groaned. 'How far away is it?'

'Five minutes,' Vila said, then checked Susie's shoes again, 'Ten minutes.'

'I don't think my socks are going to make it. Can't we just stay here? Keep you mum happy.'

'We're not a hotel Susie, catering for your every bloody whim.'

Susie raised her eyebrows at the harsh response.

'There's someone at the park I want to see,' Vila said, and shrugged her shoulders. 'Suit yourself, but I'm going.'

She headed off downstairs, and we lifted Susie and gave her support on either side while she tried to only step one in three. I hoped she didn't feel pressured by my height. It had never been mentioned before, and I'd only just started to feel relaxed about the situation myself as finally other girls had started to achieve the same height.

It was hard to know what was in someone else's head though. I couldn't read Susie's envy just like she couldn't read my awkwardness. Until the age of ten I'd felt like I was made up mostly of elbows and knees.

'Boy trouble, I bet,' Susie said as we made it to the bottom of the staircase. She shook me and Melanie off, and sat down to remove her shoes again. 'My sock's'll be ruined, but I don't think I'll make it otherwise.'

'I didn't think Vila had a boyfriend,' Melanie said.

'She doesn't,' Tracy answered. 'But I think I know who she'd like to have.'

'Tell, tell, tell,' I joined in the chant and we tugged at Tracy until Vila looked back over her shoulder to see what was happening. To avoid suspicion we all immediately fell silent.

'*Come on*. Do I have to drag you there myself?'

'Tell us later,' Melanie whispered, and ran to join Vila at the door. 'You couldn't drag me if you tried, love. You may be Samoan, but you're not a bloody rugby player.'

Vila swiped at the side of her head, but in play. She seemed to be relaxing now we were starting to move according to her timetable.

'Thanks for the food,' I called through to Vila's mother. She was standing in the kitchen looking down at the kitchen counter. She started, and turned and gave me a vague wave then resumed.

I wondered how awful it'd been for Vila in this household for the past couple of weeks. And, good friend that I was, I'd known nothing of it. I really should pay more attention to other people.

I ran to join my friends at the door, and Susie rolled her eyes at me as Vila complained loudly once again about how slow we all were. I took her shoes out of her hands – they weighed a ton – and rolled my eyes back at her as we set off, laughing.

***

There were some kids in the park already. There was one boy smoking near the poplar trees. He pinched the cigarette between two fingers, and his eye was in a long wink against the smoke. He inhaled, then exhaled with speed. He spat to one side, and then repeated.

A small gaggle of girls were kneeling in rapt attention in front of him. No matter how many health campaigns were run there was no changing the irrefutable fact that smoking was cool when you were a teenager. Not to mention the sign of someone who could lie successfully about their age, and had money to burn. Literally.

I saw Vila give a narrow look in their direction, and then she turned back to us and clapped her hands together. 'Where do you want to sit?'

Her voice was brittle and loud, and I wasn't surprised to see Tracy giving Melanie a subtle nod in the boy's direction.

'On the swingset,' Susie announced, 'I want to sit down.'

She picked her way through the loose bark and sat down with a sigh. Her shoes dropped to her side.

'That's better,' she said and swung her feet up so they weren't touching the ground.

I sat down on the short wooden wall that surrounded the playground area. It was too narrow and the rough wood started to insert its presence into the underside of my buttocks within a minute, but I stretched my legs to splay my weight a bit further and placed my hands on either side so I could lean on them and it felt a bit better.

The merry-go-round, with its flat disc surface and cold iron railings, was a popular spot, and as more kids drifted into the park its space was quickly filled. More took my example and perched awkwardly on the fence;

others stood and lurched above us like giants in comparison.

'Well, here's my contribution to the party,' Melanie said and pulled out a hip-flask of clear liquid. Vila's eyes lit up, and she pulled out one to match, pale golden in the twilight.

'What's in it?' Susie asked. I thought for a moment she was being incredibly naïve, but then Melanie listed the ingredients and I realised the need.

'Vodka, gin, tequila. I tried to get the little worm, but it always floats to the side of the bottle.'

'They'd notice that missing in any case,' Vila stated with authority, and there were nods of agreement. 'Mine's vodka, brandy and whisky.'

My mouth filled with rancid spit at the thought. I'd long given up harvesting the dregs of the various glasses left strewn around after one of mum's parties. The taste still lingered on in my imagination however, and my stomach lining.

The bottles were passed around in a tight circle. Tiny sips and attempts to hide grimaces of distaste behind forced smiles of enjoyment.

When it got to me I handed it straight back to Vila.

'Not fair, Harrow. We're all meant to have a drink.'

'Sounds lovely, Vila. But I'll pass this time.'

She handed the bottle back to me with a frown creasing its way down her forehead.

'No skipsies. Take a drink.'

I left her with her hand outstretched. 'No. I don't want one.' I kept my voice quiet, but there were still a few looks from around the park. Sideways under lashes, then snapping back into previous positions to hide the gesture.

Vila stepped close into my space, and leaned down. She pressed the bottle into the middle of my chest, but I was having none of it. 'Sod off, Vila. You've seen my mum; you know why I don't want one.'

'You're hardly gonna turn into an alkie overnight, Daina. You're spoiling the party.'

'I'm not the one ruining everything lately, Vila,' I said, my voice even lower. I tried not to notice the winces from the girls around me as the import of that one landed. 'If you don't want me to stay then you can ask me to leave, but I'm not having a drink just because you say I am.'

I wanted to jump to my feet for this stand-off. I felt the disadvantage of height at the wrong end of the scale for the first time in a long time, but to stand now would be to give in, and I wasn't about to go there either.

I'd had enough of bullies for the time being. I wasn't going to have it from my supposed friend.

Vila's teeth gritted together, the muscles at her jawline working, grinding. Then she stood back to her full height and shrugged her shoulders. 'Whatever. More for the rest of us.'

She took another swig of her horrible liquid, a big one, and blinked to hide the tears forced to her eyes from the burn in her throat. She smiled widely and passed the bottle to her right, to Melanie who took it from her and then awkwardly sipped at it, and then held it a moment longer. She still had her own bottle in her hand, and looked like the world's youngest tramp for a second in her torn jeans clutching handfuls of booze. Then she put her own down, working it into the bark so it wouldn't tip, and handed Vila's onto Susie.

'We've got all night to go,' she said as Susie stared uncertainly into the mixture. 'Take it slow if you want.'

Vila sat down on a swing. Her hands formed tight fists around the chain-links on each side.

I looked over at the boy who'd been smoking earlier and saw that he now had one of the girls from his fanbase up against the fence, and working his tongue hard inside her mouth. Revolting.

I stared at the bark in front of me, felt the imprint of the fence on my butt, started hoping that the evening would soon be over.

***

The tension started to leave our group as the alcohol took effect. It departed entirely when a group turned up with an old-style boom-box radio with gratuitously large speakers, and laid down a few beats.

Susie pulled me to my feet with the firm instruction 'You're the man,' and then started gyrating around me. I fulfilled my role as the man by dancing with awkward abandon.

Even Vila let me give her a twirl before the batteries started to run down and the party moved down a notch again. But the ice was broken, people formed and re-formed into little groups of gossip. I moved from one group to another. For the first time not self-conscious that I barely knew anybody, because I knew some, and that was enough.

Being teenagers, there were a lot of groupings which reduced down to just two and sank into the deepening pockets of shadows around the park; getting down to the true purpose of their evening.

And then a hand grabbed me out of the twilight, and someone pulled back my arms.

For a moment I laughed. Someone was playing a game. And then I realised I couldn't move. My arms were twisted up behind my back until my left shoulder started to scream. I tried to shake free. I tried to twist free. I tried to drop to my knees and out of the grip, but that caused more pain in my shoulder.

I lunged forward. Panic tapped a beat in my throat. Red bled into my vision. Pulsed in my eyeballs. Blue dripped through it like tears in blood. The ground swarmed into an army of green soldiers and marched away.

I screamed in fear, pain, panic. I could see the sound leaving my mouth, but it dropped flat on the ground in front of me. Dead and alone.

Michelle stood in front of me with a knife. The Cheshire cat grin was back. A metre wide. A mile wide.

I pushed back hard into my captor, and then tried to

lunge forward again. The arms continued to hold mine back. I couldn't free myself.

Michelle leaned in close to me, her breath stroked my cheek then darted needles into my flesh. Bright needles that imprinted on my eyeballs and turned into a dance of fire. They tasted like barbeque sauce and bitter almonds.

'I think you need to learn a lesson about privacy,' she whispered, and then grabbed my silk blouse, my mother's silk blouse, into a bunch in front of me, and slit it through with the knife.

For a moment I thought she'd cut me. Every physical sensation in my torso changed at once. But it was the cool night air hitting my exposed body.

The knife again and my bra was hanging from my shoulders, cut through the front. I could feel where she'd poked too far forward and the knife had pierced my skin and drawn blood.

A thump shook my eardrums with furious memory. My whole body stiffened. My mind went blank with terror. *Not that. No – not that again.*

No one else reacted. My clothing continued to be cut from my body. I tried to twist. What I'd thought was panic before was now all encompassing dread and fear. I screeched, a wordless morass of sounds that fled to all corners of the park and hid.

The forms around me twisted, turned, disembodied then embodied again. There was a flash of light, lightning, bolts of dazzling white that split my vision and rendered me blind.

And then I was pushed to the ground. The clothing that still fastened at wrist, at neck, at waist, was torn and cut away. I could feel something pulling me over. Flashes again.

I felt the thump this time. It ate into my body like cancer. My consciousness paled, and then disappeared altogether.

chapter six

Coroner's Court 2014

The sad little progression of people from my past stopped today as the pathologist took the stand. She's quite young. Compared to the many other adults in the courtroom she looks fresh. Still, she must be in her mid-thirties at least.

'Mrs Harrow, as you've already received the information that this witness will present to the court, you may be excused if you want. I understand this could be painful for you to hear in detail.'

My mother furrows her brow and sets her lip. Her head is shaking even as she stands up in the courtroom.

The coroner must have expected that she was about to take his invitation and leave. Instead she announces, 'I've never received any of this information.'

There's a noticeable pause in the room, and then the coroner makes a swipe motion to a clerk at the back.

'We'll take a break here then, for a few minutes. We'll reconvene at two-thirty.'

There is a hum of low whispers in the room, and the coroner makes his way round to where my mother still stands.

He talks to her in quiet tones, and then she follows him out of the room.

Somebody's in trouble my mind sings, delighted. This is far more interesting than the entertainment on offer so far.

It is less than ten minutes and then everyone is back in the room. The coroner looks flustered. It's weird, as he still remains completely calm and in control, but something has thrown him for a loop. There he'd been, all polite and stuff, and police incompetence now means he has a grieving mother in his courtroom hearing every detail of her daughter's death for the first time.

Nice one, guys. A sterling job.

My mother is made of strong stuff but I doubt this is going to be easy. In the room the coroner'd pulled her into he'd offered her the chance to go through the materials on her own. That way she could learn about them at the same time as the court room, but in a private setting where she could express her grief freely.

My mother declined.

I understand her decision. If someone's going over the nitty-gritty of your daughter's death, and there's the chance to ask questions, you take that over a private room with some official documentation. To do anything else would be to do a poor job, and mother never was one for half-measures. If a question didn't get asked here, it would stick in the back of her head for the rest of her life. Along with the knowledge that she could've asked it, if only she'd been brave.

The coroner opens proceedings again.

'I was called to the scene by Detective Senior Sergeant Erik Smith of the Papanui Police Station. They had found the remains of a body at a building site in Redwood. I arrived at the scene just after ten o'clock.'

'Could you explain what your role is?'

'I'm a forensic pathologist. My role is to perform post-mortems on patients who have died unexpectedly, or in unknown circumstances. My findings can be used to determine whether a case is criminal in nature, and if so provide evidence to the court.'

'And what were your findings in this case?'

'When I arrived on scene, I recognised that the deceased had been in the position she was found for a long time. Her clothing had rotted from her body. The natural fibres were completely gone. Some remnants of man-made fabrics remained.

'Most of the flesh had decomposed to an advanced state. Many of the bones of the deceased's limbs were clearly visible. She was lying on a plastic binder full of files, and there was a vial inside the bones of her right hand.'

'Inside?'

'I think she had been holding it, or had her hand placed on it when she died,' she said, her hand curling around an invisible object. 'There were no apparent signs of injury, but there was so little flesh left that it would've had to be an obvious trauma to show. I examined the area around her, and determined that she had died at the scene.'

'What evidence led to that determination?'

'There was evidence of bodily fluids in the wider area surrounding the body from samples taken from the scene. There was also physical evidence...' She trails off and looks nervously at the coroner. He glances at my mother, who is staring at a fixed point in the middle of the room, her features still and set. He turns back to the witness and nods.

'There were signs showing that she'd attempted to escape from the area under the house. There were scratches and dents which appear to have been made by the deceased prior to her death.'

'And what was the cause of death?'

'Judging from the evidence that the deceased was alive at the time she became trapped in the area underneath the house, and the lack of any other results from our toxicology and tissue samples, I determined that the most likely cause of death was by terminal hypohydration,' she glanced sideways at the room, 'Sorry, that's dehydration. It would've led to organ failure and death.'

'Are there other possibilities?'

She nods. 'Due to the advanced state of decay, I'm unable to find a confirmed cause. There may well have been soft tissue injuries, for example, in the decedent which we have lost the chance to determine. There's no evidence from the post mortem of any significant trauma affecting bone structure, there was no residue to indicate excessive blood loss at the scene. The form of her body as found also leads me to the conclusion that it's unlikely the deceased suffered from extreme bodily injury at the time of death.'

The coroner nods, and pauses for a moment. He turns back to the room, his gaze lingering on my mother before passing over the remaining attendees.

She's still staring straight ahead, her eyes fixed on an invisible point. A dampening at the side of her right eye gathers enough moisture to form a tear that rolls down the side of her nose and then trembles on her upper lip. She licks it away, and swallows, her jaw clenched, the muscles forming tight little lumps on either side.

'You mentioned that Daina was found with documents and a vial of some type. Would you be able to tell us some more about those?'

Her eyes widen in surprise and she shakes her head. 'I didn't examine them at the scene as they weren't relevant to the post mortem. I suppose they are held in police custody.'

The coroner nods and announces a recess.

My mother continues to sit still as the court empties. Once the last of the attendees had gone, and it is only her and one clerk, tidying up the room, she puts her face into her hands. She is silent, but her shoulders shake, and after a few moments she has to pull a tissue out of her bag.

Watch her now. Watch closely. She's crying over the death of her little girl.

Would've been nice if she'd spared me a second thought while I was alive.

***

Daina 2004
I tried to roll over in bed. I had a thumping headache and it felt like my shoulder was three times larger than normal. Three times larger, and three times hotter. For some reason my bed was hard and cold. Hard, and cold.

I've fallen out of bed. I felt around me for the trailing edge of a blanket to pull down. I felt too sore to try to get back up. I must be getting a fever I felt so cold. Coming down with the flu, I hope Mummy looks after me, I don't feel well at all.

There wasn't any blanket within reach. I'd have to move, but I dreaded it. My head was pounding so much it seemed like my skull must have shrunk, and my brain would soon be spilling out my ears. Maybe that was why my left one was blocked. Blocked and dribbling something onto the ground. *Onto the ground?*

My head jerked up. But the clanging that erupted inside it as a result left me breathless, and I rested it back down on the ground.

I was naked. I could feel the cold night air sweeping across my body; across the swatches of bare skin that should always be covered in public.

My eyes wouldn't open first time. They were gummed shut and felt as though they extended a full foot in front of my face. That would stop me running into anything now, wouldn't it?

I touched my right forefinger against the side of my right eye and swiped it with care across the lashes. I presumed the gloop I could feel was blood and I tried to open my eye again. It worked, a little. I used my forefinger to pry my eye open, and then stroked across the left and did the same. My vision still pulsed with colour. I closed my eyes. The colours remained but went dancing around the screen inside my head. I opened them again and the colours continued, then faded away.

There was the sound of traffic from a road somewhere. With only one ear working I couldn't place the direction. I could pick out another sound as well. Like a slap, then a grunt. Then nothing. Then a moan.

Was there someone else there? Someone else hurt? I tried to move again. I kept my head low and rolled onto my stomach. My shoulder and head swelled with pain again, but this time I stayed still, in place, and waited for it to subside. I heard the snick of a buckle behind me; the

111

small rasp of a shirt being tucked into jeans. The pain receded and I moved again, hitching my body up to my knees, paused again, and then to my feet.

Pinpoints of light spotted my vision, but I could make out where I was with the light from the growing moon above. The play area was in front of me, empty. I turned, careful to make the motion as slow and smooth as I could.

There was motion in the corner of my eye and I jerked around, triggering a light flash and further pain. When the lightshow subsided, I saw a man standing next to a park bench.

Fear crept down my body; raising hairs on my head, my arms, my stomach, my legs.

'You okay?' the figure asked.

I recognised the voice, and in the relief I felt like crying.

'Paul? Is that you?'

'Yeah. They all left. I left too, but then I thought I'd better see that you were okay. You were out cold.'

'Thanks,' I said and realised again that I was naked. I tried to hide my breasts with one hand, my bush with the other.

'You can borrow my jacket if you like. To walk back home.'

'That'd be great,' I said and moved towards him. He didn't take his jacket off, just continued to stand there, looking at me. Some of my fear returned. 'Thanks Paul, can I take it now?'

Paul swept one foot in front of him, leaving a line of concrete exposed under the bark. 'It's really expensive,' he said. 'It's real leather. I'll never be able to afford another one.'

The relief tried to come back, but I wouldn't let it. 'I'll give it straight back to you after, Paul. You know I will. Or, you could walk me home and I'll give it to you when we get there.'

He nodded, his face hidden under a lock of his long, scruffy brown hair. 'Yeah, I could do that.' Instead of moving to take the jacket off he swept his toe through the bark to expose another line of concrete. 'The thing is...'

His voice shrilled upwards on the last word and he shut his mouth, tight. Vila and I'd mocked his breaking voice a few weeks back. It seemed innocent enough fun.

'What's the problem?'

If I hadn't been exposed I would leave, now. My fear levels were climbing again, and I looked down at my feet and swallowed hard to keep control. There were scraps of my mother's blouse still encircling my wrists. The small pearl buttons that held the cuffs together were still fastened in place. The fabric above them gone. Cut. Torn.

I was still wearing my socks and shoes.

'The thing is, I think you owe me something, you know. For the jacket. I came back to check on you...' he gestured vaguely around the park so I could see the monstrosities his kindness had saved me from. The trees. The empty park. The darkness.

My fear climbed a notch into horror.

'They kicked you in the head when you were unconscious, you know. I wanted to make sure you were safe. I was the only one who cared.'

'I can pay you, if you want. If you take me home you can have all the money I...' I broke off as he reached out and tugged at my arm. The arm crossed in front of my breasts.

'You don't need to pay me. But, you know, you've been lying out here all night naked. I think you know what that does.'

Horror into cold terror.

'Don't worry about it Paul. I'll just wait here for a while then make my own way home. Thanks for looking out for me, but I'll be right now.'

'No, no. Don't be like that. You don't have to do that,' He tugged at my arm again.

There was a hot buzz in my head. My left ear cleared all at once, and I could hear the sounds of the night in full stereo.

And like a light the terror flicked into resignation. I

could barely stand. I was naked except for scraps and the victim's war-paint of my own blood. I was injured, maybe badly, and I was in no fit state to fight or negotiate my way out of here. If I didn't submit he would hurt me. Or worse.

I lay back down. My head protested with a low pulse, and my shoulder squealed two octaves higher in harmony.

With me eyes closed I felt his weight on me, and stared at the colours that danced on the inside of my eyelids. Where the swelling was bad the colours were more vibrant. They flowed into each other and glowed into merging shades. Doughnuts of light pink swallowed up with bubbles of deep violet then glaring into white.

With so much pain in my body already I didn't think it would compete, but when he thrust his way in there was a knife to my insides, and then raw irritation like a wet finger being rubbed on a scraped knee.

And then he got to his feet. I thought for a minute that he would go and I would be left all alone again in a worse state.

Instead he pulled his trousers further down and stepped out of them. 'Here,' he said and gave them to me. His boxers were almost knee length and either deep blue or black. They looked like shorts.

I stood up and stepped into his trousers. The legs were short by a few inches but I could get the waistband closed. He handed me his jacket, and started to walk away.

He was at the edge of the park when he turned back. 'I'll get that back from you Monday,' he said. And then he jogged along the footpath in overlapping ovals of street-lamp light until I couldn't see him any longer.

***

I walked to the safety of people. The lights of Northlands Mall with its surrounding pubs, clubs and restaurants provided me with a feeling of safety. There was a double bench not far from the main entrance, the seats back to back, which was in the shadows enough to feel hidden, but exposed enough to feel safe. I sat on the side that faced the small garden rather than the street.

In Paul's jacket pocket was a small plastic envelope of service station napkins. I tore the packet open, pulled one out, and used it to wipe some of the blood from the side of my head. It was soaked through in seconds and I pulled another one free.

If I could clean my face then it didn't matter about the rest of my injuries. People couldn't see them. I could get inside, into the safety of a mall bathroom and take proper stock of myself. But not if my face was dripping with blood.

I licked the tough tissue and rubbed it over my entire face this time. There was more blood, unexpected, from my eye. The eyebrow had split. An image popped into my head of Michelle drawing back her dainty foot and smashing it into my unconscious face and I felt a wave of pure hatred.

I'd only been trying to help.

I touched the side of my head. Even a light prodding caused enough pain that it made me want to vomit. I tried to arrange my hair so that it would cover some of my injuries, but it was tangled and matt with blood and dirt. I wanted to cry. But I couldn't. That would hurt too much.

A man sat behind me on the bench, and I flinched away to the very corner of mine. *What the hell?* Did he not notice me here in the shadows, or was that the reason why he'd chosen this seat?

'It's Daina, isn't it?' he said, and I turned to examine him with caution.

He hadn't turned in my direction. He'd spoken while staring out at the road. He was grey. Everything about him. His sports jacket, his trousers, his tie, his complexion. Grey. 'You've been hurt. You need to get help.'

I gaped at him for a moment, then turned and faced

back into the garden. Two could play at this game. 'I'm okay, I just need to get cleaned up.'

'You're not okay.'

I stared at the scrappy lavender and stubby tussocks that made up the garden. It was based in bark, just like the park playground. My mind shied away from the comparison. 'I can look after myself. I just need to get cleaned up.'

My fear had dissipated. I didn't know why. I was stranded alone in a strange place after being attacked talking to a strange man who could be there to do me more harm and seemed to know far more about me than I knew about him which put me at a disadvantage. But I felt safe.

'We both know that you need to do more than get cleaned up.' He paused, and then spoke again, his voice deeper and rougher as though the words were hard to get out. 'You need to contact a rape clinic. You need to get real help.'

I thought of protesting again, but I couldn't. I didn't want to meet any more people tonight. I definitely didn't want anyone to poke or prod me in areas that had already had far more contact than I'd ever wanted. But I did need help. 'Can you take me?'

'No Daina. I'm sorry, but I can't be seen in public with you. And you can't tell anyone about me. You can go to a phone booth from here. There's one just down the street, you passed it while you were walking here. They have a phone book and you'll be able to call the clinic from there. They'll pick you up or tell you what to do.'

I crossed my arms over my chest and leaned forward even though it hurt my head. The need to become smaller was greater than the pain.

'Why are you helping me? What do you want?'

There was a long silence. He shifted his weight on the bench and for a moment I thought he was going to go, to leave, to walk away. But he didn't. 'I need you to do something for us.'

I curled my legs up onto the bench so that I was

almost in a ball. It felt safer. I wanted to ask who "us" was, but I didn't want to know the answer. So instead I asked, 'What do you need me to do?'

'You need to get some information from Vila's dad. I'll give you details later when you're in a better state.'

I tried to put this into some sort of context but my brain wasn't functioning to its full standard, or it didn't make sense at all.

'Oh,' he said, and turned to look at me for the first time. 'Don't eat anything they give you, okay? They've been lacing your food with salvia, that's why you've been hallucinating. They're friends of Michelle, not yours.'

The pain from that betrayal hit me harder than anything I'd experience so far. I hadn't even had time to wonder why my friends hadn't stayed behind to help me. Hadn't wondered why they left me naked in a public park where anything could happen. Where anything did happen. *They're friends of Michelle.* So I had no one.

'You need to keep up the pretence for the time being. Otherwise we won't have an in with Vila. I know it'll be hard, but I think you're strong enough to do it.'

Strong. No, I wasn't strong. I was weak and tired and battered. 'Why are you talking to me? Why did you choose me? Why me?' The last a plaintive cry. I didn't want any more. I was filled up to overflowing.

'Oh Daina,' he stood up from the bench and turned back to the street. 'You know why.'

He walked away.

***

Daina 1994

The picnic spot was empty. Her mother had told her it would be nice and sunny and a good place for their lunch and a bit of a play and she was right. There was dense forest surrounding them; the lush bush that grew when showered well with heavy West Coast rain, but today it was warm and sunny.

There was a lake which swished against a pebble

beach. The stones were warm, but they hurt Daina's feet. Still, she suffered the pain just like the Little Mermaid to get to what she wanted.

Her mother had told her not to go in the water. She was never allowed to go in water if she was alone. Even the tub was out of bounds unless her mum ran it for her and then listened out from the next room. There'd been a brother once. The water had killed him. Daina didn't remember him but she had pictures of him holding her when she was a little baby so sometimes she imagined him and had him act out scenes in her head and pretended they were memories.

Daina sidled up to the edge of the water. She almost overbalanced as she also turned her head to check that her mum wasn't about to swoop down on her with loudness and guilt, but she must still be in the car. She'd been drinking; not the raspberry cordial that was Daina's favourite treat but which her mum didn't let her have too often because it was "loaded with sugar" but a clear drink which made her smell, and made her sleepy.

The water was clear right near the edge, but further out the wind picked up little wavelets so that it was a shiny blue-grey instead. But here, here at the water's edge, she could see the smooth pebbles right through the water. They looked bigger and smoother than the ones she stood on. Softer than the ones she stood on.

She stuck a bare toe into the water, just the tip. That wasn't really going in the water now, was it? It wasn't really disobeying.

The water was cold. The opposite of the sun which was hot and dry. The water was cold and wet.

Daina held her arms out to each side to keep her balance. She almost never fell over these days, she wasn't a baby, but sometimes gravity pulled on her in unexpected ways and she would fall and feel stupid and clumsy. If she did that in the water her mum would think she'd disobeyed her and she hadn't. She really hadn't.

She put her whole foot in to see if the stones in the water were smoother to stand on than the stones on the beach. At first, they were. The cold of the water ran around her foot and calmed the sole so it felt bigger and lighter. But after a minute she could feel the round unforgiving hardness of the pebbles start to dent their way into the sole of her foot again.

Maybe if she put both feet in? After all, she was leaning on her foot in the water; that could make it seem like it was still sore. If she put her other foot down next to it maybe it would be better.

Daina pulled her dry foot level and dipped it down slowly, slowly into the water. The cold on her foot was as delicious as the heat on her head. She put her hands on her head to feel where the warmth of the sun had turned it hot, hot.

Delicious.

The thump was loud. Loud. Daina pulled back from the water, guilt flooding her little frame, and overbalanced. She fell, her bottom hitting hard on the stones of the beach.

She scrambled to her knees. Her whole body was adrenalin. She'd done something wrong, something forbidden, and she was about to pay the price.

But her mother wasn't in sight.

Daina stood upright. Her bottom was in the shock stage of pain. She knew it was coming, but it hadn't quite organised its troops to deliver the full attack yet.

The thump would swim through her dreams, her nightmares, for a decade to come. It would echo in the back of her mind every time that something went wrong, and every time she would feel the flush of guilt, of being caught out.

But that was all in the future. For now, there was just the silent gap where a large noise had been.

Daina climbed up the short bank that led down to the lake and ran back to the car. She could tell her mum was still asleep from a distance, her snores were a reassuring low rumble, but she still checked on her. Just

119

in case. Her mum was lying on her back on the front seat, her mouth open. Her tongue was whitening, so she must have been that way for a while. Daina didn't want to wake her, wasn't even sure that she could. Sometimes her mum was reassuringly alive, the sounds she produced confirmed it, but she wouldn't respond even when Daina pushed and pulled her. And even if she did she would be cross.

She turned and looked out across the expanse of the picnic area. It had seemed small and lovely when they first arrived, but now that she was alert and cautious it seemed larger; there were more places for trouble to hide.

There was no memory of the direction of the sound, so Daina headed off towards the edge of the forest on her right, the inevitable draw of the right-handed. There was nothing there but the wooden bench and table – one unit – that they'd eaten at earlier.

As she walked the perimeter and found nothing Daina relaxed. It was nothing. She crossed the lakeside, walking on the grass of the bank this time rather than the stones of the beach, and everything was as it had been earlier. No monsters hiding anywhere.

The smell went from hot midday sun, baking grass and warming water, to a stench that was even worse than the time Daina had stood in dog-poop and trodden it into the carpet in the front room.

Her stomach recoiled, and her mouth filled with saliva that she swallowed once, twice, the internal liquid quelling the worst of her gag reflex. Daina started to breathe through her mouth, and turned to look at the car. But her mum wouldn't appreciate being woken, wouldn't understand that something bad had happened while she was out cold.

For a moment Daina was torn; she almost ran back to the car anyway, the comforts of a cross mother a welcome known factor instead of the creeping dread in her stomach. But she was a big girl now. She was in kindergarten and next year she'd be starting real

120

school. She didn't have to hold her mum's hand at the supermarket any more – although sometimes she still liked to – so she'd go and look at the source of this horrible smell by herself.

And if it was fun and interesting she'd tell her mum about it later when she woke up naturally, and she might earn a soft caress of her mum's hand on her head, or maybe even a kiss.

A hug and a kiss!

Daina pinched her nostrils shut with her forefinger and thumb and walked into the first line of the forest. She wouldn't go in too far – you could get lost and never, ever find your way out again – but that was the direction of the smell.

As soon as she pushed her way between the second bush and tree she could see where something had come down. Something had fallen from the sky. There was a gap in the trees where some branches used to block out the sun, and the ferns were crumbled and crushed.

Daina jumped over some low bushes and nearly slid over. Even at this far edge the forest retained enough moisture to have a film of moss over the leafy debris that littered the ground. For a second she pulled her hand away from her face to help balance. Her nostrils held shut for a moment, glued together with a thin film of drying mucus, then they pulled opened and the stench assaulted her once more.

She did wretch this time, and clamped her nostrils shut again to try to stop the reaction. Lunch had been thick slices of ham between springy white bread – a treat that made her wish her mother didn't know that brown bread was healthier – along with her cordial and an orange for dessert. She didn't want to lose that to the forest floor. That was her picnic, her day out with her mum, and she was keeping it.

When her stomach settled she moved forward again. Daina no longer wanted to see the source for that smell. She no longer wanted anything but to go back or forward in time to a place that was nice and

121

safe and this was never begun or over.

But she kept going forward because she also had to know. Curiosity And she wanted to know if she should still be scared. Her muscles were knotted and her neck was starting to hurt. She didn't want to stay like that forever.

An object had punched down through the trees, punched down through the ferns, punched down even into the leaf strewn ground. When Daina crept forward enough to see what it was she almost breathed a sigh of relief. And then looked again.

It was a man.

A man lying on the ground.

Daina looked back to see if she could still see the edge of the picnic area. It was already dim in the forest even though she'd barely come in any real distance, but she could see through the forest to where the sun was still shining. Still in view.

She pulled the tall ferns back to get a better look.

It was a man, but there was something wrong. Something wrong with the shape of his head. It was wide and flat. Like a squashed peach.

He was dressed in a shirt and trousers, but the cloth had torn apart in the middle. Where the flap of his shirt should tuck neatly into the waistband of his trousers a morass of thick magenta and brown worms were tangled together. There was a splattering of deep maroon radiating out from there, Daina could see a sticky wet drop of the colour on the fern right by her face. She didn't need to take her hand away to know that was the source of the stench. That was the source of the evil scent that was still coming into her body with every breath, no matter how tight she pinched her nose.

One of the trouser legs had split. It was easy for Daina to see why. The man's thigh was nearly twice the width of the trouser. It wasn't just the cloth that had torn. Daina stared in horror at the beige-yellow fat that showed through where the man's skin had burst like a rotted fruit. Burst like when you squeeze a tomato in *your hand.*

The vomit came up. Her stomach contents emptied in one regurgitation, fighting to get out of her body. Daina took a step back. She wretched again but there was nothing but thick bile which she spat onto the leafy ground even though it wasn't ladylike. Daina didn't feel ladylike. She may never feel ladylike again.

It was the thump that made her turn and run. Her head replayed it, pitch perfect, as though it were happening again right that second. The first perfect recall of sound. It wouldn't be the last.

Daina heard it, felt it, and the thin film of fascination that had held her in place burst wide open and the panic spilled out.

She turned and ran. Fell on the slippery leaves. Scrambled on her knees until she gained purchase to stand. Ran again. Ran out into the bright light. Blinding white light.

She fell to her knees again. On the clean grass. Grass that had never witnessed the horror that lay just metres to its side. Grass that she lay on, put her face on; rubbed her cheek on. Clean grass.

And when she heard the small click, heard the man clear his throat, saw his shadow fall over her. When she looked up to see the small circular barrel of a gun only centimetres from her face, it was clean grass that her bladder emptied itself on. Her mind spinning away, out of control, fleeing the scene like a drunk driver fleeing the scene of an accident.

part two – spy

chapter seven

Daina 2004

The clinic picked me up. I stayed next to the phone box until they did. Every time I heard approaching footsteps I hid around the other side, moving from one wall to another as the footsteps progressed past, then back into the safety of the box itself.

My heart was beating faster and faster. The pain pulsed in my head and my shoulder, and at one stage I had to crouch down when the world took on a greyish tinge.

When the van parked next to me on the street I thought I would faint. My brain was tearing itself apart – of course it was the clinic, they'd said they were coming – of course it's not the clinic, it's a trick to hurt you more.

'Daina,' a woman's voice called out softly. The tearing feeling became worse, not better, but I forced myself to walk out of my telecommunications cocoon and respond. Not because I wanted to, any more than I'd wanted to call them in the first place. Because the Grey Man had told me to, as if this course of action should be obvious to anyone, and I didn't want to disappoint him or appear stupid.

Mary drove me to the clinic. There was soft jazz on her car radio, and apart from checking that I was okay for the moment, and glancing at me every two minutes, she drove on without engaging me.

I leant my head against the window. The cooling night air had made the glass chilly and it felt soothing against my swollen face.

'This is us,' Mary said, as the vehicle came to a stop. Her voice was low and soft. I wondered if she spoke like that naturally, or if she put it on so that I wouldn't be startled. She came around my side and opened the door for me. I stepped down and followed her inside.

The clinic wasn't anything like one. There were soft sofas and cheerful paintings, quiet areas for private chats. I'd been expecting rows of hard wooden seats and a receptionist encased in a glass and concrete booth.

There was no escaping the examination table, the feet together and let your knees drop exposure. Careful coaxing didn't stop my face burning, my eyes tearing, my throat lumping.

I lay on my side on the table afterwards. My eye had been examined and cleaned and there was a butterfly plaster holding the raw edges of my split eyebrow together. It was late, I was tired but also wired. Tonight didn't feel conducive to sleep.

There was some cajoling to report the events. I kept insisting that the assault wasn't related to the rape; the rape hadn't been me screaming, 'No.' At one point I explained that since I had accepted the terms it probably didn't even count as rape and I was wasting everybody's time. I had exchanged sex for clothing. An even trade.

It was the only time that there was an edge of anger to the voices in the clinic. Emphatic denial that any trade existed, that coercion was rape, that fear of being hurt was assault, that threat of assault to force capitulation was rape. There must be ease in knowing you're right.

A large part of me wanted to give in and report this to the police. I wanted to please the people who had so painstakingly helped me for no return. Who had given me the tools to make sure I wasn't pregnant, wasn't bleeding, wasn't infected.

It wasn't the arduousness of a prosecution that put me off, but the thought of the Grey Man who'd helped me, that stopped me short of saying yes. I let their arguments run dry, and let them bundle me home with warmth, safety, and caring.

But I didn't let them report it. And I didn't let them know my real name. And I didn't let them drop me off home, instead going around the back of a distant neighbour's house and knocking at a window so they'd turn a light on. Made it look like I'd walked in through the back door and made it inside.

When I heard the van drive away I scurried around to the roadside again and ran the short journey home. The motion jolted my aches and pains but I needed to get inside to the safety of my room more than I needed a pain-free existence.

I didn't disturb my mother as per her request. I went straight upstairs and got into my narrow bed fully clothed. Paul's clothing was in a supermarket bag. The clinic staff had whisked it off me and given me a t-shirt and jeans in exchange.

So much thought put into how I would feel. I felt the flush of shame again that I hadn't fallen in with their suggestions. It competed with the flush of shame that I'd caused such a fuss over nothing. Over having consensual sex with a boy in a park. Despite their protestations it wasn't so.

The door opened and let someone out of our house. Mum's visitor was gone.

I curled onto my right side and moved the pillow so a cool area touched against my swollen eye. My mind raced through a cache of images. Flicking through, not stopping. Each image as raw as the last.

When the front door opened again I jumped in surprise, and my whole body went rigid. Footsteps moved, a low hum of voices, and then my mother's door closed. Another visitor or the same? Surely the same.

As I fell into the sweet release of sleep my mind drew distant images together to form a new picture. A complete picture.

My mother's prostituting herself.

Sleep.

***

Saturday morning, I stayed in bed. Late in the afternoon I got into the bathtub, and had to force myself out over an hour later when the water had turned pink.

I'd scrubbed at my skin so hard for so long that little beads of blood dotted its surface.

Sunday, my mother caught me in the kitchen and exclaimed over the bruises on my face.

'I fell over in the park,' I explained away. 'Hit my face on the end of the see-saw.'

There were random caresses, a vague offer of arnica – never realised – and then my mother drifted off to her bedroom to sleep.

Monday passed by in a blur of dread for the following day. And then Tuesday dawned, and I had to go back to school.

Before I was halfway along the front gate – not even *inside* the school grounds – I knew that something was wrong. There were fingers pointing, a shrill of giggles from behind me, a nudge in the ribs before me.

And I had no option but to brazen it out. As my Grey Man had told me, my friends weren't my friends, but my enemies were still my enemies.

Based on past behaviour I even had a pretty good idea of what I was about to see when I entered the corridor to my home room and saw gaggles of teenagers staring at the walls.

I wanted desperately to be an adult. To have the capability right then and there to say no, and just walk away. Pack up and go like my mother had packed up and fled a dozen, two dozen bad situations, money-owing furnishings repossessed situations. Take what you want and leave.

Maybe if I'd sat down with her on Friday, Saturday, Sunday, Monday, I could've talked it through and she might have pulled me out without a second thought. Maybe. Or she could've glazed over, stroked my hair back from my forehead, and let every word I was trying to tell her fall into the black hole that replaced her memory every time she was a few hours from sobriety.

I ground my teeth together and walked on through. If I could get to class and sit down I should be fine. I could gather myself and wait for everyone to arrive and paste some semblance of a smile on my face to recognise that a joke had been played on me. Or I could start weeping and not stop.

Michelle stood snidely by the side of the English room door. Blocking my path. I turned to go back outside, I'd rather wait out there than stand near her, but a few of her friends blocked my exit; trapping me in.

There were A4 printouts of naked me Sellotaped to the walls and locker doors. I couldn't look directly at them, but my peripherals were bad enough. The whole corridor had fallen into silence, broken only by shuffling feet and low whispers.

My spirit was breaking. My body sagged as though it were a physical thing departing, no longer propping me upright, a virtual spine packing up to go.

'Everybody out!' a voice shouted from the head of the corridor. I turned and saw Ms Pearson striding down the halls looking ten feet tall and breathing fire. She clapped her hands together. 'Michelle, Daina, you stay. Everybody else get out right now. Not that way, boy,' She grabbed Michael by the collar and turned him neatly the other way, 'The door's locked. Go out the front.'

She pulled level with us and eyed down a few strays that hovered as though they might be left out of the roll-call. When one didn't move quick enough for her liking, 'Miranda, you can leave now or you'll be in detention tonight and you won't be coming out until the end of term.' Miranda scuttled down the hallway. She dropped a textbook on the floor, glanced at Ms Pearson, and decided to leave it in lieu of getting the hell out.

The door closed and only we three still remained.

Ms Pearson walked to the entrance doors and locked them shut. She strode back to us both.

'Michelle, take those photos down,' she ordered.

'I'm not the one who put them up Miss,' Michelle replied looking like butter wouldn't melt.

'Michelle, there is not a word that comes out of your mouth that I believe. Get those photos down now.' She popped her hands on her hips and gave Michelle such a glare that after a moment she complied.

Ms Pearson turned her attention to me. I could feel a list of excuses as to why it was nothing to do with me popping straight to my lips, but before I could say anything she whispered, 'Are you okay?'

There was concern in her voice. Genuine concern. A tear rolled down my face in response, I couldn't talk. I shook my head, and she placed a hand, gentle and soft, on the side of my face and wiped it away with her thumb.

'I'll get you somewhere safe in a moment,' she said, and then turned her attention back to Michelle.

'Don't drop them on the floor, Michelle. You spent time and effort putting these pieces of degradation together; treat them with some care.'

Michelle turned with her lip curled up into a snarl. 'I didn't put these up, I didn't put them together, and I'm not taking them down.' She threw the one in her hand to the floor and crossed her arms.

'You will take them down, you did put them up, and you'll get a move on, girl. I'm not unlocking these doors until they're all removed, and if Mr Fitzsimmons has to come down here to investigate why, you're probably going to be on your last day at this school. And good luck getting a placement elsewhere with this on your record.'

'You can't exclude me without proof.'

'Girl, if you think that I can't find a dozen witnesses to turn you in, you're out of your barking mind. Why the hell do you think I'm down here? Because I had a psychic flash? Your "mates" have started to dob you in already, and it'll only take one assembly to get the whole sorry pack to cough.'

For the first time Michelle's composure slipped, and she looked unsure.

'As it is, I've already reported this incident to the police. I don't know if you're bright enough to realise or not, Michelle, but we're not talking about a prank here. We're talking about assault. Sexual assault, maybe. How'd you like to explain your way out of a lesbian sexual assault, Michelle, would you like *that* on your record?'

I just stood and stared at the woman. She knew how to give a tongue-lashing. Then the words *Police Assault* processed their way through my shocked brain. I couldn't have the police involved.

'Ms Pearson I...'

She cut me off with her hand, then folded her arms again and continued to stare down Michelle each time she dared to try to stop doing as ordered. The walls and doors were soon bare, and Michelle gripped a pile of photos I hoped never to see again.

'Are there any others?'

Michelle just stood mute, her head hanging down.

'Look at me when I talk to you, girl! Are there any others? Have you posted these pictures anywhere else in the school? Are there any other nasty little surprises that you need to clean up before you go home?'

Michelle didn't look at her, but she did shake her head convincingly to the other questions. When Ms Pearson pulled the photos out of her hand Michelle took a sudden step back, her eyes wide.

'Go home, Michelle. The school will be in contact with your parents in due course. Until then I don't want to see you here, do you understand?'

At the mention of her parents Michelle looked terrified. That look reminded me that she was really no different from me. Over the days from Friday she'd grown into a monster in my imagination, occupying more and more space. Now she was back down to size.

She picked her bag up from her locker and walked to the end of the hall. Ms Pearson let her go, continuing to stand there and stare. Michelle reached the door and couldn't exit. It was locked. She'd forgotten.

I walked down the hall towards her, and it wasn't till I moved that Ms Pearson started to as well. She unlocked the door, letting Michelle escape to freedom and parental dread, and then she escorted me through to her office, away from the curious stares.

When she sat down I leaned forward. 'I can't have

the police involved, Ms Pearson. Thanks for your help and everything but I...'

Once again she cut me off with her hand. 'I haven't called the police. I can, if you want me to, but Michelle is quite right. We don't have proof that she's behind any of this. And if you're not going to make a statement, then it'll die a natural death anyway.'

My eyes closed in relief. I sat back in my chair.

'She'll be expelled though. You can rest assured on that one.'

I kept my eyes closed. 'But you just said you don't have any proof.'

'I can manufacture evidence for a school board that I can't do for the police. That girl's not coming back here, not into *my* school. Even if it gets me fired.' She sat back in her own chair and stared levelly at me. The bell rang outside.

'You'd better get to homeroom. There'll be enough talk without you skipping class as well.'

I nodded and headed off. Confused. Grateful.

chapter eight

Coroner's Court 2014

The coroner is calling a halt to all proceedings for the day. When Ms Pearson steps away from the bench she looks half-dazed. As though she's truly gone back in time, and is struggling to return.

People shuffle out, no one talking, no one together. Disparate souls brought into a group for one purpose only, and disconnecting as that purpose was tucked away for the day, ready to be picked up again tomorrow.

My mother moves slow, looks old, but her tread is light. She doesn't have a drag in her heel as she had done when she was drinking; her speed isn't slowed as she positions each foot carefully to avoid a stumble, her balance swooping away.

The room is empty.

I look around the evacuated space. The coroner's court had become a community centre hall once more. All airs of authority gone.

There are footfalls on the steps outside and someone ventures along the corridor. *A cleaner?* As the steps grew closer I pick up on the gait and know who's approaching.

The Grey Man enters the room, walks to the front bench, and takes a seat opposite the coroner's. His head held high, his eyes staring straight ahead.

'Hey Daina,' he says. His voice is low but not quiet. It carries throughout the room, echoes off the high ceiling. I could imagine its vibrations, almost see them waving through the air. 'You've been missing for a while.'

True. So true. I'd been missing for a while. Not as long as I would be missing of course. I was going to be missing for the rest of everyone's lives, and their progeny's lives, and theirs, and theirs. There were millennia yet to go when I would be missing, will be missing, would be missing, was missing. Eons.

'I never meant for things to turn out this way, I hope you know that.' He pauses, and then picks up again, his voice a low growl. 'I'm sorry that I led you into trouble. I couldn't foresee any of this happening.'

He shifts his weight on the hard bench, and then stands. He twists his grey hat between his grey hands, and I can see where his knuckles are deformed from arthritis. Odd that I'd never seen that before. Everything else about him was the same. The pressure he exerts on his hat must cause him a great deal of pain. But he still exerts it. 'I thought you were ready for this. I thought you'd be grown up enough to handle it.'

Because everyone knows fourteen year-old girls are mature beyond their years, right?

'I thought that if anything went wrong I'd be able to step in and help. I'm so sorry.'

He turns, a neat spin on his back foot that's almost a dance move. Grace executed. He slides his finger down the crease in his hat and then gently places it on his head. Tipped at an angle, of course.

His footsteps echo out from the floorboards as he walks from the room.

***

Daina 2004

Michelle didn't come back to school. We waited for a few weeks, expecting always to see her face back in homeroom, or hear from a teacher, or on the school grapevine, but no rumours came to fruition, and then all talk of her subsided altogether.

She wasn't expelled. Or excluded, as they were starting to call it for some reason. I know that Ms Pearson threatened her with it, but *that* much we definitely would pick up on the grapevine. We were teenagers, not shut-ins.

The longer the time passed from the events of the

party-in-the-park night, and the lower the expectation that Michelle would return, bent on yet another form of revenge, the easier it was for me to settle back into a rhythm.

At first, the idea of continuing a friendship with Vila, Susie, Tracy and Mel seemed like it would be too much of an ask. It would be bad enough if they straight up didn't like me and let me know, but to keep up the pretence of friendship all the while in league with the enemy was too much of a betrayal.

But I forced the feeling down, and continued on. Just the same as I forced the suffocation and bile down when Paul passed me by in the corridor and gave my arm a friendly squeeze as if nothing had happened. As if we were just friends passing by.

Forced the feelings down, and hope that one day – soon - they would go away altogether.

The rape clinic had given me the morning after pill on site, and they'd also taken blood and smears for testing. I called them back within a week for the first results, and was informed that if anything changed in the intervening six months they'd contact me.

I took protection from my "friends" as well. I didn't take any food from them that wasn't professionally sealed, and I never shared food or drink once I'd opened it. Mum's shopping habits didn't change, liquid first, food second, so I went hungry a lot of the time, but that was preferable. At times when my stomach growled with emptiness it even started to feel good, to feel clean. I didn't want anything to ever be in my body again except the things that I put there. Control. That was what I took back. Control.

And the main impetus to do any of this was the Grey Man. That was the name my mind insisted on calling him, and in lieu of a formal introduction that was going to stay. His calm delivery of what I should do, and what I should avoid, and hints at something – something important – coming, were the memories that propelled me out of bed the day after Michelle's art gallery showing, and the day after that, and the day after that.

I had only met the man once, and that at my lowest ebb, but it felt important that I be ready to follow his instructions. I wanted to please him. Like he was my Dad and I wanted to make him proud. If that was what this feeling was. I certainly didn't have any actual experience to draw on for that comparison.

I turned another year older. My birthday passed without recognition in my household, or out. I couldn't bring myself to tell people at school, and I couldn't be bothered to remind my mother. She'd only forget again. She was getting worse and worse at keeping track of anything.

I sloped home from school in a minor sulk, and that was when the Grey Man fell into step beside me. He handed me a parcel.

'What's this?'

'Open it and see.'

I shook the packet instead. There was a soft rattle inside it, like sticks wrapped in cotton banging against each other.

'Or, you could just shake it until it breaks,' he added.

He kept his gaze fixed on the footpath ahead of him. There was no avert moves to show that he was paying any sort of attention to his surroundings, but when my foot caught from looking at him instead of the ground, his arm shot out to steady me.

'What's it for?' I asked, still leaving it unopened.

'Birthday. It is your birthday, isn't it?'

I don't know that it improved matters that a stranger knew this, but my nearest and dearest didn't.

I slid my forefinger under the corner of the brown paper that wrapped it. Brown paper. This guy didn't understand the art of wrapping; I had paper still folded neatly with accompanying bows from artful presents bestowed upon me in past years. For a while the idea of Christmas presents was synonymous with unwrapping them with care so the paper and decorations could be used again next year. The package had to be good; the present was usually from the $2 shop and lacking.

'You can just tear it, you know. I won't be offended.'

I tore the paper back, and revealed a Warehouse gift card and three test tubes nestled in cotton wool in a windowed cardboard box.

'Um, thanks,' I managed. The glass tubes looked like the ones we'd used in science experiments at school, not that we did experiments often. Every time we fired up a Bunsen burner the teacher, Mr Cooley, looked like he was about to have an anxiety attack. 'I'm sure I'll put them to good use.'

'The gift card is for your birthday. The other is for a little job I need your help with.'

I flicked the gift card over – there was an amount of $50 scrawled on the inside of the envelope. 'Thanks!'

'Well, it's not every day you turn fifteen, is it?'

I could get some new clothing. Maybe even some shoes. Maybe buy a new calculator and replace the one I'd stolen so I didn't have it in the back of my head. Maybe that was the magic act that would release the terrible run of events since then.

Lists started to form in my head until the Grey Man went, 'Ahem,' and I remembered there was something else.

'What do you want me to do?'

'That friend of yours, Vila.'

'She's not my friend,' I said. I thought my tone would emerge as anger, I'd been trying to convince myself that was what I felt. Instead my voice came out sad.

He gave me a squeeze on the shoulder. 'I know. I'm sorry. But if you can stand to be around her for a week or so longer, that may not matter.'

'Why?'

He stayed silent, and I put the gift card into my back pocket, and stowed the test tubes in my backpack before slinging it back over one shoulder. He still hadn't answered. 'Why?' I tried again. 'Is it because of her father?'

'How much do you know about him?'

I shrugged and tried to think back over the first weeks of friendship. Before the park. 'I've only met him once, but Susie said he does something in medical research. At least I think that's what she said.'

'Anything else?'

I shook my head. 'I didn't spend any time with him. Her mother is around a lot, but not her dad.'

'Well, you may need to try. I want you to be in the house at the same time he is. There's something I'll need you to get if you can, but you'll need to be in contact with him before you can even try.'

'What do you want me to get?'

It was his turn to shake his head. 'First things first. Get into the house at the same time he is. Take notice, of everything. I'll be in touch.'

And he was gone.

***

I didn't want to phone Vila. True, I'd been hanging around with her at school as though nothing was the matter, but meeting her alone without distraction was a different story. I wasn't good on the phone at the best of times, not being able to see the person I was talking to was hard for me. Disembodied voices freaked me out.

So I decided to just drop by that evening. After all, what was the worst that she could do? Turn me away? So what. I could come back home where I wanted to be, and still be able to say I'd tried.

But when I knocked on the door it wasn't Vila who opened it, it was her mother.

I could hear Vila. She seemed to be intent on yelling something to the entire world. But she was doing it from another room. Her own, by the direction of it.

'Daina, how nice to see you,' her mother exclaimed and pulled me through the door. Her eyes were swollen and her cheeks were flushed. Another screaming match with her daughter.

I tried to backpedal – if Vila saw me now she would be *pissed*, but I was pulled further forward instead.

'Vila. Vila come down. Your friend is here.'

The scream from above cut off. I smiled at Vila's mother, and she gestured toward a seat and then walked off into the kitchen.

Well, this wasn't awkward at all.

Instead of sitting down, I walked to the base of the stairs. I couldn't hear Vila moving down to greet me. Maybe I should give her a few minutes to get herself sorted.

I turned in the opposite direction to the kitchen and walked out of the lounge. There was a corridor with two doors branching off. One looked to be a laundry, the other an office.

My heart started to beat faster as I moved closer to the office. Don't be stupid, I chided myself. They left you alone down here. You're just filling in time.

The Grey Man had told me that I knew why he'd picked me. I didn't, and now I wondered if he'd mistaken me for someone else. Someone brave, someone who wasn't a complete screw-up, someone who would be able to force themselves to turn the corner into a room.

I forced myself to turn the corner.

The room was empty of people, but there was a shuffle of papers covering the desk. There was a briefcase also. I walked closer on tiptoes that felt like they were made of glass, and tested the latch nearest me to see if it would pop up. It did.

My heart was now a triphammer in my chest. I could see pulses in my vision from the force of the bloodflow. I felt sick.

I popped open the second latch and pulled the case wide open.

There were more papers, a latched box. A stain leaked from one of the fabric envelopes sewn into the top.

Footsteps sounded in the corridor outside. I pulled

the lid closed, the snap as the latches refastened sounding as loud as a starter's pistol. A man popped his head around the door just as I stepped back from the desk and turned toward the photo on the wall.

'Ah, hello?'

I jumped. It was half-feigned, half a welcome release of tension.

'Hi Mr Fa'amoe, I was just waiting for Vila to come downstairs. This is a lovely photo.'

He looked behind him, frowned, and then shook his head. 'I know I left the door open, but I'd prefer it if you didn't come in here. This is my private office.'

I scurried to the door. 'Oh, course, I'm sorry. I didn't know,' I said, the words pouring out too fast but unable to stop them. 'It won't happen again. I'm sorry.'

He stepped around me toward the desk. 'No, no, that's all right. Just... stick to the lounge. I'm sure Vila will be down soon. Or, just pop upstairs to her room. Otherwise she can take a while. Make-up and... and... stuff.' He waved his hand vaguely in a presumed demonstration of "stuff" then sat down at his desk without another look at me.

I walked back through into the lounge just as I heard Vila's footsteps on the stair.

'What're you doing here?' She asked. There wasn't open hostility in her voice, but there wasn't any welcome either. I felt fed up all of a sudden.

'I wanted to see you, and talk about what happened to me the other night. In the park,' I said with force. I hadn't known I would say that until it came out, but when it did I realised it was true.

Vila paused on the stairs and looked down at her feet. 'What about it? I had nothing to do with that. Ask Michelle if you want answers.' As though she hadn't disappeared from school.

'I already know what Michelle would say. I already know Michelle's part in it. I want to know what you knew and what you did.'

'Yeah, well I don't want to talk about it. Maybe next

time you should ring before you just come around. It's rude.'

She turned and started to stomp back up the stairs.

'No problem,' I yelled up after her. 'I'll just talk to your mother then, shall I?'

She was down the staircase and in my face in a flash. 'Keep your goddamn voice down,' she growled at me with low vehemence. 'This is nothing to do with my mother. Piss off home. I don't want you here.'

'Oh Vila, why? Are we not *friends* anymore?' My voice acid. And loud.

She glared at me for a moment, then grabbed my wrist and turned to go back upstairs. 'Fine, then. Why don't you come up and we can have a talk.'

She slammed the door behind me as I walked through and sat on her bed. There was a muffled exclamation from downstairs, and Vila yelled out 'Sorry,' and then came in and sat on her desk chair. She stared at me, and then sighed. 'What do you want to know?'

'You knew that Michelle was going to be there. You knew she was going to attack me.'

Vila looked down at the floor. She shifted on her seat. But she was already nodding her head before she stated, 'Yes.'

'How long before?'

A shrug.

'Is that why you invited me?'

'Yes.'

I felt growing frustration at the response. I breathed in, a deep breath, through my nose, and then let it out slowly between clenched teeth. 'I was really hurt, Vila,' I said. I tried to catch her gaze, but she kept looking down. 'I'm not on the floor,' I yelled out.

She looked up, her eyes locked with mine for a second, but then she turned to stare out the window instead. Her cheeks were turning warm red. Her neck was flushed. 'I didn't hurt you. I didn't touch you.'

'No, you just invited me to a party knowing that someone else would. And you tried to get me drunk

143

beforehand.'

'It's still not on me. You should've known better than to go out. You must've known that Michelle was out to get you.'

'I didn't know that *you* were.'

She shook her head, but her neck flushed to a deep crimson. It was like an allergic reaction. An allergic reaction to facing up to herself.

I thumped my fist on the bedspread. The sound was muffled, the sheets wrapped up the blow and took it away, but the movement caught Vila's eye and she jerked back.

'Why didn't you warn me? We were meant to be friends.'

'It was just a prank,' she yelled at me, all composure gone. 'It was just a prank, and you should've known it was coming. You're so *thick* sometimes, Daina!'

'Is that what you want me to tell the police?' I yelled back at her. 'Do you want me to tell them that you tricked me into going, despite knowing what they'd do to me? What do you think they'd say about your prank?'

'And what're you going to tell the police? That someone stole your clothing in a park? What am I, accessory to a clothing heist?'

'You're an accessory to rape!' I yelled, and burst into sudden hot tears.

Vila shook her head in disbelief. 'That didn't happen. She just kicked you a few times. You can't say that shit – that's serious.'

'You left me unconscious in a park, naked.' I stated, and stared at her in mounting fury. '*What the hell did you think would happen?*' I yelled, and jumped up to shake her.

I wanted to punch her and kick her. I wanted to drag her down through the mud and make her pay. Instead I pushed her back into her chair and stood over her, my tears clogging up my ability to speak. Snot running down my face until I wiped it away.

'You left me alone in a park with no clothes on,

completely unconscious. How do you think I got home?'

Vila shook her head. Instead of being fascinated with the floor, she was fascinated by me. Her eyes wouldn't turn away.

'Who did you leave there?'

'Nobody,' she croaked, then cleared her throat. 'Nobody stayed,' she repeated. Then she turned her head slightly to one side as though an invisible being was whispering something to her. 'Paul was hanging around at the entrance to the park. He thought someone should check on you.'

'Yeah, well. He checked on me all right.'

Vila put her hands over her face. 'I don't believe you,' she stated, her voice firm. 'You were fine when I left,' she added.

'When you left me unconscious,' I corrected.

'It was just a prank,' she said softly.

I felt so tired. All I wanted was to go home and get into bed. I couldn't remember the last time I'd eaten anything of substance. My stomach growled, and the pain felt like a low glow in my belly. 'Why did you do it?' I asked. My voice was low and flat. I didn't even know if I wanted an answer anymore. I couldn't trust anyone to tell me the truth.

'I cheated on a maths test,' Vila said in reply, just as I thought she wasn't going to answer. 'I cheated on a test and Michelle found out.'

'When was this?'

She looked to the corner of the room, as if there was a slideshow of memory hanging there. 'It was at mid-term. Just before. There's an assessment that was worth 20% of the total mark. I couldn't pass it on my own.'

'You're talking about April?' I clarified, and she nodded.

'So that's the only reason you ever talked to me?' I continued. 'Michelle wanted you to be friends with me just so she could play a prank?'

Vila's eyes widened. 'No! God, no. She only told me the week before. I swear.'

I tried to read her, but I didn't know anything anymore. No one was as they seemed. No one should be trusted. I nodded however, this was a way back in and I was conscious that I couldn't break this down just because I wanted to kill her. 'So why did you leave me. You could've come back later.'

'I couldn't. Michelle made me leave. She told me if we didn't get out of there she'd really hurt you.'

I looked at her. The colour was starting to fade from Vila's face. Her neck was returning to its usual warm brown. She met and held my eye. I could probably believe her. I wanted to believe her.

They're not your friends. They've been lacing your food.

The thought carried so much weight that I swung backward before catching myself. Vila was still looking at me, so I forced a smile onto my face and nodded. Her expression filled with relief.

'It was an awful thing to do. I'm so sorry. If I'd known...' She trailed off as she didn't know what it was she would have known.

I wasn't about to fill in the details for her either. I'd talked about that once – never again. I held out my hand to shake. 'Friends, then?' I asked and she grabbed hold and gave me a shake and then a fist-bump.

'Friends,' she said. A smile lit up her face. 'Would you like to stay for tea? Mum's cooking about three times the amount we need at the moment.'

My stomach lurched. Hunger, or fear. I rubbed the middle of my collarbone where the nubby ends were now protrusive. Surely her mother wouldn't...?

'No thanks. I need to get home to Mum. She'll be wondering where I am.'

The lie rolled out easily enough, but Vila's small frown showed that it didn't ring true. She let it go and tossed me a two-pack of Toffee Pops.

'Have these then. You look like you haven't eaten for days.'

I couldn't remember if I had or not.

146

'Do you want to do something together tomorrow, then? Maybe go to the mall?'

People. Crowds. Noise.

'Sure, that sounds good. I'll drop by at ten?'

She nodded. Her smile was now all teeth, and I had to look away.

As I walked through the lounge I saw the shadow of Mr Fa'amoe. He must be standing just outside his office door. Making sure that I left? My stomach lurched again.

***

The Grey Man fell into step beside me as I turned out of Vila's street. There weren't any words spoken until I turned into an alleyway that was a shortcut through to my road.

'Hard, was it?'

I nodded and looked up at him. His face was hard to read. Closed off. I turned back to scanning the alleyway floor for broken bottles and twisted cans. When I was in standard two Jamie Sullivan had cut himself - through his *shoe* - on metal in an alley and had to get a shot as a precaution. I'd been hyper-vigilant ever since.

'Tell me what you learned?'

'I'm not cut out for this. That's what I learned.'

There was silence in response. It dragged out so long that we almost reached the end of the alley, and then I couldn't stand it anymore. I stopped, and he stopped next to me.

'I looked in his office. There were papers and a briefcase.'

'What was in the briefcase?'

'How do I know?'

The silence again. It was uncomfortable, and mean. But then I didn't know why I was reluctant to tell him. After all I'd forced myself to pry against my better judgement. Why wouldn't I now tell him?

Because he'll make you do more. Because he's mixed you up with someone else, someone who could do

147

this.

'There were more papers. That's all. More papers, and some sort of stain. From his lunch probably.' I forced out a laugh, but there was no humour behind it. I wanted to go home. No. I wanted to feel *safe*. And where felt safe now?

'What else?'

There was nothing else. There'd been nothing else I'd seen. But my mouth kept moving. Words kept forming. Information kept relaying. 'The documents in the briefcase were different to the ones on his desk. His desk has something about the new vaccines for the 'flu season coming up. There's also a summary of results from the first area to be vaccinated with the new MeNZB™ vaccine. Against meningitis. There were some bad reactions, but an estimate of a drop in expected meningococcal disease that far outweighed the side effects of the vaccine.

'His briefcase had documents about chromosome structure. Or a particular chromosome structure.'

I rubbed my forehead briefly. It seemed like information had just been placed there by a foreign body. I understood the words I was saying, not in depth, but in principal, but as to how I kept forming sentences and saying them I had no clue. I thought of the knowledge rays in *Battlefield Earth* – the entire history of knowledge beamed into your head with no effort to learn – and wondered if there was something aimed at my brain right now.

'What chromosome structure?'

I shook my head this time. But just as I was about to say *I don't remember* I instead swung my bag off my shoulder and rooted around inside it. There was a small pad – an offering from a real estate agent, as though we'd ever be buying or selling property – and a pencil with the nib worn down.

No pencil sharpener, but I bit into the wood on either side of the lead and splintered off enough strips for me to be able to make a mark. I drew a quick sketch of two oblongs joined together; one long, one short. Referenced bands marked their way down the capsules.

I tilted the pad towards him, and he stared at it for a minute, two, not saying anything. Then he looked around us to make sure we were still alone, and flipped the paper over so that the drawing could no longer be seen. He nodded at my backpack, and I tucked the pad and pencil back inside.

'What was the stain from?'

I frowned, and then brought up the image of the briefcase once again. The words, *I don't know* were almost out of my mouth, when I closed my eyes and concentrated harder.

'There was a small bottle, or vial, tucked into the top pocket. I could see the outline against the fabric. It had broken. Leaked. That was what caused it. The fabric was black so I can't be sure, but I think that the liquid was blue in colour. There was a tinge of blue on one of the papers. It may have splashed it at some point.'

The Grey Man tapped me on the arm. 'You've got a knack for this. Even if you don't feel right about doing it.'

The sun was getting low in the sky. It hurt my eyes to keep trying to look up at him, so I stared down at the alley floor again instead. There was lichen: khaki, yellow, and grey. It grew on the rough concrete where the fences either side stopped the sun from shining. Life was so frivolous it would grow anywhere, whether it was wanted or not.

'I don't understand why you want me to do this. Why can't you get someone else?'

'There is no one else Daina. Only you. We wouldn't,' He paused, '*I* wouldn't put you through this if it wasn't necessary. It is necessary.'

'Why me?'

His shadow in the alleyway showed him staring at me. I kept looking down. 'Daina, you know why.'

I shook my head, and felt tears welling up. My throat constricted and my eyes burned. I closed them and kept shaking my head.

'You know you've seen me before Daina. You remember, don't you?'

A thump sounded that reverberated through the soles of my feet, and I reached out with my eyes still closed to grab hold of the corrugated iron fence to my right. The metal dug into my palm. *This is not happening. I am not remembering. I have never seen this man before.*

'Daina, you need to get hold of those papers. You need to get a sample of whatever he's carrying in his briefcase.'

I swallowed past the lump in my throat, and opened up my eyes. Colours flashed and burned and solidified in front of my eyes. The schematics changed; the road shrank and the pavement grew. A sparrow flew by, its tail elongating to a metre long, two metres long. The length of a rugby field.

That's not fair – I didn't eat anything she gave me.

But that wasn't true. I'd eaten a biscuit from a sealed packet. Vila must have caught on that I wouldn't eat anything open so she'd injected the drug into a sealed packet. A tear slipped from my eye. And I'd thought she would tell me the truth.

'Daina. Do you understand me? It's vital that we get those papers.'

I shook my head. 'I can't. He'll catch me.'

'You have to think of something. Kill him if you have to.'

I jerked my head up, and caught his grin. Arsehole. 'I can't do it,' I repeated and turned out of the alleyway into my road. 'You'll have to find someone else.'

'There is no one else Daina, I've told you. You're the only one who can do this.'

I shook my head and carried on walking. He stood still at the mouth of the alleyway.

'You've got the wrong girl,' I whispered. 'I've never seen   you   before.'

chapter nine

Daina 1994

For a time it seemed like she was going to faint. There were spots in front of her eyes just like there had been the previous summer when she'd refused to wear a hat outside to the A & P show and ended up in the St John's tent with little memory of the day. She'd been looking forward to seeing the sheep, too. And maybe a lamb as little as she was.

Daina sat down, her bottom falling straight into the warm wet patch that she'd created beneath her. The gun barrel still faced her, but now it was above her head.

Her mother would be along soon. She'd sort this out. Whatever this was.

She began to cry. The smell from the dead man was still in her nose. The taste of bile still strong and acid in her mouth. She'd been promised a nice picnic. A nice lunch in a nice place. As a treat!

This wasn't a treat. She wanted to go home. Right now.

'Stop that,' the man said above her. But it was too hard to stop. Daina's shoulders shook with the sobs. Her face streamed with tears and then her nose started to swell up and block. She sniffled to try to clear it, but another wave of bile caught her as a result and she started to cry harder. Opened her mouth to let out a wail.

'Now then, little girl. There's no need to make a fuss. Where's you mommy and daddy then?'

That just made Daina cry harder. Her daddy was long gone, she was no longer even sure if she remembered him. And her mum was probably still asleep in the car.

Earlier this had seemed like an added treat. She would be able to sneak away and do what she wanted to do. But the lake water had long since dried off her feet, and now she wanted her mother, and her mother wasn't here.

'Come on, there's a good girl. You can't be out here all on your own, can you? Where's your mommy?'

His voice had a thick American twang. Some of the words sounded so strange that it took Daina a moment or two to sort them out in her head. He was like the actors in the show on telly that she liked. The one where they got to go swimming all the time in little red bathing suits.

Daina's tears started to dry up. She knelt and then stood up again. Her mouth and nose screwed up as she registered the warm cling of fabric. She'd wet herself and it had been years since she'd done that. She'd been three years old and in a mall and her mother had yelled at her. She'd yell at her again today.

If she was still here.

The thought made Daina's throat close up again.

Her mother had been in the car. The man must have come past the car to get here. If he didn't know where her mummy was then either she wasn't in the car, or the car wasn't there either.

What if her mother had left?

What if she'd gone home and forgotten about Daina? It wouldn't be the first time. Daina remembered her mother taking her to a friend's house and making her go into Emma's room to play. She didn't like Emma, and she certainly didn't want to play with her.

When she went out of Emma's room later, her mum's friend was surprised to see her there. Apparently her mother had left – some time ago – and had forgotten that she'd brought her daughter over.

She was driven home by a tight-lipped woman, and Daina was well aware that somehow this was all her fault. After that Daina hadn't seen the woman again, and Daina's mum didn't ever seem to go out to meet any friends anymore.

At least in that situation there'd been a woman, however angry she'd been, to drive Daina home. Who would take her home this time if her mother had left? The man who was still pointing a gun at her?

She shook her head. She didn't know. The gun wavered and then dropped to the man's side. Daina felt better about that. She'd seen guns on television a lot, but never in real life before. She knew that when they made a bang sound the person facing them fell down and sometimes they didn't get back up. It didn't seem like they were nice things to point at people, and that meant that this was not a nice man.

The man knelt down so that he was looking her straight in the eye. Daina didn't like that at all. She tried to look away, look back to the lake which had the pretty sun glinting off the surface of the water, but he grabbed her upper arm – hard – and she turned back to him.

'I don't want to hurt you,' he said, but Daina thought that was a lie. His smile was tight, like Bruno in her kindergarten. He always told the teacher's aide that he didn't mean to hurt anyone. Once he'd told her that after taking Daina's forearm in both of his hands and twisting them in opposite directions. The Chinese burn had been done with such force that a trail of blood blisters popped to the surface, and there had been glee on Bruno's face.

'I don't want to hurt you, but you need to tell me where your mommy and daddy are.'

Daina started to cry again. Big gulps of air were needed to keep up the momentum. She wasn't really sad. Usually she only cried when she was sad. But right now she was scared. Very scared. That helped.

She knew in the back of her mind that tears usually caused a reaction in adults. They'd either get all concerned and start treating her nicely – maybe give her a hug – or, they'd get all concerned and look for someone else to take over.

But the man in the grey suit did neither.

He levelled his gun at her face again, and jerked the barrel back towards where the car had been parked earlier. Daina stopped crying. He jerked the gun again and Daina started to walk in the direction he indicated. She walked down into the dip where the gravel took over from the asphalt.

She could still see the indentation where she'd jumped from the car, lost her balance, and fallen down. Her hands had scraped away the gravel from the hard soil beneath. Her worst fear was true then. This was where the car had been. And wasn't now.

The man was staring in all directions. His head turned from the treeline, to the lake, to the picnic tables, to the treeline on the other side. His head jerked from position to position just like the chicken at the farm that Daina's class visited early in the year. She giggled at the memory. The head jerked to look at her again and the giggle went away.

'Where are they? No one leaves a little girl all alone in a park by the roadside. Where are they?'

Daina just shook her head, and the man bent down and grabbed her upper arm again. He jerked it up, and twisted it, and Daina cried out with the pain. It felt he was twisting it right off.

'Tell me where they are, right now!'

There was a rustle, and then the thud as a wooden bat hit hair, skin, and bone. The grey man crumpled to his knees. His eyes no longer focused on Daina's. One pupil slid out to the far edge of his right eye, while the left stayed in the middle. Then he fell face forward.

Daina's mum stood behind him with a cricket bat. The force of the blow had split the bat along an old crack secured with red electric tape. One big splinter hung separate from the main bat, the tape the only thing holding it together.

Her mum was breathing hard. The little curls in front of her ears were tight with sweat. She was shaking.

'Mum,' Daina yelled. She ran to her and hugged

154

her legs. She was sure glad to see her. Of course her mum would never go off and leave her, she was daft to think it. She'd just gone so she could surprise the bad man, and make sure Daina would be safe.

'Come on, honey,' her mum said. There was a shake in her voice, like there was some mornings when there'd been a party while Daina was falling asleep. 'I've just moved the car into the shade.'

She pointed, and Daina saw it almost hidden behind a thicket of bushes. No wonder the man hadn't been able to see it. That made sense too. If Daina's mum slept in the sun for too long in the afternoon she always woke up cranky.

'Go and get in the car, that's a good girl,' she said and pointed again.

'Are you coming?'

'I'll be there in a minute,' she replied, kneeling down beside the man in the grey suit. His skin colour had changed with the blow. It was now almost as grey as his suit, and his hair.

Daina leaned her weight on one foot, and curled the other up the back of her leg. 'Are you sure?'

'I'm sure honey. Go and wait in the car and I'll be right with you.'

There was an edge to her voice this time. An edge that said, do what I say right now or there'll be trouble. Daina started to back away slowly.

Her mum bent over the man and put her fingers on his neck. It was strange. That was nowhere near where she'd hit him. Daina could see the spot even as she edged further away. There was blood pumping out of it and shading his hair and the ground around his head. His neck hadn't been hurt at all.

Daina came to a stop and just stared. Her mother caught on within a second and gave her a look. Daina started to step backwards toward the car again.

That was when there was a whining sound above. It grew louder and louder. Louder and louder. And then there was a wrench of twisted metal. A boosh of water *being displaced. The ground shook again beneath Daina's feet. She watched twisted metal skip on the surface of the water just as she couldn't get stones to do. A large wave wet the stones on the beach well above the waterline, and then went back out.*

And a plane was sticking out of the water. Mangled wreckage. Heat shimmers above it.

Daina ran back to the safety of her mother. She forgot about the car.

***

Daina 2004

Mum threw another party that night. I fell asleep to the domph, domph, domph of a bass beat and woke in the night to silence. I ran my hand up over my rib cage. I could feel the individual ribs sticking out through my thin flesh. Skeletal. After the biscuits early today I hadn't had anything else to eat.

Tiptoeing downstairs, I clung to the left-hand wall to balance. I paused at the bottom, my head tilted as I tried to make out any sounds in the stillness. A faint growl of a snore, a rustle as someone turned over. The sounds of unconscious souls who'd fallen asleep in position after a night of hard-drinking.

Reassured, I crept through into the lounge, and then further into the kitchen. There was a half-empty greasy package of cold chips, and a couple of slices of pizza with the hated anchovies coating the surface. Mum loved these little fish in theory, but tended to spit them out with dismay when the reality arrived.

My stomach leapt and turned with excitement at the sight. I bundled them together and sat down at the table. From this vantage point I could make out three bodies lying in the dimness of the lounge. There was a sharp tang of stomach acid in the air; someone had thrown up during the night and it hadn't been cleared away. Let's hope *that* disappeared before I got home from school.

I stuffed a couple of the chips into my mouth and

156

chewed. There was something wrong. The sound of my jaw working carried into my brain in amplified fashion. I tried to ignore it, to continue eating, but the compulsion to get the food out of my mouth grew too overwhelming and I spat the sodden mess back out.

My stomach turned over, and growled with low fury. It demanded to be fed. Even the sight of the half-eaten food wasn't enough to stem my hunger.

I picked up a piece of pizza and tried a small bite. Once again the sound filled my head. Swelled. I opened my mouth and let the food drop back onto the plain wrapping.

It was the sound of poison. That was the thought that arrived full-blown in my head. The noise of chewing was the noise of the drugs that laced the food entering my bloodstream. It was the sound of hallucination being manufactured in my brain. Somehow, someone had been at the food. It was adulterated.

I tried to force another chip into my mouth. Tried to chew. Tried to ignore the sounds and the compulsion to spit it out. Tried to swallow.

The slow progress of the mouthful down my epiglottis caused a wave of violent nausea, reversed trajectory and came straight back up. I walked to the sink and grabbed a handful of water from the tap. The normally sweet taste of Christchurch's pure spring water was tainted with acid. Smelt like death.

I threw the water back up as well, and then clung to the side of the bench as my head forgot where my body was and span in circles. I retched again, and again, until at last my mouth and stomach felt clean. My hunger had gone.

Slowly, my dizziness left. Once I could trust myself to balance without the aid of the bench I walked through back into the lounge. One of the occupants was sitting up with a lamp shining on a work in progress. A spoon, cotton wool, a lighter flame.

Great. Now my mum's friends are shooting up.

The door opened and my mother walked through

157

into the room. She saw me standing in the corner and gave a faint wave, then sat cross-legged on the floor next to the cook.

***

The mall was packed. The constant crush of people in motion made me feel dizzy after a while. I couldn't imagine why anyone would suggest this as a form of entertainment. Vendors occasionally leapt out from the middle of the level to thrust various creams and concoctions in my face. I felt I needed to keep my hand up at all times, like a boxer in the ring.

Vila moved from window to window, examining and exclaiming over the displays as though they held some meaning. When I saw an empty bench to one side I took the opportunity and plonked myself down. She didn't notice for a whole shop window, so I yelled out, 'Vila!'

She turned, and I waved, and she came back and sat down next to me. Her colour was high, and she twisted the ends of her long ponytail around her finger.

'It's a pity we don't have any money,' she said, 'I could just see myself in a pair of those jeans.' She pointed to the next window over, and I looked at the pair of wide-leg jeans. Seems that bellbottoms were on the way back in. Or not. Nobody walking past was wearing them, only the shop mannequins.

'I do have some money,' I exclaimed as I remembered the Grey Man's gift. I searched in my pocket, but couldn't find the card. What had I done with it? I pulled my bag off my shoulder and searched through there instead. It was tucked inside the front pocket and I pulled it out with a victorious cry.

'What's that from?'

'Birthday present. Do you wanna see what $50 can get us?'

Vila was already running ahead. I chased after her and almost crashed into her back when she stopped short.

'When was your birthday?'

'Thursday,' I said, taking the card back out of her hand.

'You didn't say anything.'

I shrugged and walked past her into The Warehouse. The concrete floors were stacked everywhere with items that appeared to all be entering a sale, or just about to stop being on sale. Apart from the everyday low items.

The clothing section was on the left-hand side of the store. I disappeared inside there, and Vila joined me a moment later.

'Happy birthday for Thursday, then,' she said. 'I'll shout you an ice-cream after.'

My stomach turned over itself at the thought, but I shook my head.

'What?' she asked. Her mouth pursed.

I can't eat with you because you keep poisoning me. 'Teeth,' I blurted. 'My teeth can't handle anything cold at the moment. I'll take a raincheck though.'

'Raincheck. You sound like my nan,' she scoffed, and turned back to the more important task at hand. 'These,' she said and held out a long skirt in bright yellow and a white crochet top.

'I don't think yellow is your colour,' I said. It was a relief to be honest about something.

'Not for me, you dick. For you. It's your bloody birthday present!'

She held them up against me and nodded. 'What, you're a size ten?'

'Twelve,' I said from habit, but she shook her head.

'No way are you a twelve. Try it on.' She pointed me to the changing rooms, and I laughed and complied.

The skirt hung off my hipbones. I handed it back through the curtains and said, 'Size eight. They must size these ones large.'

She held the skirt up against herself, and her forehead creased into a frown. I let the curtain slip back into place and looked at the top in the mirror. It was

159

pretty and had ties at the back so I could pull the waist in.

Vila's hand popped back in through the curtain with a smaller skirt. 'Thanks,' I called and pulled it on. It fit better than the last one. The colour went well with the white blouse. I took them back off and checked the price tags. $44.90 for the two of them.

Why not?

I pulled back the curtain just as Vila stuck her head through. 'You didn't like them?'

'I loved them. I'm gonna get them.'

'Put them back on. Let me see.'

I shook my head and laughed. 'I'm not putting them back on again. You'll have to wait.'

'Do you want to come back to mine? Then you can show me.'

I nodded and went through to the checkout. 'As long as you promise not to perv.'

'You know me.' Vila narrowed her eyes and let her tongue slip through her lips. 'Just pull them a bit higher, little girl.'

I pushed my elbow back into her ribs and laughed.

The girl scanned the items and I handed over the card. She ran it through the machine and frowned. She ran it through again.

'There's no credit on this card,' she said handing it back. 'That'll be $44.90 please.'

'Try it again,' I said and gave it back. 'I haven't used it at all, there should be fifty on there.'

She didn't take it from me. Just shook her head. 'There's nothing loaded on it. It's just a blank card.'

She pointed to the display at the end of the counter. There were cards hanging there, and a sign above *Load with your own value!*

I looked back at the card. 'But it's got $50 written on it. There must be some mistake.'

She glanced at it, and then looked back at her till. There was a blush spreading across her chest, and she rubbed the keypad. 'That's just handwritten. We don't write anything on the cards at all. Just in case they get stolen. That's why you have to keep the receipt when you get them loaded. Do you have a receipt?'

I shook my head. 'It was a present.'

She shrugged. 'I can't help you then,' she said and reached for the bag.

I pulled it back over the counter. She turned to look at me then, her eyes widening. I didn't know what I was going to do until I saw the astonishment on her face. And then the expectation. She expected me to be a thief.

So I was.

I tugged hard on Vila's arm and then broke into a sprint. There was a crowd of people in front of me, blocking the exit gates. I pushed one of them, hard, and the rest cleared a path. There was a flash of light and sound and then we were out of the shop and running through the seating for the ice cream shop and café.

My feet hammered the ground, and I skidded around the corner. Losing traction for a second on the hard tiles. The recovery. I ran for the mall's side exit and then was forced to stop as my speed exceeded the automatic opening function. Vila slid to a halt beside me, and we turned to see an enormous security guard jogging to a halt.

I darted forward on one side, Vila ran on the other, and we both made it past. We fell into step again, side by side, and ran back through to the other end of the mall. There was a constant flow of people in and out. The automatic doors never got a chance to close.

As we neared the exit I felt the world fall away, and my vision shrank a narrow spot of light. It was as though I was flying, and when the floor rushed up to meet my face, it was like burying my head in a pillow.

***

Coroner's Court 2014

There's a moment when the next witness is called to the stand and I have no idea who it is that I'm going to

161

see.

The name Mr Davies is so bland it could be anyone from anywhere, but when he's sworn in and faces the court, I realise that I have seen his features somewhere before.

'Can you tell the court where it is that you worked in 2004?'

'The Warehouse in Northlands. I was the duty manager there.'

It makes sense, but I'm surprised nonetheless. How many shoplifters trawl through his department in a week? In a day?

Why the hell has my face stuck in his memory?

It's a question that the coroner puts to him more politely when an old CCTV recording is produced and the clerk has to find a machine as elderly as the video to play it on.

'We kept the recording because the girls threatened to go to the police about James's actions on the day in question. Sorry, that was the name of the guard on duty, James McWallace.

'I didn't think he'd done anything wrong, and so I kept the recording separated in case they followed through.'

The coroner doesn't bother to ask him why he's still got it in his possession when he's left the employ of The Warehouse, but I presume that's to spare embarrassment. Who really wants to delve that deep into the sticky belly of a duty manager's home life?

'I've also kept a recording of the day we think that Miss Harrow stole the giftcard she was trying to use.'

I feel properly aggrieved at that one. I didn't steal the bloody thing. Worst. Gift. Ever.

When they wheel an unstable looking arrangement of a video player and monitor through into the room, there are a few stifled snorts. The screen looks like it was old at the time it was first hooked up. Used to the flat offerings of a later decade the curve of this tiny box seems ridiculous.

The video itself is in no great shape either. Grainy footage with far too much squeezed into the frame. Someone wanted to skimp on security by the looks, so there's far too much in view to cut down on the number of cameras required.

'You can first see Miss Harrow and Miss Fa'amoe in frame here,' He points at the screen.

There's a collective intake of breath when I emerge from the dressing room. My collarbones stick so far out from my sunken chest they seem like a sculpted necklace. My face is gaunt. If it weren't so animated I'd look like death on legs.

My mother turns away from the view. No change in behaviour there.

There's shots of us in the clothing area. Not inside the changing booths; some standards of privacy are in motion, but the film changes to a difference camera to pick us up at checkout.

When she served me all I saw was the disdain. On camera the checkout operator draws her core back and her face leans forward. There's distress and pity visible even through the poor picture quality.

When we run, she hesitates. She turns her head back to her line, maybe to check if anyone else saw. Her shoulders slump as she picks up the people shuffling to get a better view.

She grabs the microphone and calls it in. The security guard had clocked us anyway. He's running through the frame before she had time to finish.

The show ends.

***

Daina 2004
'Yeah, well if you *do* want to call the police then I'm quite happy to tell them what I saw. And what *I* saw was your gorilla tackling my friend. My friend who is now covered in blood with her head split open. So you go right ahead and make that call.'

Whose head was split open?

I opened my eyes and saw Vila in full stomp. She looked furious and confident. Something that the manager did not.

'You were stealing.'

'We had produced payment. Your checkout operator refused to accept it. And then when we try to leave quietly, you set security on us so we had no choice but to run.'

That sounded perfectly logical to me. I smiled and opened my eyes.

'Sir I... I didn't...'

'James do you want to take your break now? Then resume your post.'

'But I didn't...'

'I know. We'll talk about it later.'

I heard the man leave the room, and felt a bit sorry for him. I couldn't work out what had happened, but I didn't think he was responsible for my current state. At least I hoped he wasn't. That would be a waste of my pity.

Vila's face appeared in front of mine. Her face relaxed as I blinked my eyes.

'What's going on?' I whispered. 'Where are we?'

'We're being held unreasonably by the store manager after his security thug assaulted you,' she said in a loud voice. Then she leaned forward and whispered, 'You fainted and the guard caught us. Next time I think we should just leave the bag, okay?' She giggled and poked me in the ribs.

'Help me up, would you?'

She looked back over her shoulder at the manager, then turned to me. 'I don't know if you should be moving about. You knocked yourself pretty badly.'

'I feel fine,' I replied, and tried to sit up on my own. My head swirled, and then pain set in. I gritted my teeth and forced a smile.

'Whatever,' she said, and grabbed my arm to help me down off the bench and to a chair instead. 'You don't look fine. I think he's calling you an ambulance.'

'I don't need an ambulance! Sir? Sir?'

The manager turned around to look at me. He wasn't even on the phone. Vila giggled again. 'I told him not to,' she whispered, 'There were half a dozen people said he should, but I just told them all you're epileptic and falling down was the normal course of business,' she giggled again. Her breath was sweet and hot in my ear. 'They couldn't get away from you fast enough after that.'

'I think I should call your parents,' the manager said and walked over to us. 'Given the circumstances I'm happy to let you go with a warning, but I won't release you to go about the mall on your own. What's your parents' number?'

'My mother won't be there,' I said quickly. Vila rolled her eyes. 'She *won't*,' I repeated and poked out my tongue.

'You can call my dad,' she offered. 'I've got his number here.' She dug in her handbag and pulled out a tiny pad. She flipped to the page she wanted and handed it across.

'Wouldn't your mum be better?' I asked softly. Vila's mum was generosity and happiness and baking. Her father was trouble.

'Like I want that bitch driving us home from here. There'll be enough lectures in the coming weeks. I don't need a preview just now, thanks.'

'Are you sure you wouldn't prefer a doctor?' The manager asked, looking at me. 'Your head looks like you bumped it quite badly.'

I put my hand up, and then jerked my fingers back as they encountered a sticky lump full of pain. 'Nothing a couple of aspirin won't cure,' I said. When he continued to look at me I followed it up with a big smile. He turned back to his desk and picked up the phone.

***

Mr Fa'amoe didn't say a lot in the car on the way

home. He expressed some initial concern over my state, but I had a bundle of tissues the store manager had given me that now contained most of the obvious damage. They were screwed up in the front pocket of my bag where I hoped they wouldn't leave a stain.

I could've thrown them into the nearest rubbish bin, but I felt a bit weird doing that considering they were covered in my blood. Were there rules on human waste? I didn't want to just chuck them in with the lolly packets and general mall detritus.

Vila gave me an occasional nudge of solidarity, but her enjoyment of our situation seemed to have passed. She stared out of the window at the queues of traffic.

Her father had picked us up when he left work. Why he was working on a Sunday I didn't know, but Vila didn't seem all that surprised. We'd withstood supervision until he arrived, but the timing meant we were now in a snarl of traffic as everyone's weekend drew to an end.

'Come into the house,' Mr Fa'amoe ordered when I got out of the car, and turned towards the street to walk home.

I hesitated. 'That's okay, I'll just walk home. Mum'll be wondering where I am.'

'We'll phone her. Come into the house.'

He turned and walked inside, and I looked at Vila. She gave a shrug but followed quick on his heels, so I did the same.

I felt nervous walking inside. Even more so than I had the day before. I'd never been caught doing anything bad before, and I didn't know what to expect. If it was just me then I don't think it would've mattered half as much. But I'd dragged Vila into trouble as well.

Vila's dad crossed through into the kitchen calling his wife's name. She popped her head out, frowned and started toward me, but he caught her by the upper arm and pulled her back through.

I shuffled closer to Vila, and she did the same. I could hear muffled voices, which suddenly raised in tone. I rubbed my hands together, and picked at a fleck of dried blood on my hand.

'I'll just blame you, if that's okay,' said Vila suddenly. After craning to make out what was being said in the kitchen, her voice seemed unnaturally loud. 'They'll be perfectly happy to think that you've led me astray, and it's not like your mother's going to care one way or the other, is it?'

I stared at her. My face forgot how to work properly, and my chest squeezed a tighter grip on my lungs. I shook my head, and she burst into laughter.

'Oh, your face. Classic!'

A laugh bubbled up in my own chest, but it was overcome with another wave of dizziness, and I stumbled.

'Sit down,' Vila said as she gripped my elbows tight. The pinch brought me back into myself fully, and as I took a seat the world went back to its usual vibrant colours.

'You're too skinny. You need to eat something.'

'I need some aspirin. My head's pounding.'

'Wait there,' she said and left for upstairs. I listened to her thump about overhead. I wasn't about to attempt to go anywhere else. The day felt used up.

I pinched at the worn cotton of my jeans. There was a fray at the side seam by my knee. Not the casually wrought tears that were specially commissioned in your designer jeans, no. This was from normal wear and tear. Not just from my use, but the person before me. Maybe even a person before that. It just didn't look the same.

My stomach turned over. Then turned over again. I stood up, even though the motion jolted my head.

My stomach rolled once more, then just kept on going. Saliva flooded into my mouth. I turned and ran into the side corridor. There was a bathroom to the left-hand side. I popped the door open and fell to my knees in front of the bowl just in time. Bile and stomach acid regurgitated through my mouth. I wretched once, twice. The world greyed out and I clung to the porcelain. Slowly

167

it came back into focus.

I flushed the toilet without rising from my knees. I didn't feel safe to stand. My stomach gave another twist, but then settled. I put my forehead on the cool smooth surface of the bowl and closed my eyes. My backpack felt twenty kilos heavier, and I pulled off one shoulder strap so it lay half on the floor.

The voices in the kitchen had quieted, not just through my new distance. I heard Vila's light steps come back downstairs, and then the pause as she stopped in the lounge.

'Daina?' she whispered. I opened my mouth to reply, but the wave of nausea recurred and I closed my lips tight and fought the urge to wretch again.

A door slammed open further inside the house, and I heard Vila's parents voices again.

'Where's your friend?'

'I think she's gone home. She wasn't feeling very well.'

A pause, and then, 'Come through into the kitchen. We need to have a talk with you.'

I smiled at the cliché, and then gripped the bowl again as another cramp of nausea gripped me. It let go a minute later. *Should I go through and tell them I was still here?* From the tone of voice I thought it may be a better idea to lay quiet for the moment, and sneak out. If they caught me I could explain.

The walk home seemed like a very long trek. I got to my feet and had to steady myself against the wall. Maybe I should just stay here, and then at least get a ride home. To be driven rather than have to walk seemed an impossible luxury.

But to be lectured, then driven home, seemed like a bit too much to bear at the moment. I wondered what impulse had taken over me that made stealing seem like a good idea. If I'd ever seriously considered shoplifting, doing it secretly seemed like a better bet. Rather than a full-fledged sprint from the checkout counter. I smiled at the memory. Stupid, stupid, stupid.

I walked out into the hallway, my hand trailing the wall for guidance. When I glanced into the lounge I could see the kitchen door was shut, and the murmurs from behind sounded low and intense. Probably a stern warning about the company that Vila was keeping.

The door to Mr Fa'amoe's office was shut. I swept the palm of my hand over the fake wood surface. It was made up to look like oak, but was more likely MVP and cardboard. I knew about the strength of doors from many parties that ended with firm kicks at the wrong target.

I turned the handle and slipped through the gap. I left the door ajar so that I could hear if footsteps approached and crossed to the desk. My heart started to pound. When I looked down I could see it shaking my chest and collarbone.

Just do it quickly and get out and then it will be over.

The thought did little to calm my nerves. My hands shook with more violence, so when I reached out to try the latch on Mr Fa'amoe's briefcase my fingers slid off to one side and I had to move them back.

I pulled the latch, but it didn't pop open.

The combination lock had been set. Catching me in here once may have made him more cautious.

I tried 0000, then 1111. They didn't work and I sat down in the office chair to take a look at the blotter pad. There was nothing written there.

I looked around the office for any clues. Four digits – I'd never be able to stumble upon the code. I was not a lucky person.

There was a small picture of Vila's Mum in an ornate frame hung on the wall behind me. On the cabinets were pictures of the family at the beach, at a park, around the dinner table. A picture of Vila as a child, grabbing a pink balloon in her arms, with a smile so wide it almost used up her whole face.

Vila's birthday party. I entered in 1/9/89 into the lock and the latches popped open. That easy. She'd joked

169

back in September that her birthdate was her birth year. Maybe I was a lucky person after all.

I skimmed quickly through the documents located in a manila folder in the top. There was the same sketch that I'd seen previously; tables of data, graphs, patient records. I'd never be able to recall all of this.

I pulled open the top desk drawer: pens, pencils, an evil sharp letter opener. I pushed it shut and pulled open the second. Drop-files stuffed full of manila folders. I pulled one out, then another. Some sort of report. I couldn't fathom what would or wouldn't be a good disguise. I shoved the first one into the briefcase and pulled the backpack fully off my back.

At first the manila folder caught on the edges, and the leading edge pushed back threatening to spill the sheaf of pages inside all over the floor. My heartbeat shut off my hearing and my throat tightened, tightened.

I pulled it back out, adjusted the angle. Tried again. This time it slid in. I fumbled with the front zipper and pulled out a test tube. One more thing. One more thing.

My vision was strobing along with my pulse. My hands felt like I was operating them from a metre further away. I clenched my fists. Hard. The long fingernails on my right hand split the skin of my palm. My nerves relocated themselves.

I pulled the fabric folder at the top of the briefcase, and a small bottle of liquid fell into the briefcase. For a second the sun reflected off the glass and I thought for sure I'd broken it. But it didn't spill. It wasn't even cracked.

I unscrewed the lid, and poured some of the liquid inside into the test tube. I banged the rubber stopper back in place, and pushed it into my bag. The zipper stuck halfway across and I fumbled it back and forth, making a small cry – uh, uh – through clenched teeth. It unzipped all at once, and I was able to pull it back across in one smooth motion. Done.

My elbow knocked against the open bottle in the briefcase, and liquid spilled over the folder inside. Shit! I grabbed and got it upright while there was still some left. I started to screw the top on and paused.

There was a bottle of water on the windowsill, warming in the sun. I stood up and undid the top and spilled a capful, then two, inside the case as well. I left the top half-unscrewed. Put the bottle back in the fabric folder. Snapped the briefcase shut.

I pulled my backpack onto both shoulders. There was hardly any extra weight in it. Certainly not enough substance to cause the adrenalin still rushing through my veins.

As I placed the water bottle back on the windowsill I heard the tread of footsteps in the corridor outside.

Caught.

Caught red-handed.

My heartbeat stopped altogether. My vision clouded and wavered. I was fainting. For real this time. Not just dizziness.

I crunched the heel of my shoe into the top of my foot. The pain made me stagger, but my eyesight cleared and my heart started to thump again.

The footsteps stopped. I'd left the door ajar. They could look straight in and see me. If it was Mrs Fa'amoe then I might be able to talk my way out of it. If it was Vila's Dad I was in trouble.

The door closed. The footsteps sounded again, and then another door closed. Someone had come through to use the bathroom. That was all.

I crossed the room in two strides. There wasn't time to pause at the doorway to listen. I pulled the door open, stepped into the corridor, and pulled it shut behind me, trying to cushion the snick of the tongue with my forefinger.

There was the sounds of footsteps heading upstairs; I could recognise Vila's tread no problem. The toilet next to me flushed, and I jumped with fright and moved quickly through the lounge.

Empty.

I reached the front door, turned the handle as

gently as I could, and then pulled the door wide open. I lunged outside to freedom, closed the door with less care than before, and ran down the drive to freedom.

chapter ten

Coroner's Court 2014

When Vila returns after lunch she's more subdued. I can tell why: The stuff this morning was just about her and my behaviour. The stuff this afternoon is going to cut deep.

She pulls her long black hair out of the tie holding it back, scrapes it from her forehead, and re-secures it. The end of her ponytail still falls well below her shoulder blades. Definitely in the find-a-hairstyle-and-stick-to-it club.

My mother has new company, a welcome addition to Mr Anderson. A woman in her fifties, her face bright and alert, takes the seat beside her. She reaches across and gives my mother's hand a squeeze and then turns back to face Vila in the stand.

Her name is Christine Emmet. She works as a victim support officer. She's helping my mother, as the police are now determining that I committed suicide. Because that's normal, isn't it? A fifteen year-old girl traps herself in the foundations of a house and starves to death while clawing to get out.

Yeah, suicide.

Forget that I had papers in with my body that the police have now lost. Oh, did you not see that happen? Yeah, they bypassed that one pretty damn slick, didn't they? Forensic pathologist saw them, knows they were there, but then they disappeared on the way to the evidence room. Along with the test tubes.

Still, at least my bones made it through. I wonder if someone else would've found them first if they'd have gone AWOL as well. I owe the first-attending some gratitude for that at least.

Vila's eyes have teared up. She's not gonna cope at

all well with the next hour or so. All those painful memories, and ten years isn't really that long a time to come to grips with them. Not even her version of them, and lord knows that nowhere near the whole truth.

I do wonder if she truly knew what happened with her dad, if she'd be better off or worse? Is anger an easier emotion than grief? Probably. But it wouldn't just be anger, it'd be a mixture of them both.

Having someone to blame though. Knowing someone ripped the person you cared about from your life and handed you an empty space in return; maybe that would offer fulfilment.

Watch her now. Clearing her throat and trying to keep control. Imagine that she was fuelled with righteous fury. Her eyes wouldn't tear up, they would burn. Her throat wouldn't thicken, it would climb the registers.

But who amongst this lot is going to tell her the truth?

I couldn't even convince her father, and he knew more about it than most.

I couldn't even convince her father, and Vila – I'm so sorry – I tried.

***

Daina 2004

Aspirin, damp flannels, a long drink of cold water, and I started to feel human again. There was even a packet of rice crackers on the living room floor – half-full – that I made into my tea. They settled my stomach, tasteless but substantial. No wonder women in the throes of morning sickness kept crackers handy.

I couldn't bring myself to look through the file I'd stolen from Vila's Dad. I checked that the vial of fluid wasn't about to leak out, but then left everything in the corner of my room. I didn't want to know. Didn't want to acknowledge that I'd just broken a bond of trust.

No matter that Vila had broken mine. I still had my own moral compass to live up to, and it was pointing in the other direction on this one.

I wondered how hard it would be to see her in school tomorrow. Bad enough that I'd got her in trouble and then abandoned her to her fate. Worse that I'd stolen from her father. For some reason the theft from his briefcase registered far higher on my internal scale than the attempted theft from the mall. Not just because I'd gotten away with one, either.

I wanted the Grey Man to come by and pick all this stuff up and then just leave me alone for ever. Not only that, I wanted to tear a strip off him for giving me a gift card that wasn't. Nice trick to play on a teenage girl. Indignation riled me, and prevented the long evening slumber that my body cried out for.

So I was already awake when the pebble hit the window.

The sound jerked me off the bed and I pressed myself flat against the outside wall. For a moment, a long moment, I was convinced that Vila's Dad had discovered my theft, and had come around to seek retribution.

Why he would alert me to the fact by tossing a stone at my window was a second thought that was a long time coming. When it did, I peered around the edge of the curtain to try to make out who or what was outside.

The dim shapes of the evening all melded together. Trees, the half-collapsed wooden shed/playhut/death trap, the ivy-laden fenceline. Then I saw one shadow move and separate out.

Even from this distance and this time of night, the Grey Man managed to look grey. The thin moon reflected enough light to shine off his suit jacket, and illuminate the planes of his face.

He made some sort of hand gesture, but I couldn't see what. Presumably to indicate I should come down to him. I waved and stayed where I was. No way was I running downstairs to his command after the shit he'd put me through today. Gift card indeed.

The gestures grew more frantic, and then he whispered, 'Can you come down?'

175

I smiled in the shadows and leant out the window slightly. 'No. You'll have to come up.'

He shook his head, and I shrugged my shoulders in response. The hand gestures again, but I just turned my back on the window and laid down in bed.

Stuff him. If he wanted me to do his bidding he should pay me like an employee.

There was a series of pops as another pebble hit the side of my window, and bounced down the wall back to earth. I stayed where I was. Then there was a sharp crack as something larger hit the window followed by a thud on the floor near me.

What the hell?

A note wrapped around a stone.

I looked at the window and saw a line spreading out from a chink in the glass. The arsehole must have tossed it up on the inside of the open window. Its size had caused it to actually crack the pane.

I unwrapped the message. *Come down. I need to see you.*

I wrapped it back around the stone and threw it straight down out of the window. Not aimed at his head exactly, but not aimed away from him either.

'I'm not coming down. You come up.'

'Your door's locked,' he replied simply. When I didn't respond he moved a step closer to the side of the house, 'This isn't a game, Daina. You need to come down here now.'

No it wasn't a sodding game. A game was fun. A game had excitement and laughter, not fear and nausea. A game gave you a feeling of achievement at the end, or a try harder next time mentality. Not a feeling like you just wanted everything to go away.

I pulled on a sweatshirt to counter the chill of the evening air, and walked carefully downstairs. Timing each step to avoid all possible creaks and squeaks was a difficult job, I had to move slowly, slowly, but he could wait.

I turned the key, twisted the knob on the deadbolt,

and let myself out the back door. I turned towards the back of the house, then gave a gasp as a hand gripped me on the upper arm. He must've snuck around the side. I pulled my arm back.

'What?' I asked. I didn't bother to whisper any longer.

'Do you have the stuff?' he asked. And when I didn't immediately reply he moved to grasp my upper arm again. I danced back out of his reach.

'I have it,' I said and shoved my backpack at him. 'Help yourself.'

He shook his head and wouldn't take the bag. 'You need to hide that away. You're in danger if you keep it with you.'

His voice had so little inflection in it that it took a moment for the meaning to register.

'What danger? From Vila's Dad you mean?'

He moved towards the street. After a second I followed, and he answered when we got to the footpath, his face lit by the streetlamp overhead. Strained. Wary.

'Not from Mr Fa'amoe, no. In fact he's in danger too. There are other people about who may have twigged to what he's working on. They may have found out he's been digging around into things he shouldn't.'

He stopped and looked up and down the street, then set off in the direction of the Main North Road. When I caught up with him he was turning his head, scanning in all directions. That made me more nervous than what he'd said.

'Where are we going?'

'You need to hide that away. There's a new subdivision near the old people's home. We'll be able to store it somewhere safely there for the meantime.'

'Wait,' I said and stopped walking. 'Don't you want to have a look at what I got before we *hide* it?'

'I know what you've got. So do some other people.' He turned back to me and for the first time I saw real fear on another person's face. An adult person. A chill ran down my backbone and lodged in my kidneys like a

177

cold stone. A cold ache.

'What other people?' I whispered. It felt like all my blood was pooling at my feet. A whine started in my ear, so like a siren that I jerked my head to the side before I realised it was a sound for me only.

He shook his head and started to walk again. His long stride ate up the distance with ease and I had to skip a little to keep pace. The backpack rubbed against my shoulder-blades, its weight more noticeable now that it had attracted danger.

We walked in silence for twenty minutes. The Grey Man led me down some backstreets, and then the crowded suburban roads started to be dotted with empty sections, and then fields. There was a house with its frame finished, but everything else wide open. A tarpaulin flapped where it had been tied to protect the wood. The frame looked skeletal in the wispy moonlight.

'Through there,' he said and pointed at the floor inside.

'Where?' I said as I followed his finger, and found nothing but plywood floorboards on top of cold concrete foundations.

'There's a manhole through to underneath,' he said. He pulled himself up onto the floor as well and scuffed his foot back and forth in a semicircle. I did the same and felt the edge of a wooden slat that didn't quite fit level.

I knelt and located a small recess in the wood where my fingers could get purchase, and lifted. There was a half-metre square hole that dropped through to the ground beneath. My fingers slipped, but I stuck my foot in the gap, then got my hands underneath to tip it over.

The sound echoed off the trees at the far edges of the fields. I looked around, but there was no one anywhere around. Sound travelled, and we would be able to hear anyone out there who was moving around. There was no one.

'Do you have a torch?' I asked with faint hope. He shook his head. I tried to peer into the hole, but I

178

couldn't make out a thing. Just darkness. Possibly with spiders.

'Move it into another room. Into a corner. We don't want anyone accidentally stumbling across it.'

I snorted in derision. The house may be half-finished, but it had been that way for a long time. The tarp may keep the worst of the moisture out of the house, but there were still wide waterstains spread across the flooring. Christchurch didn't produce that much rain in a year. This had been abandoned for a while.

I turned so my back was to the hole, and then dropped my feet down in the blackness. My skin crawled at the thought of what could be lurking down there, but I forced myself to take off my backpack and kneel down on the cold ground.

I stretched a hand out in front of me and swept it back and forth. As I crawled forward I kept doing it until I felt the beam of a wall join in front of me. I pushed the backpack through a gap, and then felt out the outline and squeezed myself through. My head scraped on the rough wood, a splinter lodged just above my hairline. Shit.

The hand supporting my weight on the ground found the edges of something sharp. I tried to sit back on my knees, but my head banged on the floor above me.

I swore as I picked up the backpack and pulled out its contents. They weren't protected in any way, I didn't even have so much as a supermarket bag with me, but the area was so dry I figured they'd probably be okay.

With the test tube inserted into the manila folder, I pushed it as far along as my fingertips could reach. I started to move backwards, trying not to hit the sharp object with my knee again, then worried that the papers would blow away. I felt around me, and located a piece of stone or brick, and moved back in the direction of the folder. When I could brush against its outside edge I tossed the stone.

There was a soft tinkle, and I remembered the glass tube inside. Too late. If it was broken then it was already gone.

Reversing myself I strained in the darkness to see where the manhole had gone. For a moment I thought that it had been closed. That the Grey Man had played another trick on me and I was trapped. The squeeze of claustrophobia pushed the air out of my chest.

Then I made out the slight glow that differentiated the hole. I moved toward it, more quickly now that I was on my way out. When I got to the edge I popped up and levered myself up onto the floor, gasping.

I lay on my stomach for a moment, then rolled over onto my back. I tiled my head back, the world appearing upside down, but I couldn't see the Grey Man. I flipped the cover back into place and stood up, wiping my hands on the front of my jeans. Frayed and now filthy. He wasn't there.

For Pete's sake. First he gives me a crap gift. Next, he scares me half to death with hints and implications of the trouble that's following me. And now he buggers off altogether leaving me alone in the middle of the night to make my own way home.

Man really knows how to treat a lady.

My mind flashed back to the night in the park and I pulled my sweatshirt closer around me.

I was miles from anywhere where people would congregate. What if someone had followed? I couldn't even run the length of a mall without passing out, how would I run twenty minutes back to a main road?

'Get it sorted, did you?' came a voice behind me, and I cried out. My body flooded with relief, and then flushed hotter.

'What the hell do you think you're doing, creeping up on me like that? You scared the shit out of me.'

'Where did you think I'd be? Hardly creeping.'

'Well you're certainly a creep!'

I sounded like a small child, and I stamped my foot in frustration, adding to the image. 'Why did you give me that card? There was nothing on it. It was embarrassing.'

And damn if he didn't back further into the shadows. I couldn't see his face. Couldn't make out his expression. If he had any expression at all. The guy had a blank look at the best of times.

'Well?'

He stepped back toward me. 'This isn't the time.'

I took a step closer as well. 'It is if I say it is. I've done everything you asked. There was no need to do that to me, it didn't matter. I don't understand and I want you to explain it.'

'We need to get you back home. It's late, and you need to get some sleep. You've got school tomorrow.'

'Explain it quickly then. Explain it as we go.'

'Daina, I...' He trailed off and shrugged again. 'I just didn't have time to get it set up. I thought it would be nice, and then I forgot.'

'You went to the shop to pick up the card, but you didn't have time to top it up? What does that take, a minute, two? Stop bullshitting me.'

He pulled me forward by my upper arm, and force marched me to the footpath. 'I'll explain it someday, but right now we need to go. We need to get out of here.'

'Why? What's the rush? We're in the middle of nowhere.'

'There were two men tailing us until we got across the Main North Road. When we cut through the alleyway we lost them, but they're not going to stay lost for ever. The longer we stay here the more chance we'll be found.'

I followed along behind him feeling muddled more than fearful.

'Why are there people after us? Why are you so scared? I don't understand.'

'You don't need to understand.'

'I do. I can't stand this. Tell me!' My voice had risen steadily and the last was a shout in the darkness. If there really were people on our tail then they'd have a pretty good idea of which direction to try next.

'Daina, there are forces at work here that are outside of your control. You're not going to be able to know everything, or even part of some things. Every piece of information places you in more danger, and I

181

don't want the murder of a teenage girl on my head.'

He walked a few paces in front of me, his hands shoved deep in his pockets. Then he span on his heel. 'I only agreed to get into this as long as you were kept as safe as possible. I'm not going to be the one to break that promise now. We need to go. We need to go now. And I'm sorry but I can't tell you why or how or what or who. Just trust me and come with me.'

'Why on earth would I trust you?' I called back to him, my vision starting to wobble. 'You turn up out of the blue and make me do things that I hate myself for doing, and then you won't even tell me why. I don't know you from Adam and you expect me to trust you?'

'I told you I'd come back for you Daina. Here I am. I kept my word. Trust me just on that.'

I shook my head to clear it. Nothing he said made sense.

'I've never met you before. What are you talking about?'

He came back, pulled me by the elbow, and this time I trotted next to him to keep pace. 'You remember me Daina, I know you do. But just keep quiet for a while. We need to make sure we get clear of this area.'

We walked at a quick pace until we reached the inner-suburban housing again. And then the Grey Man made a series of weird roading choices until we were back outside my house.

'I won't see you for a while. It's best we stay clear of each other until I'm sure that no one's looking.'

He took a step and I called him back.

'If I'm in danger, does that mean Vila's Dad is in danger too?' It had been bad enough stealing from him, I didn't want to get him in trouble too.

'Don't worry about him, Daina. He's old enough and knowledgeable enough to get himself out of anything he's landed himself in.'

'What about what *I've* landed him in.'

He patted me on the shoulder. 'You haven't landed anybody in anything. He's taking risks for himself.' He moved away again, his hands swinging softly against his coat.

I wanted to call after him again. I wanted to find out more. But he wouldn't tell me. My arms were shaking, though whether from the cold night air, or a holdover from my earlier collapse, I couldn't be sure.

I wished for a moment that I'd kept the files from the backpack with me. Maybe I could have deciphered something in them, worked out how much trouble I'd just stolen for myself.

Then again, I was tired and my brain didn't seem to be sorting information in the right order. I slipped in through the back door to a house that didn't even notice that I'd been gone. All I craved was sleep.

As my eyes closed and I started to drift off I felt a shot of anger. *It's not fair,* my mind thought as though it were independent of me, *I didn't tell anyone about the secret.*

***

Coroner's case file number 46782
Council Complaints Report 4th November 2004
Type of Service: Property
Body of Complaint: Caller identified as Mr Wilbur Burton called to complain of unlawful activities taking place in a sub-division site, lot 47, land parcel 6674. Remains of an unlicensed fire, items of clothing, empty drink bottles and cans were located in the property. He and nearby residents would like the property secured so that it can't continue to be used for squatting and/or parties. Caller expressed concern that underage drinking and/or drug use may be happening at the property. Recommended to caller that police be called if an urgent response is required.

Response: Council site inspection ordered
Status: Non-urgent – expected date 6 weeks

***

183

Coroner's case file number 46782
Council Complaints Report 24th November 2004
Type of Service: Property
Body of Complaint: Caller identified as Mr Wilbur Burton called to complain of unlawful activities taking place in a sub-division site, lot 47, land parcel 6674. Further to a previous complaint he has noticed youths in the area camping out at the property. He is concerned that the underfloor area is being used as a site for unlicensed fires, and sleeping area. He would like the property secured. Recommended to caller that police be called if an urgent response is required.

Response: Council site inspection ordered

Status: Non-urgent – expected date 6 weeks

***

Coroner's case file number 46782
Council Complaints Report 16th December 2004
Type of Service: Property
Body of Complaint: Caller identified as Mr Wilbur Burton called to complain of unlawful activities taking place in a sub-division site, lot 47, land parcel 6674. Further to previous complaints he has once again noticed youths in the area using the house as a base for parties and people sleeping rough. He suspects there is drinking and/or drug use at the property. Caller revealed that his son had been involved in a party at the property in which he was hurt falling through the manhole cover. He would like the property secured. Caller said that if no action was taken on his request he would take matters into his own hands. Recommended to caller that police be called if an urgent response is required.

Response: Council Site Inspection Ordered

Status: Non-urgent – expected date 6 weeks

chapter eleven

Daina 1994

They stood hand in hand staring out at the lake. Daina could see what the thing was: the distinctive shape of a wing, the curve of a tail. It was a plane which flew in the sky. Or it had been. As she watched it settle lower into the water Daina didn't think it would fly again.

There was a gurgle from behind them, and Daina was pushed behind her mother as they turned to look at the man. With the blood and the bat, and the way his body had collapsed on the ground she thought he must be dead, but he groaned. After a moment, his eyes popped open.

They were no longer staring in different directions. They were both focused straight ahead. They were both focused on her.

'Get to the car,' her mother whispered. She stood with her feet planted apart, wider than her hips, steady like she wanted to stand strong for a fight.

Daina looked over to the car. It was so far away. The man was right there.

'Get to the car,' her mother said again. Loud this time. She gave her arm and shake and pulled her forward. 'Daina, go to the car now!'

That was her mother's last voice. The last voice before the next thing. And the next thing wouldn't be the soft-option time-out, or the quick hurt-but-then-it's-over spank. No. This was the last voice before the bad punishment.

Daina started to run. Her feet forgot how to, and she tripped over them and fell. Her face landed a foot away from the man. His eyes were still fixed on her. They glared. They burned. He reached out his hand –

185

straight to her – and Daina forgot how to breathe.

Where was the gun? He'd had a gun?

The hand reaching out was empty. Daina sprang to her feet, and jumped back a step. Her eyes flicked from side to side. Looking. Searching.

There it was!

On the other side of his body. It had fallen wide of where he'd landed. A metre away. Half a metre away. Daina looked him in the face so he couldn't tell she'd seen it. He was trying to get up on his elbows. Trying to move so he'd be able to reach for her again.

There were six steps between her and the gun. She had to run around the top of his head. Far enough away that he couldn't seize her. Close enough that she didn't waste time.

Six steps.

At one, he got to his elbows. At three he stretched his arm and brushed her ankle. At five he was on his knees, his body turned to keep track of her. At six she stretched out her hands and grabbed hold of the gun. Its body was greasy. Her hands were slippery with sweat. Her body was off-balance. Daina fell.

She fell and she rolled, and she held onto the gun. It squeezed and it squirmed, but she used both hands and it stayed close to her.

She rolled again. Away from him. Then she dug in her elbows, levered herself to her knees, stepped to her feet, and ran to the car.

There was the crack of the bat. Once. Twice.

When Daina reached the car she looked back. The man was grunting. His arms were at strange angles. Her mother held the bat, but it was useless. The splinter had fallen. The tape was flapping loose. The handle was more substantial than what was left of the bat.

Her mother knelt down, and Daina felt her heart beat too loud. Her throat pulsed. She clutched the gun to her chest with both hands and pressed her back against the door of the car. What was her mother doing?

She said something to him. Daina couldn't hear.

She was too far away. Her mother was whispering something that only the man was meant to hear.

He shook his head. He was saying something back. The sounds carried on the wind, but the words were distorted, lost.

Her mother thrust the handle of the bat into the dirt next to the man's face. Daina gasped. The man did too. For a moment she'd thought it was going to go straight into him.

She leaned in close; too close.

Daina knew how that felt. When her mother had something to say and she wanted to say it so it wasn't misunderstood she would place herself so her nose was almost touching Daina's and then say it through gritted teeth. Daina could see the bunching at the side of her mum's jaw which meant her teeth were clenched.

She'd feel sorry for the man if he hadn't deserved it.

Daina turned and opened up the passenger door of the car. She put the gun on the seat, and then used both hands on the glove compartment. She had to press her thumbs really hard into the metal button, otherwise it wouldn't open. Her mother could do it with one hand, leaning across from the driver's side, but Daina couldn't.

The latch clicked and Daina could pull it open. She held it with one hand, and picked up the gun with the other. It was enormous in her hand.

On the television they always talked about a safety catch. It would be on when they wanted to fire and it would stop them. Or, it would be off when it shouldn't be, and the gun would fire accidentally.

Daina couldn't see anything like a catch. There was the smooth curved length of the barrel, and the pebbly grip of the handle. There was a quarter-circle metal curve with a button that Daina knew would fire the gun. There was another trigger on the top corner of the handle that was pulled back.

There wasn't anything about it that looked safe.

Daina placed it carefully into the compartment.

She had to turn it a few times until she was sure it would fit. When it was positioned correctly she pushed the door closed until she heard the latch click into place. Only then did she take a deep breath in and feel safe.

She turned around to look back at her mum. She was walking back to the car. She opened the door and Daina scrambled up onto the passenger seat. She pulled her own door closed just as her mother inserted the key and turned it to start the engine.

The man was lying on his back. He was awkwardly cradling his arms together. They looked askew. They looked painful.

Daina smiled. You don't mess with me, *she thought.* You don't mess with me or my mum'll get you!

When they were home and it was dark outside and Daina was being tucked into bed, the bedclothes pulled all the way up to her chin just the way she liked it, she asked her mother what the man had said.

At first she didn't answer, and Daina started to think she wouldn't. Often she asked her mother things and the only response she got was 'I'll tell you when you're older.'

No matter how old she got!

But after a few minutes her mother smoothed the top of the blankets and bent to kiss Daina on the forehead. 'He said that as long as we keep today a secret, we don't need to worry about a thing.'

Daina smiled at her mother. She wasn't worried. She hadn't been worried since her mother drove her away from the park. What an exciting day out it had been. She hoped the next one would be uneventful.

'And what if we don't keep it a secret?'

Her mother looked her straight in the eye. She wasn't smiling. 'If you don't keep it a secret, then one day that man will come back. He'll come back when you least expect it. He'll come back,' she poked her finger at the tip of Daina's nose so she screwed it up. 'He'll come back and he'll make you sorry.'

***

Daina 2004

When I woke the next day the phone was ringing downstairs, and the sun was high in the sky.

It took a few minutes for me to click, and when I did I sat immediately upright in bed. Scared that I would fall asleep again and sleep in even later.

I scrambled on the side table for my clock and looked at it with disbelief. The alarm had gone off. The alarm that was set to ring at 7.30am and would continue for ten solid minutes so there was no chance you could sleep through it. That alarm. It had gone off five hours ago.

The ring of the phone ceased. Not through being answered. The caller had just given up.

The uniform I'd laid out the night before so I wouldn't have any excuse to run late mocked me as I walked past it to get out my jeans and sweatshirt. There was no use turning up at school now. Better to just forge a letter and turn up tomorrow looking pale and giving an occasional cough.

The phone started ringing again. This time there was the clear sound of motion from downstairs, and I ran down the stairs quickly to listen at the door. Was it the school? Is that why they kept trying?

That, or the world's most persistent telephone marketer.

Mum's sweet lilt was rendered into a croak by the booze and H. She used to be so good at hiding it, her lack of sobriety. It showed how many rungs down the ladder she'd slipped recently. Only someone with a complete lack of imagination could possibly believe she was in a fit state now.

There was an outburst of swearing, and then the phone was slammed down. And slammed again. And again. Seemed there'd been upsetting news on the other end.

'Daina!' my mother yelled. There was the sound of a

189

stumble, some more swearing, and then the yell again. 'Daina!'

I slipped out the back door. There was no need to add to Mum's misery by confirming her suspicions. If I was going to be called out for wagging, it could at least score me more than a morning's sleep in.

There was brilliant sunshine outdoors. Within a few minutes the top of my head was warmed through, the hairs hot as fire, and I felt good for the first time in a long time.

I pushed the sleeves of my top up so my arms could feel the heat of the sun. They immediately plumped into goose pimples, but I waited them out, and after a minute they relaxed back into place. It was funny, but my arm hair seemed longer and in better supply than ever before. I stroked it gently with my finger. It felt like the belly of my old teddy bear.

Even with the sunshine and the walking my body didn't seem to heat completely through. I gave the school a wide berth, but otherwise retraced the same steps I'd taken last night. In the back of my head was the thought that this was nothing if not dangerous, but it seemed such a silly proposition in the middle of the day.

Was that why the Grey Man had chosen to arrive at night? It made it so much easier to sell fear when you couldn't even make out the everyday objects around you.

The journey didn't seem to take half the time it had before. Part of that was daylight, part of it the good sleep I'd finally managed, part of it familiarity.

Once again the housing gave way to sections which gave way to fields. As I approached the section of the half-completed house with its tarpaulin top hat I wondered why someone would have got so far with a structure and then abandoned it. There were always tales on the news of property developers, a phrase that seemed to be spat out rather than said, going bankrupt and taking everyone's fortune with them.

Who would buy a half-complete structure anyway? Would it cost the same as half a house, or the same as a section, or priced at a discount as you'd probably need to clear it away before you built your own dream home?

I walked past the property to see what was on the other side. The empty section was starting to overgrow, although someone must have cut the grass back recently. It was no more than two inches high. The daisy faces were struggling for sunlight amid the long grass-stems, but the dandelions had no such worries. Not the most exotic of wildflowers, but they were pretty in their own way.

There was the scuff of footsteps. For a moment I couldn't work out where they were coming from, the street was empty, then I saw the movement near the wall.

Someone was in the house. Two someones. Now that I was alert for the sound I could also hear the low hum of conversation. Two different voices. And they were standing right by the wall. One more step and they'd be outside.

I looked around but there was nothing but field. No cars. No trees. No fences.

There was a rumble of laughter. I saw the tip of a shoe. The flash of a sleeve.

I ran across the road. The grass on this side was longer. The mower must only do one side each month. I lay down flat. My arms outstretched. My chin on the ground.

When the men emerged I tried to flatten myself out even more. I pressed my body into the earth, and tipped my head to one side so the top of my hair wouldn't be so obvious. If they walked over this side of the road it would be patently obvious there was a tall teenage girl lying on the ground. But if they stayed where they were...

There was another burst of laughter. I could barely see from the angle I was in, but I didn't dare to raise my head. Even if my hair didn't make me more visible the motion surely would.

Up to now I'd thought that the Grey Man was overstating the problem. I thought he was making stuff up. Maybe for kicks. Maybe for control.

But instead he was right. There was no way these guys were out here on a house inspection. You don't dress in a dark suit so you can trek around a half-finished building site that's been left empty for months, if not years.

No. You only come out here dressed like that if you've got a tip-off. If you're in a hurry. If it's something that's more important than your tailored suit. If it's something you're desperate to shut down.

And you didn't do that because a teenage girl stole a file. You only did that if the file was something that a lot of people a lot more important than you wanted.

What the hell was it that he'd set me up for? What was it that I'd stolen?

I could hear the voices more clearly. If I concentrated harder I could even make out individual words. *Payment. Clean-up. Fa'amoe. Dead.*

No, no, no, no, no. *You're making it up,* I thought to myself. *This is just a dream and you're making this shit up.*

The voices continued. The sun warmed one cheek while the other one pressed into scratchy grass. I didn't wake up. This wasn't a dream.

Footsteps sounded, but I couldn't tell if they were coming closer or moving away. I closed my eyes. Maybe I could pretend that I'd fallen asleep here. If they caught me I could pretend I'd walked twenty minutes away from the city so I could fall asleep in a field on my stomach.

It was worth a try.

I tried to calculate how quickly I could get to my feet if I needed to. I hadn't seen a car nearby so they must be on foot. Could I outrun two men who were caught by surprise and dressed in suits?

Probably not. But that was worth a try to.

I tensed up my calf muscles. I pressed the palms of my hands into the ground, ready to leverage.

And the footsteps grew fainter. And fainter.

Aware that they would have a view for a good long

while, I stayed where I was while I counted to one hundred over and over. I waited until the shade from the blades of grass nearest my face grew longer. I waited until I was sure.

By the time I moved, my body had locked into position and my muscles groaned with the change. I slowly got to my knees and scanned the street. There was no one in sight. There was nothing.

I looked over at the half-finished house. I'd come all this way in order to retrieve those files and read through the information I'd soiled my morals to get. But I no longer felt like looking through them. In fact, I was quite happy to let them rot in there.

Whatever they contained was important to someone. More important to them than I would be. If those men came back, or a new set arrived, there was no way my luck would hold out again. Better to be on my way.

I chose to walk further away before crossing over the back line of a field, and doubling back on a parallel road. The last thing I wanted to do know was meet up with those men.

Mr Fa'amoe. Whether I'd really heard the other words I thought I had, I had definitely heard his name.

The Grey Man was scared. Two men had patrolled a site that they should've known nothing about. They were talking about Vila's Dad.

When the Grey Man told me that Vila's Dad was old enough to look out for himself, I'd accepted it. But that had been when I'd only half-believed there was any sort of trouble. That was before I'd heard his name in the mouths of men who scared the shit out of me.

What if he didn't even know about the trouble he was in? What if he was just going about his daily work and his daily life and his daily grind and he didn't realise that full-blown trouble was on its way?

What if he met with trouble and he relied on the documents that I'd stolen to get him out of it?

What if I was the reason that trouble would find

him?

I started to jog along the road. When I reached the Main North Road I started to run. The fear and the confusion spilled into endorphins that fuelled me, until I had to stop, gasping for breath, dripping with sweat. But calmer. Certain.

I would go to Mr Fa'amoe and tell him of my fears for his safety.

And once I'd told him he could be old enough to take care of himself. And maybe at the heart of the impulse I thought, *And maybe he'll take care of me.*

***

I didn't think that he'd be home that early. When I arrived at Vila's house there was a flood of students on the roads. School had let out so it must only just be after three.

I expected to walk past her house and carry on to Nunweek Park. I could find a bench and sit myself in the shade, or the sun. I could try to reason myself out of my panic. Try to think of what I needed to say to make myself understood. There was no use in me talking to him if I sounded like a bumbling paranoid fool.

I expected it so much that I was almost past the turnoff when I registered that his car was in the driveway. He was home.

For a minute I almost walked past. I could continue on to the park and take the time I'd promised myself. Sort my thoughts into order. Sort my speech out. Sit down and take in the end of the day.

But then I might miss him. If he was home early I couldn't trust it would be for the day. He may be paying a flying visit before going back to work. He may be changing to go out for the night. He may be doing a thousand different things with a hundred different time limits, and if I left now to gather my thoughts there may be no one left to distribute them to.

I pulled my hands through my hair to make sure

that it was free of any grass. There was little I could do about my frayed and stained jeans, or my tatty sweatshirt, but I pulled them into line so they were at least as neat as they could be.

When I drew back my fist to knock I hesitated. There was no way he would believe me. This was a useless exercise. There was no point.

But I forced my knuckles to tap on the door. I held my hands to my side, and locked my knees so my legs wouldn't turn and run. I waited while no one answered the door, and then I made myself knock again. Louder.

This time there was a response. Mr Fa'amoe opened the door and his eyebrows raised when he saw me. Then his smile fell away, and his brow furrowed into anger.

'Vila's not here, and to be honest I don't think you should come around here any longer. You're not welcome.'

He made to close the door, and I forced my foot forward, to jam it open.

'I'm not here to see Vila. I was here to see you.'

The force against my foot didn't decrease. 'To apologise,' I added. 'For my behaviour. And for getting your daughter into trouble.'

The pressure on my foot eased, and the door opened wider.

'Well, I really think that you should apologise to Vila instead. She's the one that you hurt with your actions.'

'I will. Tomorrow. I just wanted to apologise to you first, and make sure that you were aware it was my fault. Vila didn't know what was happening.'

Mr Fa'amoe moved his hand further up the doorframe, and leant his forehead on it. His body was still using the door as a shield between us. He still didn't invite me in.

'That's very odd. Vila said yesterday that you didn't know what was going on and none of it was your fault.'

I stared at him, but if he was lying then he hid it well. Vila was protecting me, even lying to keep me out of trouble. I didn't understand.

'But, I...'

'We didn't believe her. In case you're wondering. We've worked very hard to make sure that Vila gets a good shot at life. That she gets a fair shot at being anything that she wants to be. We know that she would never get into trouble like that by herself. *Stealing*. Carol and I raised her better than that.'

I felt the slap. In another situation I would've responded to it. But it paled in comparison. There were bigger stakes at hand.

'I'm sorry. I didn't know that she'd said that...'

'That's because you ran away yesterday when I specifically said to stay here because we wanted to talk to you.'

'I wasn't feeling well. I needed to get home and lie down.'

'I could've driven you. It would've been safer. Instead you just up and walked out and left Vila on her own telling us a bunch of... a bunch of *baloney*.'

'I'm very sorry.'

'You've said that. Was there anything else? I need to get back to work.'

I stared at him. The words that I needed weren't there. I should've gone to the park and practiced after all.

'There was something...' I started. But then I couldn't think of where to go with it.

Mr Fa'amoe stood in the doorframe, his eyebrows raised. He was flushed from his outburst. There was a line of sweat clinging to his brow. He didn't look like someone who wanted to listen.

'Funny you should mention stealing,' I said. As soon as the words left my mouth his face pulled into itself and darkened. 'I think you've been stealing something too.'

The words had come out wrong. I'd meant to say *I'd stolen something from him*. But when I tried to correct them my mouth refused to say it.

And there was something weird going on with Vila's Dad. I expected he would grow even angrier, but instead he pulled back. His head nodded forward. Not in a determined way as the result of thoughtful action. More like an unconscious response to a truth.

'I haven't stolen anything in my life,' he said quietly. His posture relaxed against the doorframe. He even opened the door wider and gestured me inside. It didn't make sense. I'd said completely the wrong thing, and instead of slamming the door in my face he was making me welcome.

I walked into the lounge, and took a seat on the couch. The pale floral covering was beautiful and unsullied. Too late I thought of the grass-stains and dirt that covered my jeans. I tried to sit lighter on my bottom so it wouldn't press my grubby imprint on the clean fabric.

'I haven't stolen anything,' he repeated as he took a seat next to me.

'Where's your file on BRAC1?'

He looked at me and his lower lip was trembling. 'I really don't think you're in a position to ask me about my work, young lady. Not after the trouble you've been causing.'

'Except it's not your work, is it? That's why you've got it hidden away in your briefcase instead of filed in your drawer.'

He stared at me, his gaze level. 'I think you should keep out of things that don't concern you.'

'I think that you should keep your head down. They're after you. They're after both of us.'

Mr Fa'amoe stood and paced the length of the living room. 'No one knows I've taken that file. No one.'

'Someone not only knows you've taken that file, they know that I took it off you, and they know that I hid it. And if they're onto me, they're certainly onto you.'

He paced the floor, back and forth, back and forth. And then he stopped right in front of me. 'I want you to leave. You need to leave right now.'

He grabbed a handful of my sweatshirt, and pulled me up off the couch. I pushed back at him, but he didn't let go. He dragged me over to the door and pulled it open.

'Stay away from me, and stay away from my daughter.' He pushed me out of the door, and slammed it behind me.

I turned and hammered on the heavy wood. 'Mr Fa'amoe please listen to me. You're in danger. Your family is in danger.'

There was no response, and I tried again. My hands flat against the surface, both slapping in time on the wood. 'Please, you have to watch out for yourself. You're in danger. They're coming to get you.'

A window opened off to my left. He was in the kitchen. He had a phone in his hand. 'Get off my property or I'll call the police. I'm serious.'

I opened my mouth to call out a warning again, but he waggled the phone in his hand and my words stopped short of forming.

'Get off my property,' he said again. His voice was a low growl, and he held the phone like a weapon.

I turned and got out of there.

***

Coroner's Court 2014

Vila adjusts her shirt. She pulls at the collar and fiddles with the small pearl button that holds it closed.

'I was quite angry that she had just left like that. Without a word. And then she didn't turn up at school the next day and I started to get worried. She'd really hit herself hard when she fell down. I wondered if she'd ended up in hospital or something.'

She jerks her hand away from her throat and sits on it. She's staring at a point on the floor in front of her; it's where there's a divet in the floorboards. The hall used to be used for musical recitals. The divet formed in front of the cellist. A tiny chink in the floor, and the cellist found that if she rested the point there she didn't have to squeeze her knees as tightly. One year, two. She moved on to other things, marriage, motherhood, but the divet remained.

I wish I could snap my fingers and tell her to get a move on. Listening to this testimony has been alternating between entertaining and frustrating, but the emotive response has now passed through into boredom. Come on, already. I've been through this once before, so it doesn't hold the thrill of the unknown. Get to the good bits.

'She went to see my father. I didn't know it until I got home. He was riled up like I'd never seen. He'd been angry because of, you know,' she waved her right hand in circles, 'The shoplifting and stuff. I'd never really been in trouble like that before. But he was wild, just wild.

'He told me that she'd been around there sputtering garbage. Not,' Vila turns to the coroner, 'Not like lies or anything. Actual garbage. Like she couldn't form sentences or anything. He said she was just making sounds, and pointing and gesturing. In the end he'd had to throw her out. Then she just started banging on the door and yelling that he was trouble, he was trouble, he was gonna get his. Making threats and stuff, I don't know. She'd torn up some of the flowerbed where she'd stomped up to the kitchen windows. Mum cried over that; she spent ages getting that looking nice.' Vila paused and her hand popped out from under her to fiddle with the button again.

'In the end he'd had to threaten to call the police to get her to leave. He was so angry,' She shook her head in recollection. 'So angry. He had a lot of stuff going on with work and everything. We thought at that stage we might have to move to another city. And then I get in trouble, and my friend turns up and starts threatening him and yelling. He was not happy.'

Vila smiles at the memory. I sit there seething with resentment. There I was trying to do him a favour, and instead he made me out to look like a gibbering fool. Some people, eh?

The Grey Man enters the makeshift courtroom. I

199

can feel his presence before I even notice he's there. He turns in a slow circle, in that way he has, surveying everything. You can see him noting every last detail. Remembering it all for later reference.

And then he comes over and sits in the back bench. He sits in the back bench where I sit too.

'Hey Daina. How's it going?'

I look him over from top to toe. His face is still the youthful mask that the Grey Man sported when he pushed a gun into my five-year old face. Time won't ravage him any more than it can now ravage me.

'Have they started to talk rubbish about you yet?'

'They started with the rubbish. Now they're onto the complete make-believe.'

He takes my hand in his. I didn't even realise I still had appendages until I feel the warmth. He gives a low chuckle.

Watch this. See this now. A dead girl in a courtroom being comforted by her imaginary friend.

At least someone's still got my back.

***

I follow my mother when she moves into a back room. Her new friend Christine comes with her. There's a sheaf of papers in her hand. I know what that is. As part of the pathologist's recommendation, there was a forensic psychiatry assessment done. Trying to piece together my mental state at the end. Trying to pull together half-remembered incidents from half a dozen witnesses all recalling events through a filter of their actions, being seen in their best light.

And if you think that Bones has a hard job, trying to work out what killed someone from the evidence of their physical bodies, you ought to think again. These people, because no one does this job alone, these people had to work things out with no body, no physical evidence, nothing but words from unreliable sources. Conjuring up a mental state that it can take years to diagnose when you have an actual patient in front of you. Pity them.

Still, at least they weren't under the gun on this one. You should see them try this game when someone's been in their care. That's a graceful dance if ever I saw one. Don't step there, that's blame. Don't step here, that's an oversight.

And now my mother needs some help to understand. Because there she's been, blaming herself for all of my downfall, and there I actually was, a victim of her genetics.

Christine pulls her into a side room and they sit down on a bench to look over everything. A break in proceedings after Vila's testimony. My mother expected to be here the whole day, so she's using this time. Christine assigned as well. At least this one will come easy to her. She trained in psychiatry. She knows what all these words mean.

There won't be a witness for this one. The coroner will read the report and enter it into evidence that way. There'll be people in the courtroom who will never know what's written down here. They could ask, but they don't know enough to. There'll be conclusions made that they'll be completely in the dark about.

My Grey Man stays close by. He's my protector and my challenger. My friend and my enemy. The person who is best for me, and my worst influence.

He is the kindest person that I know, modelled on a man who threatened me a little girl. His guise is just that. Not a clue to his internal makeup. Not a pathway to enlightenment. A mask that he wears because he has to wear something, and looking in the mirror is a hard task for a teenage girl to master.

I listen as Christine explains my symptoms. She doesn't know about the flashes of colour, and how I could taste them and smell them. She doesn't know that my Grey Man told my friends were giving me hallucinogens, so I could explain them away.

She doesn't know why I stopped eating. The fear I had of being poisoned. She only knows that I did stop.

201

That I did stop and I lost weight and I started fainting and my body hair grew thick and lush to try to shelter me from the cold.

She knows these things because other people saw. Other people reported these symptoms. And none of them did anything about them. They just stood back and watched me fade away. Watched as my speech turned to gibberish, and my actions turned erratic, and my responses became unhinged.

They watched in so much detail that they managed to fill up twenty pages of a psychiatric report. *Twenty pages*. And at no time did anyone reach out a hand to me in help.

My Grey Man enfolds me in his arm as my mother listens to a report into my mental state that means absolutely nothing, a decade too late. Its only usefulness in knowing how to treat someone, to bring them back from the brink of insanity.

You can't bring back a dead girl.

chapter twelve

Daina 2004

I spent the next day avoiding my mother. Not as hard as it might seem. She was passed out when I slipped down the stairs in the morning, fully intending on going to school. When I ducked back home a few hours later she was in her room – with company. When I headed out again she was asleep on the living room floor. That was the only worrisome one.

Her gear was still by her body, the tourniquet still in place, though loose. I stepped as close as I dared to make sure she was breathing. Her chest rose and fell, rose and fell. It was slow. I had nothing to time it with but my own breath. She was expending only half the effort I was. But there were no hitches, no stop-starts.

She'd collapsed onto one side. It was close enough to the recovery position that I felt free to leave her there. As I walked out the front door again I could feel a mean-spirited child in the back of my head shouting – *I hope you die. I hope you overdose and die.*

But that was foolish and shortsighted. The little child didn't know half the trouble it'd be in if that truly happened. It was bad enough trying to work the system around a parent who was incapable. Try to do it with a dead body in your lounge, and you'd find out what difficulty really was. And there was no way I was going into some nasty CYPF family or home this late in the game, and no chance that Dad'd suddenly find room in his heart and his home for me.

The day was overcast. As I walked out of the house for the second time that day it started to drizzle. At least it cleared the footpaths of people, though the traffic on the road increased.

I'd fully intended to walk into class this morning; I

even had the forged note in my hand. But there was a car sitting on Langdon's Road opposite the entrance. A large black car that raised the hairs on the back of my neck, and dropped my body temperature another five degrees.

I didn't get close enough to tell if there was really anything odd about the vehicle or its occupants. I wasn't into taking any more chances. My close encounter the day before was still fresh in my mind, along with the frustration caused by Vila's dad's refusal to listen to me.

As the Grey Man had stated though, he was old enough...

I was still fighting with myself as I walked away from the school gates. Surely someone who was seriously into disguising themselves wouldn't use a car that stood out so much from the standard school traffic. If they were trying to hide, then wouldn't they use a silver vehicle, some standard import model that would just get lost in the crowd?

But the thought that they wanted to stand out brought its own horrible conclusions to mind.

I headed over to Vila's house. There were half-formed thoughts about maybe meeting her on the way and telling her to watch her back. Not a likely scenario considering I could hear the bell go before I'd reached the end of the road, but it gave me some direction.

Maybe she'd taken the day off anyway. Maybe her dad had taken my warning seriously and the whole family was now packing up ready to make a run for it.

There was no one at home. Even Vila's mother was nowhere in sight. I knew she worked part-time, but I still hadn't clocked the exact timetable, so I couldn't judge if her absence was standard or not.

I sat in the park for a while and waited for something to happen. Nothing did. My head was stuffed full of thoughts, but none of them connected, and none of them required any input from me apart from anxiety. And that I could give in spades.

Back home. No relief from the panic.

There was pressure building in my stomach. I kept

expecting something to happen. Something bad.

The thought of the files hiding under the floorboards struck me. I didn't even know if they were still there. What if the men yesterday had found them?

I checked on Mum and walked out of the house. My insides twisted in two directions. I wanted to go as far away from the half-finished house as I could. There was only danger in going out there again. Either the papers were there or they weren't. Me getting caught by some very nasty people on site wasn't going to change that.

But, but. I wanted to read through them. Commit the contents to memory. Then, if they were taken, at least I would know what they contained. At least I would be sure that all of this trouble and turmoil was worth it.

In the end it felt as though my mind would split apart if I didn't take some action. And since one option was inaction, I took the other.

The drizzle had stopped, but the day was still overcast and gloomy, even though the sun was high overhead. I was still wearing my school uniform, but at least it being midday there were less curious glances. It was perfectly reasonable that a schoolgirl might be out on her lunchbreak. I could start cursing my choice of clothing when I made the return journey. *If* I made the return journey.

There was going to be no hiding in the grass today. The blades were sodden and drooping. If I dived into them now there'd be an obvious Daina-shaped patch.

But no one came.

I crawled under the house. At one point my knee came down hard on a stone and I swore aloud, before hushing myself. The files were where I'd left them. I tried to sweep as much debris out of the path as I could, but I still found a few sharp edges as I stretched out to retrieve them.

So whatever the two men had been up to, they hadn't found them.

The glass tube was unbroken, the light amber liquid still sloshing around inside. I unzipped the front pocket and put some hankies around it so it wouldn't accidentally break in my backpack, and then placed it by the side of the house, far enough in so it wasn't sitting in collected rainwater.

Then I spread out the files. I left the manhole cover up so that if needed I could plunge back under the building. The thought of letting that cover fall into place with no one above to lift it up if I couldn't made my blood run cold. But so did the thought of being caught. Need be, I could probably kick out a grate and get out that way.

For a moment as I stared at the papers in front of me I couldn't make head nor tail of them. There were formulas, there were sketches, there was the diagram that I'd recreated for the Grey Man earlier – this week? Surely it was longer ago? No – this week. It was a chromosome. Showing a genetic marker. There was an SNP number out the side, but it didn't mean anything to me. It wasn't like I could call up a catalogue and check it out.

But the longer I stared at them the more I could read their patterns. It was like looking at a complicated algebraic formula. You started off with the part you could most easily understand, and then worked forward or back or both until the whole relationship became clear.

The first part was an isolation test. The fabric of the sample was reduced down and reduced down until only one part remained. And then there was a check to see whether the sequence of the material matched the standard sequencing formulas already recorded.

A genetic test: Isolating and then comparing a specific gene on a specific chromosome, looking for a match, or looking for a known mutation.

I could follow it up to there. I could understand the sequencing and the patterns, even if I couldn't have replicated them or known how to get this out in the first place. I could see the overall structures even though the details would take me months, years even, to understand.

But then it all changed. I could see that it was something to do with the sample I now held. I could understand that this was in some way connected with one of the mutations, rather than the expected results. I couldn't see how it fit together.

And it wasn't like I could ask anyone. I didn't even have a GP; there was no chance I'd meet a geneticist.

I pulled the papers back together. There'd been the frisson of discovery, but the flat feeling of non-comprehension wore it back down to nothing.

I swung my head back down through the hole. I swerved my eyes back and forth, back and forth, looking for the natural patterns that caught attention. There was a slight raise in the earth on the far right-hand side. If I put the folder behind there it would be more hidden from view than it had been on the left. There, it had been inconvenient to retrieve, but not impossible to see. The slope of the ground in the new position however, would form a natural hiding place. Forcing the eye to scan straight over it.

When I tried to lever myself back down into the hole, I felt a wave of nausea overtake me, and then my head spun. I sat down on the cold earth, my strength gone, my body crumpled in on itself.

My awareness didn't fade. I could feel every muscle and every inch of my skin as it collapsed on itself. I could feel the cold chill of the ground where the temperature dipped by a couple of degrees from the air above it. I could see the dim shapes of the beams and the rough foundation walls. I felt as my left leg caught and twisted under the weight of my body. The sharp hammer of pain in my head as it clanged against the floorboard on the way down. I could feel a trickle of blood at my temple, and see how the light changed as the sun came out of hiding behind a cloud.

I could see it all, feel it all, smell it all. But I couldn't move my body. I couldn't move a single muscle. And then my senses shut down one, by one, by one.

***

Coroner's Court 2014

'Are you okay to pick up where you left off yesterday?' the coroner asks Vila. She nods her head but her face is tight. She thought she'd be done with this yesterday. The pause in proceedings has spun it out too long. She wants to be home. She wants to be done with it.

The air in the courtroom is leaden today. There's no sun peering in through the windows, and the wood panelling that looks so deep and rich in warm sunlight looks heavy and dark in its absence.

'As I said, I didn't see Daina for a few days. She wasn't at school, and then my Dad had that run-in. When she wasn't at school the next day either I went by her house.' She rubs above her right eyebrow and sneaks a quick look at my mother. Judging the reception. My mother meets her gaze and inclines her head. Permission granted.

'Mrs Harrow was passed out in the living room. We'd known that she was an alkie – it doesn't take more than a visit or two to pick that up – but there was other stuff on the table,' she pauses while she feels different words in her mouth, 'Drug paraphernalia,' she chooses.

'I was scared. I'd never met anyone who did drugs, or even knew someone who did drugs. You say things and pretend things at school, but nobody *does* it. Or, if they do it's just weed or pills or something. She was *injecting.*'

My mother doesn't bow her head. She keeps her chin up and gives a short nod at Vila. Acknowledging her actions. She's come a long way. I'm so *proud* of her.

'I couldn't talk to Mum or Dad about it. They wouldn't hear her name in the house. If I'd tried to bring her up they probably would've been more likely to call the police, than to help me find her. And you don't want to do that sort of thing, not to your friend.'

She shifts her weight on the seat, and moves one shoulder in a circle to ease her back. It's stalling. There's no way she's uncomfortable – physically uncomfortable – after only ten minutes up there. If that. But the next part, she's already trying to pull away from it.

The coroner picks it up too. He has some idea of what's about to come. There were talks in hushed tones, before they made the decision to let Vila go up there and talk about this. After all, the probability is it's not relevant. And it's certainly going to be distressing.

But warts and all. That's how the coroner likes to run his courtroom. Better to have too much information than to have too little. He's already noted down a few names that he'll be calling back in here. Information that should've been provided but is mysteriously absent.

He doesn't like mysteries, our coroner. He's worked his whole life to pull all the little disparate pieces together until they make a pattern that fits. And having one loose piece left over, a large and obnoxious piece at that? It's not the way he runs things.

Vila presses her fingertips briefly to her cheekbone. The pressure leaves pale marks on her skin that quickly fill back in with colour.

'The next day was when my dad died, so I lost track of her after that.'

The bald statement hangs in the air for a moment, swaying this way and that, looking for a place to fall.

And then Vila's emotional control shatters and she bursts into violent tears. Her statement crashes to the floor.

***

When I came to, it took a few minutes to work out where I was. In the darkness my first thought was I was home, it was night. The cool hard earth registered, and I thought I'd fallen out of bed.

When I sat up, I hit my head on the floorboards above me. Flashes of light and a band of pain. But it

209

tripped my other senses, and I realised where I was.

Panic gripped me as I tried to get up through the manhole again. I could see that the cover was still off. I could see that there was a clear exit to jump out of. But panic insisted that I was trapped. That I would never get out. That I would die here, in this wide abandoned grave.

The adrenalin rush gave me enough strength to lever my body through the hole. I pushed the cover back into place as quickly as I could. I couldn't relax while that open mouth was there waiting to swallow me again. I caught my fingers underneath the closing lid, and stuck them in my mouth to calm them. I pushed myself into the centre of the room, and sat breathing hard for a minute before standing and backing further away.

I couldn't have been out for long. The light outside was still strong. The smell of the rain was still fresh. The papers were still out on the floor, but there was no way I was putting them back down under the house tonight. I retrieved my backpack and stuck them in. I felt the vial to make sure it was still okay, still whole.

And then I got to my feet and slowly started to walk the long trek home. My exhaustion was overwhelming, but there was no other option.

There was a build-up of traffic as I joined the rush of suburbia again. I'd taken so long that my uniform melded back into the flow; the last bell of classes had rung just before I swept past the school.

I didn't want to go home. I hoped that the Grey Man would catch up with me at some point, but he was staying away. Keeping me out of the spotlight, maybe. Certainly keeping his distance.

With no particular place in mind I found myself turning in the direction of Vila's house. She'd be on her way home. She'd be pissed off at me, no doubt, but if I could catch up with her I could try to issue her with a warning too. Make sure her Dad got it from both sides.

The cars were piled back to the roundabout, and then further back to the traffic lights.

Some careless dude inched his way across just as

the lights turned, and discovered that he couldn't pull his car far enough forward to get out of the cross road.

Horns tooted and someone with their window down clearly swore at him, but there was nothing he could do. Traffic stalled in two directions.

There were lights flashing on the road in front of me. Red and Blue. My first thought was construction: they were digging up the street for some reason and backing up the traffic because they had no sense of appropriate timing. But as I drew closer I recognised the familiar boxy shape of an ambulance. Off to one side was a police car. Their presence reduced the traffic to a single lane, marked out with cones and their own parked vehicles.

The dread and panic that had been my companions for the past two days compacted into a single pulsating beam. It was here. Whatever I feared, it was here.

My body tensed up, and I started to move more quickly along the footpath. A police officer was talking with a couple of people standing at the side of the road. Taking notes. Another officer had a roll of tape which he was using to mark out two vehicles.

There had been a car crash. One vehicle had pole-axed the other broadside. The hairs raised along the back of my neck. The first car was a large black saloon. Its license plate was the same as the one that'd parked outside the school. The one that stuck out like a sore thumb.

I turned quickly to look in all directions. The men who had been inside it, whom I presumed were also the men from the half-house, were nowhere in sight. The cars doors were open. The airbags inside looked like grotesque balloons. Both had inflated. There had been a driver and a passenger in the car. Now empty.

As I walked closer I recognised the second car as well. It was the one that had been parked in Vila's driveway the day before. The one that her father drove.

I continued to walk forward on legs that felt like jelly. A hum started up in the back of my mind, and my chest started to have to work to get air.

This car was empty too. But its occupant was easily located. Strapped to a gurney being loaded into the back of the ambulance. There's a manner that people have when they're working hard to save somebody. A rush of activity, but the speed is focused and productive.

The paramedics weren't rushing. They pushed the gurney into the back. No one jumped up to assist with a smooth journey. No one jumped up to keep airways open or pressure applied. Two paramedics slammed the door shut and then walked around to the front of the vehicle.

The ambulance turned its lights off as it pulled away from the crash scene.

I'd seen dead people before. But not anyone I knew. Not anybody who mattered to people I knew. Not anyone that I felt responsibility towards.

I continued to walk. Past the crash scene. Past Vila's house.

I stopped in the park nearby. Sat on a bench. Stared at the ground in front of me.

The papers felt heavy in my backpack. I could feel the movement of the liquid in the glass tube the way I could feel my blood pulsing through my bloodstream.

I was surprised when a couple walked by with their dog running joyously ahead, and didn't cast a second look in my direction. Surely there were beams of light shining out of my bag. Surely there was a sign notating guilt that pointed directly at me.

When the sun started to cast longer shadows, and my arms started to shake from the cold of the late afternoon, the Grey Man joined me in the park. He sat on the bench next to me. He faced forward. His expression set cold and hard.

'Run,' he said.

chapter thirteen

Coroner's Court 2014

With Vila finished, the whole thing is winding down. Look at all this evidence. Look how neatly it all ties together. Guilty.

Christine and my mother exchange long whispered conversations together in the courtroom. Their heads tilt in towards each other, and sometimes one of them will issue an inappropriate giggle.

Thick as thieves.

My Grey Man is now a constant companion. He doesn't talk to me though, he's too interested in his own thoughts on the matter. I can feel them pulsing at me as each sentence is spoken aloud in the room. I ignore them to form my own.

Erik Smith is hovering. This'll be interesting. Someone's "lost" something. Something important. The coroner is not happy. DSS Smith is not happy. Someone in his department looks like they might be careless. Or they might be on the take. Either way, not strong qualities in a serving member of the police force.

That's okay by me, though.

There's a whispered conference going on at the front of the room now. The coroner breaks off the conversation, and his little minion scurries away. She was ordered to recall someone yesterday and she's just told him they're back.

On with the show.

The forensic pathologist takes the stand again. She's not happy either. Had to break a date with a mouldering corpse that was dragged out of the Avon river. Dragged out with a car for a coffin intact. With a very old license plate.

Even this many years after the earthquake spewed

213

up its bounty the river still holds a few secrets. There are still a few deep pockets left unexplored. New surprises.

But instead, she's been called back to finish a duty she was told was finished once already.

Introverts are funny to look at. Their faces are blank half the time, one quarter they're deliberately animated with the expressions they think they should have. And the last quarter is reserved for the expression they can't keep off them. Expressions like, *I'm seriously pissed off because I've better things to do.* There's no one in this courtroom who doesn't know what *this* witness is feeling.

The coroner doesn't bother with the offer that he made to my mother last time. He already knows that she doesn't want to leave the room. She was the one that put forth this request. Christine prompted her to do so; whether that's just because it upsets DSS Smith I can't quite tell, even in my exalted state.

She's still sworn in from last time so the coroner just starts.'You talked last time of how the body of Daina Harrow appeared when you first arrived at the scene.'

The witness nods, and then clears her throat. 'Yes.'

'You mentioned that there were papers found with the body, and a small vial of liquid.' He's looking back through his papers, but I'm not the only one who can tell that's more to do with avoiding eye contact with the glare coming his way, than to actually reference the information.

'Yes.'

'Did you get a good look at the contents of either of these?'

'No.'

Ouch. It's like pulling teeth, Without anaesthetic.

The coroner sits back in his chair. 'Did you see anything of the contents?'

The pathologist relents a little bit. No one's off the hook, but she wants to get out of here more than she wants to make everybody pay for her inconvenience.

'I skimmed through a few of the papers. I don't know anything about the liquid, except it was amber coloured and partially opaque.'

'If you can remember, what were the papers dealing with?'

'They were concerned with research into the BRCA1 and BRCA2 genes,' she turned to the courtroom, the lecturer within her awakened, 'These are the genes that have been identified as having strong ties to familial breast, ovarian, prostrate and lung cancer. If you have a mutation of these genes, then your body doesn't produce a protein that offers protection against some cancers forming. Because of this you're far more likely to contract cancer.'

There's another pause, while the pathologist scans her audience to assess understanding.

'It's the reason Angelina Jolie had her breasts removed,' she tries. There are a few more nods of recognition at that one.

The coroner frowns. 'These were test results?'

'No. They were just research papers. I didn't see very much of them, but they were referencing a study that Dr Atlas had performed last decade. It's been widely discredited.'

I look carefully at my mother while she's saying this, but there's no reaction to see. She's looking at a pad that Christine has made notes on, but I don't really understand why she thinks that a summary of schizoaffective disorder is more important than what's happening up on the stand.

'Dr Atlas?'

The pathologist actually sighs. Well, if there weren't know-it-all pedants in the world how would the rest of us cope?

'He was a research scientist from Tennessee. He specialised in breast cancer. There was a period he worked closely with Marie-Claire King, and he'd continued on with research on how to use the genes they'd found to devise a cure.'

'For breast cancer?'

She shook her head. 'For the protein deficiency.

Where the BRCA1 and BRCA2 don't produce the anti-cancer proteins that are usually produced. He claimed to have simulated a protein that acted in the same capacity. It would basically have reduced the risk of cancer in patients with the mutated genes back to normal levels.'

There was a pause in the room, but the pathologist spoke again to break it. 'It was a load of nonsense of course. They found that out after his death. He'd fabricated the whole thing, the test results, the compounds. It was a smokescreen he was using to generate donations and grant money.'

'And the papers you saw were referencing this,' the coroner waved his right hand, trying to find the right word. 'This research?'

'Yes. I didn't get a very good look of course. I didn't realise it would be important.'

She directed a glare straight at DSS Smith, who just looked away.

'I'm sorry to press you on this, but in the absence of the actual documents...'

She closed her eyes and sat back in the chair. She didn't open them as she continued to talk. 'There were results that *I think* were reproducing the original test scope. Or what the test scope should have been and wasn't. But I just didn't look very far through them.'

She opened her eyes again, and shrugged. 'I'm sorry, but I just can't tell you any more.'

The coroner nodded. 'This doctor, you said he'd died?'

'Yes,' the pathologist said offhand as she stood from the chair. 'He died in a plane crash. In New Zealand, oddly enough. The West Coast.'

***

Daina 2004
I ran.

I cut through Nunweek Park and emerged onto the street. I kept running until I was outside the fire station. All of four minutes. I slowed to a walk to try to catch my breath. There were pinpoint flashes of light in my vision. After a few minutes' walk they began to fade.

I couldn't see anybody following me. I couldn't see any suspicious vehicles in the road. But I doubted that Mr Fa'aemoa had either. At least if I pretended that someone was hot on my trail and they weren't it wouldn't matter. The other way...

There was a steady stream of traffic as the cars ferrying kids home from school melded into the cars ferrying adults home from work. I walked until I met the corner of Memorial Street and Greers Road. If I'd been thinking straight I could've walked through to Northlands Mall and be safe in the throng of people.

There was a rattle in the front of my backpack. Where I'd stored the test tube safely away from harm. I pulled it open as I walked along. My actions interrupted by a glance here, a glance there. A movement out of the corner of my eye and I spun, but there was just an elderly gent trying to walk with the aid of a walking stick and a dog. I don't know which impeded his progress more.

Loose change was tinkling against the glass. I fished it out, some sticking in the corners as though now it had drawn my attention to its existence it was playing hard to get.

There was $1.50 in total. I walked to the closest bus stop and sat down to wait. I could get into the central city, or I could catch the Orbiter and get to Westfield mall in Riccarton. Either way there would be crowds, and crowds should be safety.

'Child's fare, thanks,' I said as I tipped my handful into the change scoop.

The driver looked me up and down. A wave of exhaustion ran up my spine, making my legs feel close to collapse. If he didn't accept me at a reduced fare, I couldn't afford to travel at all.

He pursed his lips and shook his head, weighing up my school uniform against my height, but a ticket span out of the machine. I ripped it off and moved down the length of the bus quickly. Before he could reassess.

There was a double seat in the raised area at the back. I nearly fell as the bus took off, the jolt of motion almost overbalancing me. But I fell into a seat instead. I pulled on the headrest in front to support me as I levered into the seat closest to the window. There were two men running. Along the footpath behind me.

My blood ran cold then hot. Hot then cold. They were both wearing suits. One was limping as he ran, favouring his left foot over his right. Like he'd recently been hurt. Like he'd been in an accident.

They did not look like the type of men to run for a bus.

They fell away behind me as the bus ran the length of its route down Memorial Avenue, and then turned off towards Canterbury University. A group of students, fresh from a lecture, spilled into the grounds and began to toss around a Frisbee.

The bus filled up as we grew closer to Riccarton Mall. There were a rag-bag of pupils and students, but mostly workers trying to navigate public transport on their way home or to errands.

I joined the mass exodus when the bus stopped at Riccarton. Moving as quickly as I could, I crossed the road, weaving between stalled traffic, and entered the mall through a café that smelled of coffee and cinnamon.

My mouth watered as my stomach clenched in pain. Not that it mattered, I had no money left.

I sat on a bench in the central mall and watched the crowds of people around me. No one stood out. No one didn't belong. I started to relax.

And then a hand clamped down hard on my shoulder.

**

Mrs Harrow 2014
It was nearly Rachael's turn to take the stand. It would be hard, but perhaps not as hard as listening to everyone else had been. Her life had been lonely since

218

Daina had disappeared. For long periods of time Rachael had almost managed to convince herself that maybe she really had run away, run to somewhere good, could almost see her daughter living the great life that she'd built without her.

After the disappearance, Graham had been useless to her. But then he'd always been a bit of cleavage on a bull. When Davy had died, drowned in a puddle while they each thought the other was looking out for him, she'd expected they would lean on each other to get through. It wasn't even three months past his funeral when Graham decided that grief was best got through by fucking another woman. A woman who didn't have half the features of his dead child to look away from.

Rachael had always thought of herself as too clever to make the mistakes everyone else made. Genius level IQ, always knowing the answer. It left her unprepared to face the fact that she was as inept at living as everyone she'd poured scorn upon. Hard to use intelligence to combat grief, to combat abandonment.

Daina was always there to be looked after. A younger version of her darling little Davy. Too many questions, too many demands. When Rachael started to drink heavily at least it'd taught her self-reliance.

She shifted on the hard bench. It bit into the backs of her thighs, and caused her lower legs to fall asleep and her upper legs to grumble they were doing all the work.

The plane crash had scared the shit out of her. She'd been full of threats and retaliation on the day, spitting into the face of the man who'd put fear of the loss of a child back in her heart. One child already taken, how dare you? How dare you?

For a while Rachael had been still with indecision; report everything and face danger head on, or just leave it alone and let it fade away. Time was making the decision for her. And then the picture arrived. No stamp, hand delivered.

It was a photo of Daina walking home alone from school. They were only a few blocks from the Primary

219

School, and after Rachael had held her hand to lead her there and back for a week, Daina had been delighted to make her own way instead.

Walking home. Alone.

I can get her. I can still get her.

She made her decision.

***

Coroner's Court 2014

When my mother takes the stand there's a lull in the noise levels of the room. Not respect, exactly, but care. Due to her position in relation to me.

There's little she can add to my final days. Not seeing me for days on end isn't exactly an informative stance. I stick around for a while, but it's going nowhere. I wander away.

There's a television in a side room. This is the one that my mother retreats to when it all gets too much. Open to the public, but not *too* open. A place for people to gather themselves before, and compose themselves after.

'He'll reserve the decision,' the Grey Man tells me as he walks in, 'There's no way he's going to get to the end of your mommy's speech and then render a verdict straight away.'

Whatever. The longer it all goes on the less it matters to me. Blah, blah, blah, blah, blah. Everyone just saying whatever makes them look good. And then my mother, so desperate to tell her warts-and-all truth.

'They could still find the documents,' he says. I look at him critically. He should know better than that. *I* know better than that, and he knows what I know.

He shrugs in response to my glare. 'They still exist somewhere.'

Yes, they still exist somewhere. No one set fire to them, no one shattered the glass vial to let the simulated protein spill away. Someone wanted insurance against future finger-pointing. But it's not coming their way. No one even knows they exist. A ghost. A phantom. A myth.

And a decade may seem like nothing to the Earth. A decade may seem like nothing to the Universe. But to a roomful of human beings, a decade is too long to start chasing up leads that were buried deep to start with.

My mother is still going on. I wander back through and watch her for a while. Her teeth are the thing that give away her past the most. Age may have brought her a serene beauty, but the dentures – no matter how well-fitted – draw her cheeks in too deeply. They tell the story of use and abuse. Of years of ill-living that no amount of yoga and self-discipline can wipe away.

'When did you first notice that your daughter was missing?'

Oh good. Wouldn't want to miss this recollection of a drunken haze.

'The school had rung early in the week. I knew that Daina was around because her clothes kept changing. I could hear her running in and out even if I could never catch up with her.'

My mother comes to a halt, and pushes the side of her cheek in with her middle knuckle. She's using her dentures to bite through the top layer of skin on the inside of her mouth. She'll nibble at it, wearing and tearing, then swallow and start again. A remedy for boredom expanded into a habit.

'I was still taking clients. There was one, he was always interested to know what my daughter was up to. I shouldn't have allowed him into the house really. But he was a regular and he was a good payer.

'He was the one who noticed that she was truly gone. He asked me about her, and when I said she was around; he pointed out the ways that he knew she wasn't.'

She laughs, but there are tears in her eyes as well. 'If he hadn't been creeping around my house and looking, it may have taken a bit longer. But the school rang on the Monday or Tuesday; he noticed she was gone by the Friday.' She bites away at the inside of her cheek again,

221

pressing her forefinger below her lower lip so she can nibble across the bottom in a line.

'I didn't believe him at first. When he'd gone, I checked her room, and looked through the whole house. I thought I'd find evidence that would contradict him. But there wasn't.

'I hoped that she'd just stayed a few nights overnight somewhere. Her backpack was gone. She didn't go anywhere without that grubby thing. I sat in the living room and waited for her to come home.'

I wonder how long I lasted while she was waiting. There wasn't that much of a window of opportunity to reach me, and considering how long it took anyone to find me in the end, the reporting time didn't matter. Doesn't matter now.

But still, I count back the hours, the ones I can remember. I count back and think of what I tried to do to get out of there. How many times I picked at things that were never going to give, picked my fingertips bloody. How I'd kicked and yelled. Even when I was told to be quiet.

Kicked and yelled and screamed in full-blown panic. While my mother had to have a client tell her that I was missing.

'When it got around to Monday again, I knew he was right. She wasn't coming back. I went to the police to report her missing, but they wouldn't really take an interest. A fifteen-year-old from a bad home. They just thought she'd run away.'

And maybe they didn't want the old drug addict stinking up their pristine lobby. Maybe if you'd cleaned yourself up they would've paid more attention. But no, you had to make it so obvious that you were someone that any teenager would've run a million miles away from.

'I called Graham in the end. I couldn't think of what else to do. It was news to me that she'd been in trouble at school. He should've told me.' She wipes at the corner of her eyebrow, trying to still a twitch. She gives a little smirk. 'Although I understand why he wouldn't want to.'

The self-discovery arriving a bit too late for me.

'I stopped using while I was waiting for her to come home that weekend. I gave up drinking a week later. I answered the phone once so drunk that the person on the other end hung up on me. Even in my state, I realised that wasn't going to help Daina any, so I stopped.' She laughs, a tight hard sound. 'I found out later that it's one of the most dangerous things you can do. Stop drinking without medical supervision. But nothing bad happened.'

My mother shrugs her shoulder. 'Nothing apart from the bad you'd expect. Graham's comments got me worried all over again, so I went down to the school and talked to Patty in the office. She was the one who got the police concerned enough to really start looking. She pointed out that the bullying had been against my daughter, not caused by her.'

She coughs, and rearranges herself on the stand. 'Patty was the one who suggested that the police look into Mr Bond.

'That worried me. That Daina had been harassed and bullied, for months, but had never felt confident enough to tell me. Some of the things that happened...' My mother shakes her head. 'You don't expect your daughter to have to go through that at all, and to go through it alone.'

'Patty came along with me to the police station again and again. She helped get the message through that with the end-of-year examinations about to start up in earnest, there's no way that Daina would've moved on. She was smart; she passed exams whether she studied or not, and she'd enquired about scholarships based on her results. She wasn't going to run away and risk her future, not when she'd lived with the status quo at home for so long.'

'I've read through the police reports at the time, and they're submitted into evidence,' the coroner interjected. 'I can assure you that the police were looking for your daughter from the moment she was reported missing.'

My mother waves away his comment. 'There's looking and there's *looking*. And what they were doing before Patty got involved wasn't nearly enough.'

I find it strange even with all of this knowledge that the woman who started off as my nemesis became instead my champion. Look at her sitting there. Still prim, still with her hands neatly folded in her lap and her legs together. Not crossed, only whores cross their legs – or women who like their calves to look fat. She still looks like she wouldn't take any prisoners, or suffer any fools.

I wonder, if I'd survived, if I would've developed some of her same defence mechanisms. Wearing tweed like armour plate. Waving my wit like a sword.

There are worse things I could aspire to become.

This is all very boring and depressing. I don't understand why the coroner is allowing it anyway. He's meant to be determining my cause of death. My mother's belated discovery that I was missing in no way contributed to that. It just stopped any chance there was of preventing my eventual death. And that only if I'd been found.

And let's face it. Both me and the Grey Man went to great lengths to make sure that I wouldn't be. Mum being a drug user didn't contribute to *that*.

So maybe that's the only part of the story left to tell. There's no correction to be made here because there's no testimony to correct. Only I know what happened. There's a couple of spooks who could lend perspective. If they were found and were willing.

They're as likely to make an appearance in this courtroom as the papers I tried so hard to find and keep safe. And for the same reason.

So while my mother witters on the stand about how terrible she was – no contradiction arriving anytime soon from this quarter – I'll take you through what happened to me while she was still waiting to notice. Waiting to notice I was gone. Waiting to notice I was in trouble. Waiting to notice I was dead.

***

Daina 2004

When the hand clamped down on my shoulder I bit my lower lip clean through. Blood swelled and tipped down my chin while I tried to stem it with my hand.

'We'd like you to follow us,' the man behind me said. I turned to look at him. His face was blank of all expression. Just a skin holding all the parts together. Just a working Joe doing his job, and not stopping long enough to consider if he liked it or not.

That was the part that was frightening. It didn't even look like he was giving what he was doing consideration. A few hours at most since he'd killed a man in his car, and he was stopping me in a mall in public to take me somewhere and do something similar but he wasn't even going to check it against some moral compass before he went ahead.

If he had a moral compass to check against, that is.

His companion was nothing more than a blur to my side. The blood was still dribbling from my lip.

The panic grew too much for my body to take. There was a flash of light, and then my whole body was calm. Everything snapped into focus. My heart seemed to pause between beats instead of racing at a trot.

I wiped at my chin again, but instead of cleaning the blood away I smeared it over as much of my face as I could. Then I opened my mouth and screamed.

'Help!' I jerked back as though the man's outstretched hand had been holding me instead of resting on my shoulder. I stumbled back, and turned so the shoppers could clearly see my bloodstained face.

'Help me, please. I don't know this man!'

That turned out to be the magic phrase. A domestic dispute, or a parental admonishment, instantly coalesced into a man assaults woman, or man assaults child.

I pulled at the bottom of my school uniform and curled over to hide my height. With my hair hanging

225

down either side of my face, my face covered with blood, I hoped I looked younger. I hoped I looked like the child I wished I still was.

There were hands helping me to my feet. I pretended to be limp so that I didn't have to straighten up. Activity was on all sides, and then a security guard arrived.

He assessed my condition, and picked up his radio.

Before the crackle of static could clear into an open channel the two suited men faded back into the crowd, and walked briskly away. The guard started to follow them, but as more concerned people gathered, his way was blocked so they escaped outside.

He returned to me. 'Are you okay? Do you want me to call an ambulance?'

I shook my head. 'I think I've just cut my lip. I'm sorry to make such a fuss.'

More magic. A cluster of womenfolk reassured me that, 'You're not causing any trouble,'

'Don't you worry,'

'It's not your fault,'

'You just sit and rest.'

I allowed them to seat me, and clean up my face. There was a lace-edged hankie offered, and when I hesitated at its intricate needlework, it was pressed to my lip by old-age-pensioner hands.

'Let me see,' said a kind voice further back. A woman stepped forward, and knelt to examine me. 'It looks like you'll need some stitches. Is there a doctor on site?' she asked, turning to the guard who was still standing and fiddling with his radio.

He shook his head. 'There's a doctor's surgery down the road. I can give them a call.'

'You should call the police,' said another voice, and there was a chorus of agreement.

I saw the Grey Man edge into the cluster. He shook his head. I understood. Police would take time, and they would take effort, and they would more than likely divine that the state of my life wasn't quite up to scratch.

Group home. That was what the police meant. Group home.

So now I needed to find the magic words that would let the group disperse.

'The surgery's nearby?' I questioned. The guard looked relieved to have a solid question to answer.

'Just down the road. Opposite the McDonalds and a few doors further down.'

'Well?' said the woman tending to me. 'Are you going to take her?'

'That's not his job,' I interjected. 'If it's that close I can easily walk there.'

'I'll walk with you, and make sure you get there okay,' the woman said as she stood. 'We can't have you fainting out there and doing more damage.'

There were a few mutters, and the crowd began to disperse back to its shopping.

The guard hovered as the woman helped me to my feet. 'Can I call someone for you? Your mum or dad, maybe?'

'They'll be at work,' I answered. 'Thank you,' I quickly called as I saw the old lady who'd donated her hanky was moving away. I turned back to the guard, 'I'll let them know once they're home. If I'm not back by then anyway.'

He nodded, and started to move away, and then came back.

'It's on CCTV,' he said waving his hands from one camera to another. 'I'll get operations to set aside the tape in case you change your mind. About the police. It'll be here if you need it.'

'I think that's a good idea,' the woman said. Then took my hand. 'I'm Marjorie. What's your name?'

'Daina,' I replied as I let her lead me out of the mall doors. 'Daina Harrow.'

***

There was a wait in the doctor's office. I wasn't

enrolled with them, or with any PHO for that matter, and with no appointment I would have to wait. The medical receptionist mentioned twice that I could visit the emergency room, or the after hours clinic on Bealey Ave.

Poor thing. She didn't know that a long wait in a brightly lit, safe environment felt like heaven to me at the moment. Her anxious glances upped my panic levels until I moved seats so my back was to her.

Marjorie stayed for a while. In the end I had to fake a phone call to my mother *who was coming right now* before she felt able to leave.

I stayed on for another half-hour. Relaxing in the soft comfort of the waiting room. I even felt peaceful enough to check my backpack to make sure everything was safe and sound.

When the receptionist was tied up with a patient checking in and another paying her invoice I slipped back outside. I hoped that my disappearance gave her a breath of relief, instead of inducing more anxiety.

The late afternoon sun was hitting the tops of houses and shops, making them glow with red undertones. There was the sound of twittering birds overhead, starting to sort out their evening sleep arrangements.

I walked up the road towards the intersection of Riccarton and Clarence. If I turned there, I had pretty much a straight line home. It would take an hour, an hour and a half maybe, and then I could put this day to bed.

My lower lip throbbed, and I could see it out of the bottom edge of my vision. Swollen. It would be black and red tomorrow. I wondered if not getting the stitches would result in a scar. I could be a badass. I smiled, but the cracking of my lip dissuaded the action.

It was the rapid movement that alerted me to the men. They bolted at me from across the road.

I turned and ran down a sidestreet. I cursed as I did so. I'd chose the wrong path. What I needed was lights and action, instead I'd chosen silent suburbs. Their residents at work. Their children at after-school care.

I tried to increase my pace. Although my energy output increased, I didn't move any faster. I was already at full tilt.

I rounded a bend. There was a park to one side. The Grey Man was at the gate, pointing further in. I turned, almost overbalancing in my speed. I could hear the pounding of the men's footsteps closer. Closer.

I skidded behind a house. Ran up the side path. It opened out onto concrete grounds. A showhouse. A display house. The Grey Man was in front of me again.

'Quick, through here.'

There was a set of doors leading into bush. I ran through the first as he held it open. There was a second door. I closed the first and pressed the button. It was a predator gate. It wouldn't open if the first door was still ajar.

It seemed to take an age, but the jamb clicked open, and I was through.

I took off my backpack, holding the door ajar with my foot. The men arrived at the other side. Pulling at the door. Pressing on the button. Cursing at me.

I pulled the papers out, grabbed the vial from the front section and stuck it in my pocket. I placed the emptied backpack between in the doorway and let the door go.

It bumped up against my backpack. For one horrified second I thought it was going to close anyway, that the fabric wouldn't be thick enough to stop it. But then it rested against it. Ajar. The first door would stay locked.

I ran down the path for a hundred metres, and then dove into the bush to the side. There was swampy ground where the sprinklers maintained the climate of dense bush. My feet were instantly soaked. My canvas shoes dip-dyed brown.

I waded ahead. There was a large tree in front of me and I placed it in my line of sight and walked to it. My sense of direction was bad. I needed to be able to navigate by sight.

When I reached the tree I walked to the other side of it, and picked out another. I walked to it. Another.

I must have been angled slightly off, because I arrived back at the path. At first I had the confused thought that I had somehow walked in a complete circle and navigated my way back to the first gate. But it was different.

A sign said emergency exit only. The gate structure was the same. One door on the outside, another on the inside. And only one could be open at a time.

I picked up a piece of rotting branch from the forest floor, and opened the inner door. The wood held securely, and I breathed a sigh of relief.

Unless the men had managed to get inside first.

The thought had me backing away from the door again. Fading back into the forest.

I crouched down, my knees only just touching the top of the swampy water, and waited for my immobility to create silence.

There were rustles in the bush. The constant sing-song of native and introduced birds flittering in the tree-tops above, or rooting about in the soil for a fat grub.

I stayed in the same position for as long as I could stand it. My locked knees started to complain loudly; my thigh muscles started to burn.

When I couldn't take it any longer I stood as quietly as I could. One knee popped on its release – the sound a gunshot in the quiet surrounds.

There was no corresponding rush of activity.

I was alone.

***

I hid until I heard a man swearing in the dim light.

I stepped onto the path, ready to run if my assessment was off and it was one of the goons again. It wasn't. A man swore on the other side of the second gate.

He fished a key out of his pocket and manually unlocked the outer door. He kicked the stick out of the inner one while swearing, 'Damn kids think it's funny,' under his breath.

I waited until he'd gone, and then made my way back out through the doors.

I could hear him in the stillness of the night at the main gate. Swearing again. I made my way past the gatekeepers house and down his driveway until I reached the street. I didn't want to hang around until he put together the thought that if both inner doors were open someone must still be inside.

Instead of heading for the bright lights of the mall, I clung to the shadows this time instead.

It was a clumsy movement, with the folder in my hands, so I lifted up my schooldress and stuck it down the front of my pants. Then pulled the dress down again.

The edges of the folder caught the skin just under my bra. I moved it through the fabric, but as soon as I let go it wormed its way back there. Wearing at my skin. I let it.

I kept one hand on the top of my pocket. Scared that the glass vial would somehow leap to freedom.

I moved slowly and carefully. Trying to keep my noise to a minimum so I could hear if someone else approached.

I tried to think of the route home. Suddenly I didn't want to go there. I could see in my mind's eye the two men suited up and guns strapped on sitting in a replacement dark saloon across the road. Waiting for me to return. Waiting to spring their trap.

I decided to head for the half-house again. I should have stayed there to begin with. Now I'd come full-circle it all seemed like wasted effort. My faint. The car accident. My adventure at the mall. My chase through the wilds.

I should've stuck to the Grey Man's plan and left everything in place until the whole thing blew over.

Or I could be encountering the men at my home

231

right now, clueless and defenceless.

I mapped out the quietest street route there. Every time I approached a well lit intersection I tried instead to cut through the back of a house. To stay out of the way.

At one, I woke up a dog who thought I'd either come to feed him, or to be his food. I scurried back out of there, and risked the main lights. Hard to listen for any noise with a dog barking, a household screaming at it to shut up, and my heart pounding in my ears.

I stopped a short while later, crouching in a pagoda on a front lawn, listening for footsteps in the silence. Hearing none, I carried on.

For a while I lost the map of Christchurch from my head. Instead of a route there were blank sections with question marks. Places I'd never been, only knew the surrounding suburbs of. I spent a long time navigating around areas I probably could have walked straight through. If only I'd had a compass instead of landmarks in my head.

Then I was back in familiar territory. Close to the pinpoint.

I stopped in the empty field opposite the house, and watched it as the moon rose above the treetops, and started to trace a semicircle across the sky. It was on the descent, but still cast silver light over the scene.

When I was satisfied there was no one inside, I crossed the road. I boosted myself up onto the floorboards, and stepped as lightly as I could across to the manhole.

My fingers were stiff. They couldn't find a hold at first on the cover. Instead sliding along the ridge, mocking my efforts.

The folder dug into me as I bent lower, trying to find purchase. At last my fingertip gripped and I could lift up the cover enough to slide my hand under. Instead of lifting further, I pulled it toward me so it was free of its snug fit, then shoved it to one side.

I jumped down into the hole, twisting my ankle as my weight tipped to one side. I swore, and knelt. My ankle still protested, but I tried to use the other for navigation.

I moved the folders back to where they'd been, and then lay down on the earth to rest. I closed my eyes and the whole day spun in front of me. Each moment run through at fast forward, pausing on each horror, each fear, each fright.

It was too much risk to go home, and nowhere else that I'd be welcome. I wished again that I had the extended families that existed on sitcoms: the grandparents and aunts and uncles who were always ready to lend a hand, take you in, offer their advice.

My own father wouldn't even spend a day with me. And my mother was too out of it to notice if I was there or not.

There had been a different life once. It was so long ago it was hard to think of. A life where both of my parents were in the house. Where there was the fresh memory of a sibling.

I could hardly remember my brother at all. There were photos, tucked away in an album, travelling with us from state house to slum house. I had memories I'd imposed on myself that included him. Memories that I knew weren't real not because they didn't feel real, but because they only existed in the same timeframe as each photo. Before, nothing. After, nothing. But in the moment of the photo, a storyline complete with emotion.

It was hard to think of my childhood. There wasn't much to draw me back there; the things I'd enjoyed were gone and to think of them left me wistful.

There was a low hum outside. The sound of a car engine. At first it didn't mean much; I heard the same sound all the time. Then I remembered where I was. The edge of nowhere. This could only mean trouble.

I pushed and crawled over to the manhole cover just as a sharp knock sounded above me. I froze in fear, and then feet dropped down into the hole in front of me. I cowered backwards, but there was no escape.

The legs kneeled and then a head appeared below

233

the level of the floorboards. The Grey Man was grinning at me for a second, revelling in my discomfort, then his expression turned grim.

'Give me a hand. We need to get this cover pulled across.'

I scurried over as quickly as I could. My knees ached from their contact with the cold earth, and my ankle was already swollen and painful.

I helped position the manhole back into place, and gave a sigh of relief as it dropped snugly into position.

'Who's out there?' I asked as we both moved in tandem back into the dark edges of the foundations. 'I heard a car.'

'I don't know their names,' he snapped back. He sounded rattled. I couldn't see his face well enough to work out what his expression was, but his posture was hunched and defensive.

'What's the time?'

He turned to look at me. I shrugged. I had lost track when I was hiding in Riccarton Bush.

'It's just after eight.'

I lay back down full-length on the ground. The cold seeped into my bones, but I needed to stretch my muscles out more than I craved warmth.

My lower lip still throbbed, and I put a tentative finger to it. It felt about three times its usual size, and I could feel the scabbing split where my teeth had bitten through.

'Won't they work out we're down here?'

'They will if you keep talking.'

I blew him a soft raspberry. He covered his mouth with his hand. I hoped to keep from laughing.

I lay still and kept quiet. After a few minutes there were footsteps overhead. At first one set. Then another. After a while I couldn't keep track of the noises. It was possible there were three or four. Then I heard a grunt as someone jumped down. A moment later there was the sound of someone else jumping down from the building site, landing in the high grass.

Then footsteps moved overhead again. Pacing the floor.

So at least three.

I waited to see if the engine on the car would start. If the other two would drive away. But there was nothing to indicate the car was starting up.

There were shuffling sounds overhead. The sounds of items being moved. Then footsteps again, that crossed the floor and stopped right about the point that the manhole cover was.

Silence.

It stretched out, and I turned to seek out the comforting glint of reflection off the Grey Man's eyes. He was staring straight back at me.

The manhole cover lifted.

My whole body tensed. I felt the flow of blood through my arteries, my veins, my capillaries. My muscles grew fat on adrenalin and poised ready to run.

A torch was shone down into the hole. I tried to lay as flat as I possibly could. Think thin, think thin.

'Is there anyone down there?'

The voice sounded uninterested. Not expecting a response.

There was a shuffle of movement, and then a hand came down through the hole. It hit the ground and stretched out. The torch moved lower down in the other hand. And then a head appeared.

I stared in horror at the man. Surely he could see me. The torch seemed to be aimed straight at me.

I closed my eyes so he wouldn't see the whites bouncing torchlight back at him, and waited for the moment of discovery.

And waited.

I heard another person jump back up onto the flooring and join the one shining the torch.

'Anything.'

'Nah. I don't think anyone's been down here for a while. Why would you?'

The torchlight withdrew, and I opened my eyes; its

image still dancing on my retinas. The manhole cover scraped back into position.

'There's a whole lot of kit back here though. Better safe than sorry.' The voices were muffled by the floor, but still clear in the absence of other sounds.

There was more knocking, scraping, footsteps.

I started to relax. Whatever they were here for, it wasn't me. And it wasn't the folder. And it wasn't the Grey Man.

Just a random check of an abandoned building.

I thought of the small pile of discarded clothing, empty beercans, empty food wrappers, on the floor above. Obviously some kids used this as party central, though whether that was yesterday or a year ago it'd be hard to pick.

These guys were just checking it out. Probably would put up some signs for the kids to ignore in future.

I relaxed back into the cold earth again. I stretched my arms and legs, making myself long, in order to release the tension.

A coincidence. That's all it was. Pure coincidence.

And a benefit. If the goons did drop by they'd be frightened off by these men. We were safe as long as they were stepping about above. Probably safe even when they left.

They couldn't be council workers or they'd have knocked off work by now. I wondered if they were home-owners from further afield; the property owners of this doomed sub-division; or concerned parents whose children had left the mess above.

I crawled closer to the Grey Man. I tapped him on the shoulder, about to ask him whether we could move closer to the grate so there was more light, and then the footsteps came close to the manhole cover again.

There was the sound of a person kneeling. The scrape as he moved something into position.

And then the hammering as he drove nails into the manhole. Nailing it shut.

chapter fourteen

Daina 1994

Daina shouted the first time she saw the man on the TV. Then she remembered and she switched to another channel before her mother came running to see what it was. She waited until she'd gone back into the kitchen before she changed back, but by that stage he was gone.

She saw him again though. She saw him and her mother saw him too. He was on the news. He was on the news talking about the body of a man who'd been found in a remote area on the road to Greymouth. Near a lake, and a picnic area.

Her mother shut off the television the first time, but he showed up again and again. Daina snuck a paper out of the rubbish one day, while her mother was in her bedroom sleeping, and she found an article about him. The man she'd seen fall from the sky was a bad man. He'd misled a whole lot of people. He'd pretended that he'd invented something he hadn't. It was wrong to lie. If you did it enough, you went to Hell.

It was odd that they described the man who fell from the sky as a liar, but no one said anything about the man in the grey suit. He was a liar too. A big one. He told everyone that the man died in a plane crash.

But Daina knew he hadn't. She knew it and her mother knew it too. She wasn't about to say anything though. She didn't want him to come back.

She knew because he smelled the same way that her rabbit smelt when he didn't wake up one morning. Not the morning he hadn't woken up, but by a week later when she thought to tell someone else that he hadn't. He'd smelled ripe and he'd been bloated.

Daina thought that the man must have been dead

for that long too. He'd smelt even worse that the rabbit had, though whether that was because he'd been dead longer or because he was bigger, she didn't know.

She even checked it out with her teacher. She didn't let on that she was asking because of the plane crash man. She knew enough to know that might get back to her mother and she wasn't going to let that happen. No. She asked about some meat instead. Not a person, just meat. Asked her teacher if meat smelled so bad when it was left out in the sun because it was dead. When she said yes, that meat goes off if it's not kept in the refrigerator Daina asked her if people go off too. When they're dead. Do they need to be kept in a fridge as well?

Her teacher had screwed up her nose and given her a look. Daina knew that look well. It was when you asked a question that it was perfectly fine for another adult to ask but wasn't okay for a kid. Especially a little kid. She got that look a lot.

But her teacher had said yes. She'd also gone on to say a lot more about how children shouldn't be thinking about those sorts of things, but Daina tuned her out.

So he'd been dead before he fell out of the plane. Maybe dead a long time. And he hadn't died in a plane crash because the plane had crashed a long time later. The plane had taken so long to crash that Daina and her mother had managed to get into and then out of trouble in the gap.

So if the people on the telly were saying that the dead man was a liar, but not saying that the grey man wasn't, then maybe they had it all wrong. Maybe the dead man told the truth, and everything else was a lie.

There were signs and symbols in some of the stuff that they'd written about him. Signs and symbols that were somehow attached to the work that was meant to be a lie. That might not be a lie.

Signs and symbols that after a while Daina could have drawn in her sleep.

It was hard to hide her interest from her mother. One night she snuck into Daina's room when she was

238

already in bed. In bed with her wool blanket tucked up tight against her chin. It made her skin itchy where it touched, but if she didn't pull it all the way up the cold would get in. And if the cold could get in, the monsters could get in.

Her mother sat on the edge of her bed. She leaned her head down until Daina could inhale the weird smell that she had. It was sharp but sweet. It made her nose crunch up, but also made her breathe in deep. It was like car exhaust that way.

'You've been watching the news.' She smoothed the cover with her hand, the edge of her long fingernails scraping Daina's chin. 'I don't think you should do that any more.'

Daina squirmed deeper under cover. She didn't want to defy her mother. Up till now it had been okay because she hadn't said anything directly about it.

'I like the news. I like to see the weather.'

'You haven't been watching it for the weather. You can switch on the television for the weather, but nothing else. I don't want you watching.'

She patted the blankets, and pushed herself upright again.

Daina could feel her mother's weight start to shift off her buttocks as she began to stand.

'I'm not telling anyone about it. That was the agreement and I haven't broken it.'

The outburst over her defiance left, and she snuggled even deeper into her bedclothes as she felt her mother fully sit again. Adults only like it when adults stand up for themselves. They don't like it when children do.

'You aren't good at keeping things to yourself, Daina. I don't want you watching those shows any more. That's it.'

'I won't tell anyone.'

'And you won't ask your teacher inappropriate questions? Daina?'

'Well, can I ask you then? You already know. Can I

239

ask you about things?'

'What things?'

'Why are they saying he died in the crash? Why do they keep saying his work is rubbish? Why aren't they finding out what really happened?'

'He did die in the crash. His work was rubbish. That is what really happened.' She leaned over and kissed Daina on her forehead. Then pecked all the way from the top of her head to the end of her chin.

Daina giggled, but all the time she thought how similar her mother's answers were to I'll tell you when you're older.

'Now promise me now. You're not allowed to tell anyone.'

'I promise.'

'And you're not to watch anything on the news except the weather.'

'I won't.'

'And if you ask your teacher another question like you did today, when you thought you were being clever and I wouldn't find out. You ask anyone a question like that and there's a good chance you'll come home and find me dead. We only get one warning, okay?'

Daina stared at her mother. She tried to move her mouth to answer, but her vocal cords tangled so there was no sound. Her skin rose in tiny bumps all over. The blanket felt thinner than ever.

Her mother gripped her shoulder and shook her. 'Do you understand me?'

Daina nodded.

'Tell me.'

'I understand.'

'And you don't talk to anyone, you don't ask anyone, you don't tell anyone. Okay?'

Daina nodded, 'I understand.'

'Good girl.' She bent over and kissed Daina on her cheek, and briefly rested her own against hers. Then she stood and shook out the crinkles on the front of her skirt. *'You just forget all about this, and then we'll both*

be fine.'

Daina stared straight ahead. Even when her mother put the light out, she stared straight into the darkness.

There's a good chance you'll come home and find me dead.

Daina could see herself turning the handle. Coming through into the kitchen, full of the joy of release from the classroom. To find her mother with a hole in her from a gunshot. A hole in her belly. A hole in her chest. A hole in her head.

It was too much emotion. Daina tried to cry it out, that usually worked. But this was too big to fit into tiny little tears. It sat like a lump on her chest. It made it hard to breathe.

Coming home to find her mother dead and knowing it was her fault!

A steady pounding started in her head. Daina no longer saw darkness, there were flashes of light; there was the pulse of blood through the small vessels in her eyes.

A thump reverberated in the black. The sound of the man falling to earth. A thump immediately absorbed by the pulsing, moving, flashing of the night.

Her brain was too small to hold all of it in. The thoughts hurt to keep thinking, and then Daina imagined them growing too big for her brain to hold. They leaked out of her ears and into the pillow. They leaked from the corners of her eyes, slid down her cheeks, and were absorbed by her hair.

The thoughts and the memories and the questions flowed out of her and were whisked away by the night.

When her head was empty, the pillow was wet with the tears that came at last, and Daina fell into a long, deep sleep.

Empty.

***

Daina 2004

At first I was frozen by the sound. I couldn't move. I couldn't cry out. And then I rolled over onto my front, and scrambled for the manhole.

The Grey Man leapt on me, holding a hand on my mouth, gripping my arms to my sides.

The hammering stopped as I tried to free myself in the tomb underneath, and I could hear the men moving away.

Only when the car engine turned over, and they drove away, did he let me go.

'What're you doing?' I yelled at him. I crawled over to the manhole, and tried to lever the cover up with my shoulders. It wouldn't budge.

'Quiet. They might come back.'

I screamed as loudly as I could. The Grey Man reached for me again, but I kicked back at him.

'What does it matter?' I yelled. 'They weren't the ones after us. They were just some random guys.'

'Of course they're after us. They're all after us. You know this.'

I ignored him, turned onto my back and started to kick up at the cover. It gave me more leverage, but I still couldn't get it to move. I started to sob with frustration and fear.

'Keep it down. Keep quiet,' the Grey Man gestured with his palm down. 'Come away from there.'

I kicked again. And again. And then kicked so hard that the reverberation ran all the way up my spine and I stilled in shock.

My legs fell to the ground. I was crying. My tears falling silently now. I wanted to stop. The congestion they caused clogged up my airways. It felt harder and harder to breathe.

I rolled onto my front again. Using my elbows I hitched my way to the wall brace, and then further through to the outer wall. There was still scraps of metal, this time they dug deep into my skin, into my flesh. I noticed them but I didn't care.

The claustrophobia was on me. Restricting my vision. Swelling my windpipe.

'You shouldn't have poked your nose in. You shouldn't have stolen those papers. You got Mr Fa'eamoa killed. You'll get yourself killed. *You'll get your mum killed.*'

I tried to scrape at the sides of the foundations. Trying to slip my fingers between the planks of wood so I could pull.

I couldn't fit them through. I couldn't get a grip.

In the complete blank of panic I scraped at the wood with my fingernails trying to dig my way free. Shrieking. Screaming. Shouting.

Splinters dug beneath my nails. My fingertips grew raw, and then bloody. I gave up when the panic receded enough to feel the pain.

I wiped my face clean. I rolled onto my back and watched the light filtering through the breaks in the wood play on the floorboards above. And I finally registered what the Grey Man had said.

'They won't hurt my mother. I only did this stuff because you asked me too. I haven't told anybody anything.'

He didn't answer, and I crawled slowly back to look through the wall frame to where he was sitting.

Had been sitting. There was nobody there.

***

I worked my way around the foundations. Trying to find a gap. Trying to find a break. Trying to find a way out.

The grate that I'd thought previously I'd be able to push out in order to escape wouldn't budge. It was fixed into the concrete base as firmly as the wooden struts were. I tried to kick it out nevertheless, but I grew so exhausted from the effort that I passed out.

I don't know how long I was out, but it must have been hours and hours. The light coming in from outside wasn't from moonlight, it was from the sun. I'd spent the night in a panic or unconscious. Great.

With the new day came new hope. I made my way back to the manhole again. I waited underneath until the light was illuminating as much as I thought it would, and then I examined it in detail.

It didn't take long until my neck and back were screaming. I was propped on my hands and my head was tilted back to see the cover. The posture was torture. I dropped back down to the ground again and stretched my back out until it clicked.

There wasn't any light coming from around the edges. I could feel them with my fingers but they were flush.

If I'd been above I could've got more leverage. Using gravity and angles to gain force. From below my options were limited. Even kicking at it I couldn't get a good angle. There wasn't enough room for me to draw my legs back to gain force enough to stand a chance of popping the nails free.

I tried though.

I kicked until my legs were so sore from the repeated blows that the bones felt they would shatter.

I kicked until my lower back had dug a groove in the hard earth where it lay.

I kicked until I realised that I was never going to get anywhere with it, and my thirst was overpowering me. If I kept going I would continue to expend energy. I'd continue to sweat.

My thirst was so powerful that I knew already I was in danger. I knew that you only start to feel thirsty when you're already dehydrated. That milestone must have been and gone somewhere in the night.

I crept around my perimeter again. This time not in search of a way to freedom, but in search of a drip or a leak or a puddle that could keep me going.

Halfway through the search my vision clouded. I realised that I must have passed out and come to again. The light had shifted, changed colour. We were past the full sun so it was now afternoon. I thought of my sobs last night. I thought of my tears leaking their precious fluid uselessly onto the ground.

How long had it been since I'd taken a drink from the tap? My mouth was so dry that I left it open so my swollen tongue wouldn't rasp against my upper palate.

I thought of all the taps at home and at school. So many of them, waiting for someone to come along and turn them. Turn their taps or push their buttons and release all their cool clear Christchurch water.

I came to again. The light had faded. It was almost nighttime.

I was dying.

It was easier to roll my body than to crawl. I rolled over once, twice. There were the wall struts again. I curled and twisted through the gap. My mind greyed out with the effort, and I may have passed out again. I couldn't be sure.

The papers and vial were where I'd left them. Abandoned them. I rolled and crawled and dragged myself over to them. I took the small glass tube into my hand and curled my fingers around it protectively.

I had expended my life to keep this safe.

I tidied the papers in their stupid plain manila folder. They looked so innocent. So nondescript. I rolled my body once more until they were under my side. I pulled my legs up until my knees touched my stomach. Tucked the hand holding the tube on the inside of my other arm and folded them so it was safely enclosed by my body.

Safe. They were both safe.

The light had gone completely. Nighttime again. And this time without the benefit of a moon.

It was so dark. Almost total. Almost complete. Just enough light to let me know that I hadn't gone blind.

The Grey Man came back then. He curled himself as a protective shield around my body. He held me close as the first of the convulsions hit. He stroked the hair back from my forehead and whispered in my ear that I was safe; I was loved, I was a hero.

I would've wept into the darkness if there'd been any moisture left in my body. The dry sobs were my only release. He held me tighter and rocked me back and forth, back and forth.

'I didn't tell anybody. They won't come for my mum, will they?'

'No. You were a good girl. You didn't let your secret out. You mother will be safe,' he whispered. He blew a gentle breeze into my ear. Like my dad had done when he tucked me into bed. Before he left. Before Davy died. Before everything started to go wrong.

There was the loud thump of impact behind me. The sound that echoed through my dreams. My body didn't contain the energy to jump.

'What is it all for?' I asked into the darkness.

'You'll see,' the Grey Man whispered back to me, 'One day you'll see.'

I could feel the darkness enter me. I drank from it, and it filled me up. It made me warm. It gave me comfort. I drank the darkness in until there was no light left in me anywhere.

And the Grey Man rocked me, rocked me.

***

Coroner's Court 2014

When my mother leaves the stand it all seems a bit anti-climatic. The coroner announces that he's reserving his decision, so we can all look forward to waiting a couple of months for a long written report that almost no one will work their way through.

She meets up with Christine and they stand and talk at the side of the room as the court starts to empty out. The pathologist checks her watch, and queries DSS Erik Smith about something. He points out the room at the back, and she hurries off to it. Doesn't want to miss the news, apparently.

The coroner leaves, and soon there's only Erik,

Christine, Mum and Michelle left. My mother walks over to Michelle and touches her on the arm as she invites her out for a couple of drinks. Virgin, of course.

I haven't experienced too much in the way of emotion through this whole ordeal, but this is one step too far.

That woman, that girl, made my life a misery for months on end. She tortured me every moment she could through every chance encounter. And when I ignored it all and reached out to help her she assaulted me and placed me in a position that she knew was dangerous. And then she revelled in it, publicly. Revelled in the laughing stock she'd made of me. Revelled in her revenge for an imagined slight.

The Grey Man puts his arms around me and holds me tight.

'It's not fair,' I mutter. 'She's a complete cow and she's inviting her out for drinks as though she's her new best friend.'

'I know. I know,' he murmurs. 'She never understood you. She never supported you. Don't worry, I know what you did. I know how important you were.'

'How important?' I spluttered, almost inarticulate for a moment as rage filled me from top to bottom. 'I died alone in a large coffin protecting something that's disappeared from sight. That's never going to be followed up on. That no one will ever know about. How is that important?'

He holds me and rocks me. The anger starts to subside. I watch as my mother laughs at something Michelle says, and reaches out to tuck a strand of hair behind her ear. She used to do that with me once upon a time. The anger turns to regret.

'Wait,' the Grey Man whispers in my ear. 'Just wait.'

But surely it's too late to wait for anything? My inquest is over; all the evidence about my shabby little life has been rendered to the court and found wanting. There's nothing left for me. It's been too late for over a decade.

I follow the group of people out as they wander from the courtroom. The television is still on in the room at the back and they're drawn to it. Like people are. Still fascinated with moving pictures in a small box, no matter how long it's been in existence.

The Grey Man squeezes me tighter, tighter.

I see him on the small screen. Not my Grey Man. The real one. He looks so much older, and then I click that he would be. Twenty years older. His face is wrinkled with a life badly-lived.

I look from him to my own Grey Man. And back again. I move closer in, not understanding what's going on. There's been nothing for me about this. No knowledge admitted.

My mother is staring in fascination too. She grips at Christine's arm, and gets a wondering look in return.

I see the fear on her face. I can see her physically start to crave a drink. Her body curls towards the craving, bending inwards, crumpling her features in lust.

I stare at her, and then to the screen, and back to her.

I want to shout at her, to scream at the top of my lungs. But there's nothing I can do. Nothing except feel the expectation of a lifetime of misery and longing, and send it out to her, trying to telepath into her brain and her soul everything that I need, and needed her to do.

She lets go of Christine's arm and turns away from the screen.

I can feel the arms of the Grey Man tighter still around me. 'Wait,' he says as I start to fill with despair. 'Just wait.'

My mother looks into DSS Erik Smith's face and announces in a strong voice that I didn't know she still possessed, 'I know that man.'

Erik turns to her, not really interested. Christine and the pathologist turn as well. Michelle hovers by the door, wanting to leave.

'I know that man,' she repeats in her new loud compelling voice. 'He killed my daughter.'

248

The tension in the room breaks. DSS Smith turns to my mother, Christine places a hand on her shoulder, Michelle creeps in and curls an arm around her waist.

'I know the past few days have been tiring,' DSS Smith says. His voice hovering somewhere between pity and condescension. 'But that's the head of security for Seripina Pharmaceuticals. He had nothing to do with your daughter's death.'

My mother shakes off all of the comforting hands laid upon her. 'I know what was involved in my daughter's death,' she says, her voice quiet. 'She was suffering from a mental illness I didn't even notice she had; she was being punished simply for existing by this woman – this, this bitch - and her friends!' She points straight at Michelle, who steps back at her vehemence. 'And she had a mother who was too wrapped up in herself and her stupid regrets to even notice that she was in trouble, that she needed my help. I know how my daughter died, DSS Smith.'

Michelle turns away, and my mother grabs her arm. 'Don't you dare go anywhere. My daughter tried to help you when you needed it. She was a good judge of character, she was a good person, better than I'll ever be. And if she thought you were worth saving, then you're worth saving. And if I have to make you do it because you're incapable of it yourself, then that's what I'll do.'

'But I also know that they weren't the only ones responsible for my daughter's death. A stupid bully and going crazy wouldn't be enough to pull her down. She was stronger than that.'

DSS Smith's face sets like concrete. 'We've all heard evidence about your daughter...' he begins, but my mother cuts him off in fury.

'Yes. We've all heard evidence about Daina's death, haven't we? Except for the evidence that she was found with. Except for the evidence that she was lying on and clutching to her when she died. We haven't heard very much about *that* evidence at all, have we Detective Senior Sergeant? And would you like to tell us why?'

249

Erik backs up a step, propelled by her fury. 'I wasn't aware...'

'You weren't aware that you had a member on staff who destroyed evidence at a crime scene?'

'It wasn't a...'

'You don't know what it was,' my mother got right in his personal space and started to poke her finger at his chest, emphasising each word. 'You don't know what it was because you let it all slip through your fingers. You let someone steal away the reason that my daughter was found in that stinking hole in the ground, and you didn't even notice.'

Erik's face flushed deep crimson, but he had no comeback.

'Perhaps if you'd bothered to tell me how she was found instead of just where, I could've worked this out a long time ago. Instead of being forced to sit through this ridiculous charade.'

Christine tried to intervene then. She stepped between my mother and DSS Smith and used her own personal space to push her backwards.

'I think we should all take a deep breath. I don't think this is the right time or the right place...'

But my mother didn't let her finish either.

'That man on the television,' she pointed and they all turned in unison to the screen. 'That man faked a prominent medical researcher's death over twenty years ago. He faked a crash site to explain away his death. And do you want to know *how* I know that, DSS Smith?'

Erik gave a single, tight nod.

'I know that because he threw an already dead body out of a plane in front of me and my daughter. He or his cohorts tossed a corpse out of a plane and when he came to check that the scene looked the way it was supposed to, he found us. He found us and he stuck a gun in my five-year-old daughter's face.'

She panted with the effort of speaking a truth that she'd never dared to speak before. I felt the Grey Man loosen his hold on me and I felt like chanting at her go, go, go.

'And he said that if we *ever* told anyone what we'd seen, he would hunt us down and he would kill us. And do you know what, *Detective?*'

He shook his head.

'I let him bully me into doing exactly that. I told myself it was for my daughter's safety. The same daughter I didn't even notice was in trouble when she'd been raped and assaulted. The daughter I didn't notice had lost a third of her body weight before she died. *That* daughter. I told myself I was doing it to keep her safe.But what I really did was put her in danger.'

My mother hung her head forwards. There were tears forming in her eyes, but she swiped at them angrily with the back of her hands. 'I put her in danger because I should've known that my genius daughter who knew nothing better in the world than right and wrong would never let it go that easily. She saw a murdered man split open on the ground in front of her when she was five years old. She watched his reputation being torn apart on television every night by people who didn't even know the truth about how he'd died.

'And she died hiding a folder of documentation based on his research, and I don't know where or how or why she happened upon it. But when she did, she was strong enough to recognise it for what it was, and she made sure that it didn't disappear for a second time. She made sure that it was hidden and maintained even though it cost her her life. She made sure that whatever the true research he'd conducted was, it was kept safe so that the lives already lost by not knowing that information wouldn't continue ad infinitum.

'She kept it safe for a new generation to benefit from it. And you lost it.'

My mother is only five foot four. She barely scrapes the heights of average. But in that moment she towered over everyone in the room. She used the strength and the truth and she was a giant in that room.

'See,' the Grey Man whispers to me again, 'See how

this works out.'

He spreads a scene in front of me. Unravels the future and the past and all of the tiny pieces in-between. He shows what's followed up and revealed and researched and verified. How research notes from a lost manila folder in an unmarked grave are recovered and put to use. How they work to save the lives of people who would otherwise die. How they're used to lock up the people who did wrong, and free the lives of people who did right.

I blink in wonder as the world unravels in front of me like a long tapestry. A long tapestry that I can see my own thread in, tying together the different scenes of wonder and joy and brilliance that would otherwise have remained disjointed and worthless.

And if I had eyes I would cry, and if I had a mouth I would laugh, and if I had hands I would clap them in joy.

And instead I watch these final things unfold in my dying mind as I lie on the dirt ground underneath the floorboards of a house no one cares enough to finish, in a body no one cares enough to find.

And in my last moment the Grey Man's arms fold me tight, he beams the truth into me, I give a prayer of thanks to Mum, and I smile.

ABOUT THE AUTHOR

Katherine Hayton is a shy reticent genius
who doesn't like to be put in the spotlight.

She has lived in Christchurch her entire life,
and currently resides two blocks away
from the house in which she was born.

Skeletal is not her first novel.

*- Taut and engrossing,
    with a tough humanity -*

kirkus reviews

Found,
near water
K a t h e r i n e   H a y t o n

Made in the USA
Charleston, SC
18 January 2015